"You're better than you look,"

he murmured, winding a blazing path along her jaw and chin. Their stance was incredibly intimate.

"And you're bigger up close," she whispered.

Caught with a man alone. At midnight no less, with no chaperone to raise objection. Diana wondered if he'd planned this, touching her as if she were his to touch, wondering if this was how he said good-night to all his ladies.

"I think you'd better—" she gulped "let go of my basket."

His voice dropped to a lulling rasp. "Maybe I like your basket...maybe I like the curve of your handle...maybe I like the way your bottom engages my attention."

"Then I'll have to...slap your hand." She stood encircled and trapped in his embrace.

"To hell with it," he muttered, then swooped down to her face, crushing her mouth with his own.

* * *

The Bachelor
Harlequin Historical #743—March 2005

Praise for Kate Bridges's books

The Engagement

"It's a pure delight to watch these stubborn characters fall in love."
—*Romantic Times*

The Surgeon

"Bridges re-creates a time and place to perfection and then adds an American touch with warmhearted characters and tender love."
—*Romantic Times*

The Midwife's Secret

"This is truly a story which will touch your heart and stir your soul. Don't miss this delectable read."
—*Rendezvous*

Luke's Runaway Bride

"Bridges is comfortable in her western setting, and her characters' humorous sparring make this boisterous mix of romance and skullduggery an engrossing read."
—*Publishers Weekly*

The Doctor's Homecoming

"Dual romances, disarming characters and a lush landscape make first-time author Bridges's late 19th-century romance a delightful read."
—*Publishers Weekly*

KATE BRIDGES

THE BACHELOR

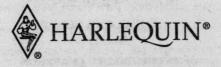
HARLEQUIN®

TORONTO • NEW YORK • LONDON
AMSTERDAM • PARIS • SYDNEY • HAMBURG
STOCKHOLM • ATHENS • TOKYO • MILAN • MADRID
PRAGUE • WARSAW • BUDAPEST • AUCKLAND

ISBN 0-373-29343-7

THE BACHELOR

Copyright © 2005 by Katherine Haupt

This edition published by arrangement with Harlequin Books S.A.

® and TM are trademarks of the publisher. Trademarks indicated with ® are registered in the United States Patent and Trademark Office, the Canadian Trade Marks Office and in other countries.

www.eHarlequin.com

Printed in U.S.A.

Available from Harlequin Historicals and
KATE BRIDGES

The Doctor's Homecoming #597
Luke's Runaway Bride #626
The Midwife's Secret #644
The Surgeon #685
The Engagement #704
The Proposition #719
The Bachelor #743

Other works include:

Harlequin Books

Frontier Christmas
"The Long Journey Home"

Please address questions and book requests to:
Harlequin Reader Service
U.S.: 3010 Walden Ave., P.O. Box 1325, Buffalo, NY 14269
Canadian: P.O. Box 609, Fort Erie, Ont. L2A 5X3

I'd like to dedicate this book to all the teachers
I've ever had. You make a difference in our lives.

To name a few: Miss H. McKay,
my first-to-fourth-grade teacher, who imbued in me a love
of life and introduced me to Jamaica. Mrs. Littlefield, my
ninth-grade English teacher, who was the first to read one
of my short stories aloud. To the authors and teachers who
have touched my life and shown me that great writing is a
craft as well as an art: Dawn Stewardson, Brian Henry,
Lynda Simmons, Rob Horgan, and a heartfelt thank-you
to Tom and Tomolynn Torrance for your support
and much-appreciated encouragement.

Chapter One

❧❧❧

The harvest fair, Calgary, Alberta 1893

"Good heavens, they're raffling off men."

With a jolt of pleasant dismay, Diana Campbell peered through the boisterous crowd to her new friends, Winnie Gardner who was speaking, and Charlotte Ford who was smiling in expectation at the handsome men lined up as prizes along the dirt midway. Horses neighed beyond them; the wooden carousel creaked.

"I think the object is to win a bachelor as a prize." From twenty feet away, Diana read from the sign above the men. An afternoon breeze, warm for September, whispered over her cheeks, coaxing her to forget about her looming problems, to enjoy the humor here.

She and her two friends wiggled through the mob to get a closer look and identify the bachelors. Through a shifting sea of Stetsons and bonnets, Diana focused on three shirtless men perched above huge vats of water, a bull's-eye target mounted above them, ready to be blasted by any participating female who plunked down a nickel.

And there were plenty of beautifully dressed women lining up to plunk.

Taller and ten years younger than her two friends, Diana adjusted her tattered bonnet. "They're Mounted Police."

"How do you know?" Charlotte loosened the cloak around her thin shoulders, exposing her faded work tunic.

"Because the sign above them says so."

Winnie and Charlotte stifled a laugh.

"I didn't see it," Charlotte confessed, bobbing in place to read. "The sign also says they're collecting money for the children's charity and that the Mountie would do your bidding for twenty-four hours."

"Well, I for one wouldn't know what to do with a man if I won him." Self-conscious of her drab clothing, Diana smoothed her clean apron and told herself she didn't care what anyone thought of her coarse, black shoes.

She steered her friends to the center of the crowd. An hour away from their three-o'clock shift at the poultry factory, wearing kerchiefs beneath their bonnets and freshly laundered work tunics, Diana knew they could easily be mistaken for sanitation workers.

"I'd know exactly what to do with one," whispered Winnie, her plump body straining beneath her blouse. "I'd make him massage my feet."

Diana smiled, mostly because Winnie, the captain of their poultry line, always complained about her aching feet. "I could use a foot rub myself."

Charlotte leaned to the other two and whispered. "*I'd* make him massage the rest of me."

Gasping, then laughing, the women headed to the center of the maze and stopped, but not before their movements attracted the gaze of the man sitting above the right tub.

Inspector Mitchell Reid.

Diana felt the muscles along her stomach tense with surprise. Her shoulders and arms stiffened. She lowered her hand as cool, brown eyes flickered over her body in equal, primitive recognition.

Although Diana and her siblings had only lived in Calgary for a month, she'd already had a run-in with the police. Yesterday, Inspector Reid had come banging on her door with her adolescent brothers in tow—Wayde and Tom—demanding an apology for their "delinquent behavior" as he'd put it. Well, staring at the man now she'd almost give her rent money to see him plunge into the brisk water. Headfirst.

The men on either side of him were well into their fifties, handsome and sporting, but something drew her eyes to the inspector. He sat taller on his plank with a tanned torso, a whisper of dark hair running along the ridges of his firm chest, his lean waist twisting toward her and long legs encased in denim pants.

What set him apart wasn't so much his youth and stature but his bold look. That of a lean, hungry renegade. His black eyebrows leveled over deeper, blacker eyes. There was an intensity to the set of his tanned jaw, the crisp shadow of his cheeks and the stubborn curl of black hair at his temples. Even here, he seemed to be in calm command.

Her senses heightened.

The rush of air felt suddenly hot. Bodies crushed her. Children's laughter from the pony rides echoed above the throng. Aromas of the bountiful harvest wove a ribbon through the air between her and the inspector—moist pumpkins, tangy apples, fresh-baked cookies. A rich harvest was something she and her family hadn't fully experienced while living in a city, and it soothed her senses.

Up until the officer had seen her, he had seemed rather bored. Now his eyes glistened with the smug assurance of a man in control. Just as he had been yesterday, ranting at her while towering above them at their splintered front door, daring her to cross him or to put up an argument. Threatening her brothers with jail in that dangerously low voice, speaking to her as if he weren't quite civilized himself.

The rudest man she'd met so far in Calgary, he'd given her only two opportunities to speak. "Are you Miss Diana Campbell?" And then at the end of his condescending speech, "Have I made myself clear?"

Yes, sir. No, sir. Thank you very much, sir. Were those the words he was used to hearing?

It was a wonder that the lineup of gawking women to Diana's right were happily tossing rubber balls *solely* at his target, whispering and hoping to win him above the others.

"Good heavens," said Winnie, spotting him, too. "It's the wild Reid brother. The youngest of the three."

Charlotte stared with admiration. "The second brother to become a Mountie. I think it's sweet that they both became policemen like their father." She added to Diana, "Their father was a copper in Ireland but is now one of the biggest ranchers in Alberta. They say he took bribes in Ireland and had to flee to America."

Diana wondered if it was the truth or a rumor. Either way, the Reid family had long roots in the community. It made her feel like more of an outsider.

They were Irish; she and hers were Scottish.

"And Mitchell Reid has broken every heart in town."

The information didn't impress Diana. How could *this* obnoxious man have the talent to break any woman's heart?

"There's the woman he's courting now. Don't know how long she'll last." Winnie pointed to a pretty redhead in the lineup who was tossing a ball at his target. "Allison Oxford."

Diana wondered what it might be like to forget about her dreary life for twenty-four hours and step into the glossy shoes of Miss Oxford, immersing herself in the company of this attentive, dark-eyed Mountie. Diana struggled to banish the thought. She had more important goals to consider, such as her interview tomorrow with the town's optometrist and whether she would get the better job. Providing a home for her family that was safe and secure would bring her peace of mind she'd never get by winning a bachelor.

Comically, to Diana's right, a photographer from the local newspaper recorded the events with a huge, portable camera. A magnesium flashlamp clicked and, a second later, covered the thin blond fellow with smoke and soot.

With a splash, one of the older Mounties fell into the water. The crowd shouted approval and the reporter took notes, but Miss Oxford argued it wasn't the target she was aiming for.

The woman was a poor shot, for she had been aiming at her beau, Inspector Reid. The inspector shrugged his shoulders and laughed, indicating there was nothing he could do to change the results. The bachelor in the water was quickly replaced by yet another Mountie as Miss Oxford left the midway with her prize.

Diana peered with curiosity at Inspector Reid's remaining flock of admirers, who were still vying for him. They were dressed in satin bonnets and smart, lace-trimmed jackets. She recalled a time when she had worn satin bonnets; when her mother had her gowns made by the best dressmakers in Toronto. Bristling with embarrassment as she compared herself to the giddy lineup, Diana adjusted her thin hemline to conceal the edge of her thick shoes. They were floppy on her feet although she wore two layers of socks.

They had been her father's shoes. The only thing left of his great fortune. The only shoes she had.

With her parents gone and buried for five years, it was up to Diana to put clothes and shoes on her sisters and brothers. She was grateful they were younger and perhaps didn't remember as well as she, the lushness of their former lives. Maybe at times such as these, their ache wasn't quite as vivid.

"Miss Campbell!" a man shouted, causing her to snap to attention. The fort's commander, Superintendent Ridgeway, who seemed to know everyone in town, chewed on an unlit cigar as he addressed her. He held a red rubber ball in the air. "Would you like to win some help around the house for twenty-four hours?"

As if she could spare a nickel for a ticket. "No, thank you." As if she'd want to waste one minute of her precious day with the irksome Mitchell Reid.

Blessedly, the commander went on to other ladies in the crowd and Diana sighed in relief.

"Diana, you should try it," urged Winnie. "You could win one of the men and split his duties between us."

"I won't be wasting my pennies on anything so silly. You could try it instead," replied Diana.

"But you're the better shot. I've seen you throw. You're always practicin' ball with your brothers. You could win and we could each get a foot rub out of him."

"I wouldn't take a foot rub." Diana returned her gaze to the inspector. He was teasing a giddy blond woman who aimed then missed her third shot. The thought came with a pang that he'd be trouble for whatever woman won him. "I'd make him do my endless pile of laundry."

The three women laughed at the ridiculous notion.

"And then," said Diana wistfully, running her slender hand along her mended skirt pocket, "I'd make him repair the ripped screen on the front door. I'd make him clean out the privy with lye and…and help Robert with his mathematics and coax Gena through her nightmares allowing me to sleep through one blessed night." She quieted, thinking of all they needed. "I'd make him show Wayde and Tom the proper way to eat at the supper table and make him explain that being a man doesn't mean you always have to fight. I'd have him carry Elizabeth and Margaret on his shoulders all day just because they're little and need the extra attention."

"But for you…what would you have him do for you?"

Mitchell Reid was bending over the water, his broad shoulders straining in the sunlight as he demonstrated to a buxom older woman how to pitch over her head.

Diana smiled, dreaming of luxury. "I'd ask him for three minutes of time to myself. To shut the private door behind me, close my eyes and do absolutely nothing. Alone and uninterrupted."

"That's asking for an awful lot," said Winnie, who, widowed in a farming accident by a runaway long-horned bull, had three children of her own to support. Her elderly mother looked after the children while Winnie went to work at the factory, dipping slaughtered chickens into boiling water then handing them to Diana who plucked them.

"Let's go." Diana thought it wasteful to daydream. "I promised to meet my family at the carousel before our shift starts. Elizabeth fell into her nap just as I was leaving the house. The older brothers are sitting with them then bringing them to see the fair."

The three women squeezed through the crowd and made their way past the lineup of beauties. Trying not to feel intimidated by their nosy glances, Diana smiled and nodded politely. But as she turned, she heard one of them whisper the awful words.

"Lovely shoes, miss."

Diana flushed. Mortified at the insult, she turned to see who could utter such a condescending thing, but the four young women closest to her quickly looked away.

Speechless for a moment, Diana realized she'd stopped walking. "In my home," she said with dignity, "I teach the children it's never kind to make fun of a stranger."

No one apologized. No one even looked her way. No one in the crowd seemed to even notice she was talking. Others continued tossing balls at the inspector, who was too far away to overhear. Diana felt invisible, as she had on so many occasions in the past five years. She felt as if she was always on the periphery, watching others make life choices, marriage choices, watching others toss balls at targets.

"Come along, Diana," said Charlotte. "These women obviously have no manners."

But something in Diana hardened. She wouldn't be invisible. She couldn't let this pass. "I'd like to try that rubber ball, Superintendent," she yelled above their heads. "To win the inspector."

The fashionable women gasped in disbelief, but they finally turned to look at her. So she *wasn't* invisible.

In the periphery the reporter strained toward Diana, then quickly adjusted his camera.

"Imagine," said one of the society women beneath

her breath, causing Diana's blood to stir. "*Her* with *Mitch*."

The accompanying laughter stung more than the words. But Mitchell Reid was someone Diana knew these women wanted. And for one desperate moment, she wanted to prove that what she wore on her feet had nothing to do with her value as a person or her ability to toss a ball. She knew her temper was leading her. It would likely lead her into deeper trouble, as her father had often warned her, but she couldn't stop herself.

"Oh, God," said Winnie. "Good luck." The three women scrounged through their bags for coins. "I'll put in two pennies."

"I've got one," offered Charlotte.

Diana dug into her drawstring purse. "And I'll chip in the other two. We'll have to work an extra half hour tonight to replace this money." They made four cents an hour, exactly half the wages of the men who worked alongside them.

"You've got one shot. Don't waste it."

Diana nodded. "If I win him, you can have him."

Charlotte's eyes widened in delight. They paid their money. Charlotte shoved Diana around to face the audience, and then the rugged, looming Mitchell Reid.

A smile crept along the corner of his lips, the first she'd seen him wear. It combined with the dangerous glint in his eyes and made her shiver.

"Atta girl, Miss Campbell," he hollered, "money for the charity then you'd best move on to find your brothers."

Diana cleared her throat, irked by his mention of her brothers as if implying that they were in trouble somewhere and needed her. She grasped the ball. "Better not get too comfortable, Officer, because you may slip off that pedestal."

A number of men laughed. He quirked an eyebrow with apparent amusement. "Come here and show us, then."

Was he aware of the pattern to their speech? When she was a child, her father, a newspaper editor, would often play a game of alternating sentences with her by starting each new one with the next letter of the alphabet. A, B, C, just as they were doing now. But no one else in the crowd seemed to have noticed, so maybe it was a coincidence.

She'd try a D and see if the officer followed. "Don't suppose you've got swimming trunks beneath those pants?"

"Easy to imagine, isn't it?"

The crowd cooed and Diana's skin tingled. It *was* too easy to imagine and he *was* secretly playing the game with her. She wondered where he'd learned it.

When his intrusive stare deepened, she felt a rousing sensation in the pit of her stomach. This game was terribly intimate, as if he were flirting with her in private but somehow out in the open. Her pulse skipped as she aimed the ball above his mocking glare. She wasn't used to flirting, and certainly not used to mocking.

"Fortunately I've got a steady hand," she continued with an F, "and nothing you can say will shatter my confidence."

"Glad to hear about the confidence but too bad about the steady hand."

The crowd laughed and she felt her blood rush. He was so quick to return her volley of words. She should stop this so that he understood she didn't approve of his cocky game.

But she couldn't. "How much time do I get you for scrubbing my floors?"

More laughter from the folks watching.

"I'm insulted that you'd waste my time with floors!"

"Just you wait and see." She took a deep breath, aimed carefully and threw hard.

The rubber ball collided with the metal bull's-eye. Boards clattered.

The rest happened all at once. Diana heard a camera click in his direction. Flecks of ash fell from the sky. Then his deep brown eyes widened in shock as the arrogant Mitchell Reid tumbled into the water with a loud, satisfying splash.

Chapter Two

Who would have figured such a slender woman could throw with such a firm hand? Hell, thought Mitch underwater, she threw better than some men.

The water was cold. Immersed for three seconds before he rose for air, Mitch heard the dampened sound of the crowd's laughter. The reporter had taken a damn photograph. Mitch's pride burned. Although he approved of the charity cause, he didn't want to be here.

He didn't want to be won by Miss Diana Campbell.

Up to this point, there'd been a chance that no one would hit the target and that he'd go home without having to fulfill the next useless twenty-four hours.

What he preferred to be doing was what he was trained to do. Ballistics and forensics. The emerging study of guns, bullets and science in criminal investigations. Having returned from the Officer's Academy in Regina last month, Mitch had been trained for a year in those specialties. Hell, as he volleyed words with Diana Campbell, there were bank robbers getting away with stolen payroll in the surrounding territory, and whiskey runners committing cutthroat murder in the south.

And he was about to waste his skills on some whiny woman. She'd likely make him take her to the dance tonight, or force him to go shopping at the mercantile so he could carry home her bags, and perhaps invite him for supper in her home where she'd cook up a big meal and hope he'd stick around next week, too, for the courting to continue.

Sliding above the water surface, he rose from the tub and planted his bare feet on soft, warm grass. Three women handed him a towel, none of whom were Miss Campbell.

She stood aloof beyond the other women, which seemed to make her all the more…*confusing*. Yesterday at her front door when he'd brought her brothers in for lifting tickets at the rail station and reselling them, she'd been withdrawn and silent, as if she didn't rightly care what her brothers took. What did the woman care about?

The friendly gals closing in reminded Mitch of a flock of squawking gulls.

"Here, take my towel, Mitch—"

"But this one's been warmed in the sun—"

"You're such a big man, maybe you should take two."

Mitch nodded and took the closest towel. He rubbed his hair and shoulders. He'd grown up with most of these young ladies—hell, he'd kissed most of them, too. They knew him as the rowdiest Reid brother, who enjoyed a good game and a good laugh. But things had changed drastically the week before he'd left for officer training. He no longer wanted to be the life of the party.

Sadly, they still viewed him that way. The commander apparently did, too, and his wife who set up the yearly charity game. "We'll get a lot of contributions for you, Mitch," they'd told him. "We insist you be a part of it this year."

Leaving the other women behind in the grass, Mitch made his way to Miss Campbell and her two friends. Her bonnet tipped upward as she followed his approach, glancing at his dripping pants, which to him felt heavier than gold.

The photographer, David Fitzgibbon, raced to his side, grinning. Lanky, with matted yellow hair sticking out from beneath his plaid cap, David looked like a scarecrow. "Could I get another photo, Mitch? Perhaps one of you and your conqueror, Miss—"

"You're beginning to get on my nerves, David. Scoot!"

David winked and left.

Mitch rubbed the back of his broad neck with the towel as he reached Miss Campbell and peered down into her sun-soaked face. Even without his cowboy boots, he was a lot taller. "Good aim."

She looked different in broad daylight than she had cast in murky shadow. Her features came alive. She looked much, much younger. She had a widow's peak of brown hair peeking out beneath the flattened kerchief. Her skin was clear, her green eyes sharp. Lips stained with the sun's kiss parted into a bemused smile. "Good splash."

Her two friends smiled in conspiracy.

Lifting a bronzed arm, he pointed to one of the shacks. "I'll go change into my dry clothes then I suppose you're going to tell me what we're going to do today."

She frowned. "You mean I have to take you now?"

"I'm all yours till two-fifteen tomorrow."

Stepping back, she nervously pointed to her friends. "But couldn't my friends arrange to start with you in the morning?"

"Your friends?"

"Yes. Charlotte Ford and Winnie Gardner." The two women, dressed in plain garb similar to Miss Campbell's, nodded hello. He'd seen them around town but only knew them by name.

"I'm leaving you in their hands," said Miss Campbell. "And—and they've got to go to work this afternoon, but tomorrow they're free."

He tossed the towel over his right shoulder. All three women followed his movement. He wondered what they were staring at. "Sorry."

Miss Campbell squinted in the flash of warm sun. "Beg your pardon?"

The rays penetrated his back, instantly evaporating the remaining drops of water and wonderfully heating his skin. "There's no transfer of prizes."

She laughed as if she didn't believe it. *"Really."*

He tilted his head. A lock of wet hair slipped to his forehead. "Look at the sign on the shack."

Three bonnets pivoted around his big shoulder. The sign read NO TRANSFER OF PRIZES.

Miss Campbell blew a puff of air. "Why on earth would you need a sign like that?"

He lifted his eyebrows in amusement, about to point out it was needed for women like her, but her stern expression silenced him. "Well, it seems that last year, Constable McKenny was won by a Mrs. Hogan, but Mrs. Hogan's husband decided to use the constable for plowing his toughest field. When the Mountie finished behind the mule there, the neighbor borrowed him to plow the adjacent field. After twenty-four hours of pulling stumps, the constable was useless as a Mountie for a week. So this year the commander had that sign made."

Alarm flashed across Miss Campbell's face. "But I

don't need you… No bachelor is going to follow… All those muscles…" Her gaze drifted to his arms again. "…And I—I promised my friends they could have you."

His voice hummed low. "If we broke the rules for you, now, we'd have to break the rules for everyone."

Diana simply stared.

With a pleasant jolt, he realized maybe this was his way out. "Of course if you don't need me, I've got a lot of important work I could be doing—"

"Oh, no, she needs you," interrupted Miss Ford. "She really needs you."

"It seems you've won yourself a man," whispered the other one.

"But I don't need…I don't want…" Miss Campbell gulped.

"You should have thought of that before you threw the pitch." He grabbed her by the elbow and pulled tight. "Now say goodbye to your friends and let's get this over with."

Diana wondered when to get rid of him. Flustered at the turn of events, she smoothed the gathers of her apron and waited in the warm sunshine outside the shack for the Mountie to disrobe. Or rather, to put his clothes *on*. Well actually, to disrobe then put his clothes on. Her fingers fluttered thinking about it.

A bachelor, one of the town's most wanted, was about to step inside her world. She wondered how much of her life she should reveal, what to share with him, if anything. She *should* send him home. They had nothing in common and came from two different worlds. He was surrounded by other officers and their wives, educated and accomplished and enjoying the finer things in life while she toiled with basic necessities. She couldn't envision an officer of his caliber and magnitude, even his physical size, standing beside her in the factory or entering through the tight door of her modest home—not that she would allow it. There wasn't enough food in the house to feed him.

He'd be entirely bored by her life.

Send him on his way, the little voice inside her head suggested.

At that moment, the shack door burst open and out strode the officer, fully dressed in blue chambray shirt, worn blue denims, black cowboy boots and a remarkable black leather cowboy hat. She'd never seen one made of leather.

Farther down his body, a holster with two guns was slung around his narrow waist.

Be quiet, she told the little voice. She could use his brawn and strength to help in her shift, even if she didn't like the man. For heaven's sake, he was *free.*

Trying to be casual, she lifted her sweaty hand and fanned her heated face. "Hi."

His charcoal eyes flickered. "Hi."

She rubbed her cheek self-consciously. How did one walk away with a bought man? "You're ready?"

"Ready."

Her eyes strayed to the top of his shirt. Partway open, it revealed the brown hollows of his throat. Remaining droplets of moisture slid along his neck. His hair wasn't quite dry and the water drizzled downward. Someone should reach up and…and rub a towel along that hair.

As he spoke, the muscles at his temples moved. "Where are we going?"

She turned and led him through the crowd, veering toward the carousel. "This way. I'm—I'm supposed to meet my brothers and sisters at the carousel."

Good grief, she realized, she'd need to get rid of him before tomorrow. She had a serious business appointment at eleven o'clock. Her whole life seemed to hinge on the success of that meeting. And she couldn't forget her secret pact with her family—no strangers allowed inside the house.

She *felt* the officer following behind her. A current of electrified air seemed to bind them. The man made her aware of her own breathing, her posture, the bonnet mended at the back of her head where the boys had ripped it once using her hat for tug-of-war before she'd reprimanded them. Tom had felt so bad about the rip he'd tried to mend it himself. And she'd allowed him because he needed to learn the consequences of poor behavior. But now as the officer followed her, she wished she'd done the stitching so that it wasn't so painfully noticeable.

Two hundred people crammed the midway. There was no money for her siblings to spend at any of the booths or games, but Diana knew the sounds, scents and colors alone would thrill the children. The fruits of harvest—corn on the cob, golden apples, bales of hay—filled every corner.

She would give the littlest ones a peck on the cheek before her shift, then the older ones would supervise the younger ones, putting them to bed before Diana returned home. Wayde and Tom each had intermittent jobs to help with bills, but their hours were carefully timed so that the younger ones always had supervision. Thankfully, their friendly neighbor, Mrs. Hillyard, six months along in the family way, filled in whenever there was a gap and Diana needed her.

She felt a hand on her elbow. The officer's touch was firm and warm. It was the second time he'd taken her elbow, and it felt strange to be touched in such a charged manner.

"Hold on. I see another officer I've got to talk to."

Diana stopped as he came to stand beside her. Lean, powerful, and with that hungry look in his eye again. Trapped between folks who jostled by, she accidentally pressed the officer's hip with her own. "Sorry."

"It's all right." His hand brushed her waistline ever so gently, sending a quiver through her stomach to her toes. He was a very demonstrative man, and no wonder, according to rumor, that he got into trouble with his hands. With women. But he was already looking toward another man approaching. The second man was dressed in the scarlet uniform and black breeches of the North-West Mounted Police.

Diana had never been grabbed by a man before. No part of her. Not her elbow, her hand or her waist. As a matter of fact, she thought with a certain amount of embarrassment, she had never been kissed. She wasn't against it—*kissing*—wasn't against marriage, either, but it was hard to be for it when no one had ever asked her. During her younger years, she'd been insulated by her parents. After they passed, her priority was caring for her family, and no man had ever been interested enough to remain in her cramped world for long.

Maybe it was *she* who was bored by her own life.

Twenty-four hours of escape. Could it be so bad? Lord, what a fantasy.

She shifted nervously from shoe to shoe. Why did standing next to this lean Mountie make her think of kissing?

"Where are you off to, Mitch?" asked the shorter man, peering at Diana.

"Miss Campbell here won my time at the raffle, but that's not what I want to tell you." He pivoted his massive body to face the painted wagons and games lined up along the midway.

She marveled at the pretty plaster prizes lined along the shelves, the colorful ribbons, the stuffed dolls.

"While waiting for my time to begin at the raffle," said the inspector, "I studied these booths. Then I was so bored sitting on the plank that my mind started drifting and I think I solved a few puzzles. About a quarter of these games are cons. I want you to take a look at the game around the corner."

"Which one?" asked the constable.

"The wooden bucket game. Three buckets are lined up and the object is to toss two balls into one and get them to stay."

"I've seen it."

"I think each bucket has two bottoms. Meshed together, they create a drum effect and make the balls bounce out. From the angle where the barker demonstrates, it's easy for him to toss the balls and make them stay. Force him to demonstrate standing where the customer has to stand."

"I'll see what I can do."

"Then take a look at the stacking bottle game. The one where one glass bottle is placed on top of two others and you have to knock all three down with one ball."

"Yeah, it's around the other side."

"I noticed that each time, the barker sets one of the bottom bottles an inch farther back than the others. When they're misaligned, it's impossible to knock them all down. Point that out to him and force him to straighten up."

"Got it."

"Then have a look at the nailing game. The one where you have to hammer one nail into a board in a single swipe."

"I tried that one myself and couldn't seem to get it in like the operator showed us. Think it's a faulty hammer?"

"No. He uses the same hammer as the customers when he demonstrates, so I suspect he's got two types of nails. A hard nail he uses, but a softer one he gives the customer which is impossible to hammer in one strike."

"Son of a—" The shorter Mountie stopped himself as he glanced at Diana. "I'll check on it."

When the other man left, Diana contemplated how sharp the inspector was in his observations. It made her fearful for her brothers. A knot of warning twisted in her stomach. Maybe she shouldn't lead this man to her family. "I never imagined that folks would try to cheat here."

"I think half the fun of attending these carnivals is knowing you're being outwitted and trying to guess how."

"Not for me."

The officer laughed softly. It rumbled at the back of his throat and made her conscious of his reputation as the rowdiest Reid brother. She mustn't get too close.

Gently pushing her through the crowd again, he grazed her waist. If she closed her eyes, she could well imagine the man behind her as a legitimate suitor, cupping her back when he thought no one might be watching, unloosening the braids from her dark hair, stealing a kiss at the back of her neck.

It was a good thing the man couldn't read her thoughts. Her drawstring purse swung back and forth from her wrist like a pendulum as they neared the carousel and she slowed down. When she turned around to speak with him, he was gone.

She spotted him three feet away with his gun drawn, discreetly thrust into the back of a gentleman's fine coat. She gasped.

The wind blew in her direction and she caught most of what Inspector Reid said next. His muscled body swayed with confidence. "Put…billfold back…pocket where you found it."

Caught with dirty fingers, the thief, almost as large as his captor, slowly turned to look the officer in the eye. Seething, the thief slid the billfold into the pocket of an older man standing beside them. The man appeared to be with his wife and they were picking up three-foot darts from a barrel, neither aware of what was happening.

Stunned, Diana drew closer. The victim and his wife hadn't even realized they'd been robbed, let alone that their billfold had been returned. The inspector wasn't motivated by accolades, thought Diana, which made him truly dangerous to confront.

Leading the man by the scruff of his collar, the inspector spoke calmly. "I'm going to lead you to the outer fence and I don't want to see your face again while the fair is running."

"Yes, Officer," the thief mumbled.

Then the inspector shoved the thief off the premises. He returned to Diana's side as if nothing had happened. "Where were we?"

She heated from his proximity. He was quick on his feet and lightning fast in his response time. What was she doing, leading him to her brothers? "I didn't even notice you'd slipped away."

"Sorry you had to witness that." He stopped before the spinning carousel, a turntable of crudely cut wooden horses full of laughing children. The youngsters were barely visible through the lineup of people swarming it. A stream of sunlight caught his leather hat and sliced his tall body in two, lengthwise. The shadows accentuated his physique. "Call me Mitch."

"Mitch," she mumbled. "I suppose under the circumstances, you may call me Diana."

He tilted his hat and said it softly. "Diana."

It rolled off his tongue in such an intimate tone that her skin tingled.

He glanced beyond her shoulders then frowned. His dark jaw tightened. She wondered what had changed his mood.

"I see your brothers. And I see they've brought their cards."

With alarm, Diana spun around to look. There they were, all six children. The oldest two had a cardboard box and were laying out blue-and-white striped cards while the younger ones were each holding a peppermint stick candy. They had promised her they wouldn't bring their cards. *They'd promised.* And if the children had candy, it meant they'd gotten it by unscrupulous means because they didn't have one spare cent at home to spend on sweets.

Collecting her composure, she spun around to the inspector. He stared hard and she fidgeted beneath his assessment. Who cared what he thought? This was her family and he didn't know a thing about them.

"Look, let's be direct." She took a step back. "You don't want to spend your day with me, and I don't want you…tagging along. I've got to go to work and you'll only be in the way."

"Work?" He glanced down at her gray tunic. "Where do you work?"

"The poultry factory."

He thought about it for a long moment. "I thought you'd want me to escort you to the social this evening. It's a big party. Don't you want to go?"

Did she want to go? How *could* she go? Without

pay? It was so obvious that they came from different worlds and he didn't understand the desperation in hers.

"You go if you like. I know you'd much rather spend your time with your friends…the other officers. Drinking and telling stories and…and dancing with Miss Oxford."

He stiffened at her comments. She wondered what she'd said.

"Officer. *Mitch*." Saying his name felt awkward on her tongue. "I'm sure you would've had more fun if one of those other women had won you. I need to earn a living and my shift is long and hard. You go on to your social and we'll call it even."

He blinked. "Why did you buy a ticket for the raffle?"

She faltered. "I wanted to prove that I could hit the target."

He took his time adjusting his leather hat. "I'm not particularly fond of socials. Besides, I'll see everyone I need to at the barbecue tomorrow."

She wondered what barbecue he was talking about. Before she could ask, he looked past her other shoulder. The harsh wrinkles between his eyes faded.

Diana turned around as Miss Oxford brushed by in fancy skirts. She kissed Mitch on the cheek, a dreamy cloud of satin and lace and long red hair.

Feeling like a woman on the periphery, Diana wished the ground would part and swallow her.

But it was not to be as Miss Oxford whisked her astonished gaze on Diana. "The winner?"

"Pleased to meet you." Diana smiled at her and her companion, the older Mountie Miss Oxford had won in the raffle.

"Likewise," said Miss Oxford as Mitch introduced them. Then she sniffed.

"We're just heading out," said Mitch, latching on to Diana's wrist and walking.

His manner was brisk. Diana wasn't sure if he was irritated with her or the other woman. And why on earth would he be vexed with Miss Oxford?

In passing, the woman lowered her calculating gaze to Mitch's fingers on Diana's wrist. Embarrassed about what the woman could possibly be thinking, Diana broke free.

But the inspector's voice was gruff, imprisoning her with its commanding tone, causing another flash of heat to tingle through her body. "Let's go say hello to your brothers, shall we?"

Chapter Three

Leaving Allison behind as he led Diana toward the carousel, Mitch wondered why, in the three weeks since his return, he always felt trapped around Allison. He dreaded tomorrow, the barbecue and the things he needed to say to her.

He squeezed past shorter men. One glance at the card-playing Campbell brothers twenty yards away, and Mitch felt his neck stiffen. He turned to Diana. "You'd better knock some sense into your brothers before they dig themselves into deeper crime."

She scowled. "It's not a crime to play cards."

"Swindling is." Although his face was shaded by the cool brim of his hat, he felt the sun's rays seeping through the crown, warming his head.

Maybe he should have arrested her brothers yesterday and thrown them in jail. He'd fully intended to, but something about seeing their sister standing at the door made him soften. He'd told her he was giving them a severe warning, but that next time he wouldn't be lax. He wondered if this was the next time.

The sixteen- and seventeen-year-olds looked more

like grown men than boys with their shaggy hair, clean-shaven faces and deft fingers. One was a muscled red-head, the other more slender with dark brown hair similar to his sister. When they called out to passing men, holding up their blue-and-white striped cards as an invitation, Mitch knew they were up to no good. And that their sister had her hands full trying to tame them.

Grumbling, Diana walked beside Mitch as they approached her noisy siblings. Mitch scanned the crowd in his usual manner. In different circumstances, he might have enjoyed the day. Families with babies strolled by, adolescent girls and boys winked at each other, older folks pointed to colorful porcelain trays lined up as prizes in a dice game and a passing hound dog gobbled a dropped sausage. Mitch watched the gorgeous dog with a slow smile. He knew if his own dog, Digger, was here, Digger would have beat the hound to it.

To their right stood a crowded drinking tent, assembled by local saloons. One of his friends, Clay Hayward, hollered from beneath the awning. "Hey, Mitch! Come have an ale with us!"

Mitch shook his head at his gang of six friends, neighbors he'd grown up with and most of them still working hard as cowboys and ranchers. There was Douglas Saddler, Vic Wood, Clay Hayward, Art Lambert, Quinn Turner and Ryan Brown. They sat around a circular table, much like the adventurous Knights of the Round Table, Mitch used to imagine when he was younger. But as they'd grown into men, some of them were living hard, serious lives. Over the years, some had even had minor problems with the law. There used to be seven of them, thought Mitch with a flicker to his heart, eight including him. They were missing one important friend. Now beneath the awning and tucked around the beer-soaked table, the empty seventh chair seemed to be staring at Mitch, silent and angry.

"I can't join you," Mitch said to Clay, the quietest drinker among them. By Clay's serious expression, Mitch never knew what he was thinking. "I'm busy."

"You said that earlier when we asked," said Quinn Turner, the best athlete. "And it's the same thing you've been telling us since you've been back. Come here and have a shot of rye. You used to down them faster than—"

"I'm working."

They grumbled. "Any word on those dangerous bank robbers you've been chasin'?" hollered Art Lambert, the joker among them and heaviest there, weighing two hundred and fifty pounds.

"Not yet!" Mitch answered to a chorus of friendly laughter. Then sadly, Mitch eyed their glasses of golden liquor. Poison. The poison that had robbed them of their seventh friend, Jack Sherman. The best fisherman.

On that black night more than a year ago, Jack had drowned, along with Mitch's ten-year-old sheepdog, Digger. Two best friends lost on the same night. Mitch hadn't been able to save either one of them.

Sometimes it slipped his mind for a moment, but it always came back. A lot of drinking, a lot of laughter. Men and women. A wild argument. A moonlight dive. A flash of lightning, waves shoulder high and five frantic minutes.

On the train back from Officer's Academy, Mitch had daydreamed how much Jack would have appreciated the fancy fishing lures the old cook there had used for catching trout. Jack had won every fishing competition in the county. The thing he'd love to do most—be around water—was the thing that'd killed him. That and the party their friends had thrown them as a going-away celebration for officer's camp. But Jack hadn't made it to officer's training. Mitch had to go alone.

He'd been back for three weeks now and still hadn't gone to pay his respects to Jack's old mother. After the accident, every time she'd looked at Mitch all she'd done was cry.

Goddammit.

Sometimes in the hours between twilight and sunrise, Jack and Digger came to Mitch in his dreams. It was always sunny then by a river that looked harmless, Mitch as a young boy swinging a bucket of worms, Jack with the poles and Digger sniffing at fox tracks. Fishing was an activity Mitch had shared with Jack more often than any of their other friends.

Maybe Mitch's attempts to save Jack hadn't amounted to much in the end, but he'd see to it that every dirty criminal, every thief, every killer, every crook who passed through Calgary paid his rightful dues. He'd do it in honor of a friend who would have made a much better officer than he.

Shaking off his thoughts, Mitch strode toward the Campbell children. The two younger girls with dark-haired pigtails, five-and-a-half and six-and-a-half, immediately latched on to their sister.

"Diana!" They whirled around her skirts, not yet catching sight of Mitch in the crowd. "Diana! Look what we got!" They held up white peppermint sticks.

"That's very nice."

The middle set of children, an eight-year-old girl and nine-year-old boy, held up a small whittled horse. "We won this, Diana! Look!"

"Very nice," said Diana, her gaze on the cards.

Her oldest brothers, red-haired Wayde and brown-haired Tom, peered up through a small group of young men who'd congregated around the card table.

At the sight of a policeman, elbows rose quickly, boots shuffled in dirt, cards flew. "Officer Reid."

Mitch pulled himself taller. "What are you boys doing?"

The other players scampered. To Mitch's personal dismay, the littlest girls finally looked up, spotted him and screamed in terror.

"For cryin' out loud," he said.

Then the middle ones huddled around the youngest, as if he were a monster. What kind of an impression had he made on them yesterday?

"Sorry," Diana mumbled at him. "You're a bad influence."

Mitch sputtered. *He* was a bad influence on *them?*

"We're not doing anything, sir," answered Wayde. "Bit of cards."

"Are you playing for money?"

Wayde, freckle-faced, glanced calmly to Tom, who was shorter and a year younger at sixteen. "No money in sight, sir."

It wasn't precisely what Mitch had asked. He turned to Diana, who swept up the striped cards without speaking.

With head bent and speaking quietly, she riveted her brothers' attention. Everyone's attention, including Mitch's. "Where did the children get the candy?"

Her brothers glanced at each other. Tom pulled the stack of cards from her clutches and slid them into his pocket. "We bought them."

For some reason, his answer seemed to upset Diana. She whispered something to the red-haired one. Mitch could only make out the last part. "…with card money?"

Tom squinted and asked his sister in a voice loud enough for Mitch to hear, "What are you doin' here with *him?*"

"I won him for the next twenty-four hours in that— that raffle. I'm taking him to work. Maybe I can do some extra reading tonight to prepare for tomorrow and he can pluck the chickens. That is, if I can keep you in order. Maybe—" she lowered her voice, but it escalated into a threat "—I should send him to keep his eye on you."

That silenced Tom and Wayde.

"We brought your lunch basket," Tom said to Diana. He swung a picnic basket up from the ground and handed it to his sister. It was covered by a thin checkered napkin.

"And your library book." Wayde handed her a leather-bound book while Mitch continued to watch. She was bringing a library book to work with her at the poultry factory? On what subject? Chickens and eggs?

He was still trying to understand that aspect of her character when the children continued talking about him as if he weren't there.

"We don't want him around us."

"No," the youngest girl whispered. "Keep him away!"

"I promise I won't bring him home," Diana replied sternly, which calmed them, but further humbled him. "Hush now."

While Diana said goodbye and hugged the littlest ones, Mitch stepped back and decided they were all a tad peculiar.

Twenty minutes later Mitch fell into a quiet step beside Diana. It felt good to be free of the crowds. Carrying her book and basket, he sucked in fresh air, his senses saturated with autumn. They walked along the main street, Macleod Trail, toward the poultry factory on the edge of town. Occasionally, his elbow brushed her upper arm. The resulting flare of tension was difficult to ignore. He stepped away to avoid her.

Her stride was smooth and long for a woman's. She was much shorter than he, but remarkably their paces fit. Her skirts swirled without a sound above her thick shoes while his boots scuffed the pounded road with a steady beat. His leather holsters creaked with the shifting weight of his guns.

So he would help her pluck a couple of chickens and be through for the day. It couldn't be difficult.

He didn't have much to say to the woman who didn't want to hear his advice about her brothers, so he looked around to observe if anything had changed in Calgary over the past year. There were more stores and several faces he didn't recognize.

Wagons overloaded with hay and vegetables squeaked by, a triumph of harvest. In the distance to the west, Rocky Mountain peaks formed a jagged outline. To their right, a herd of cattle bellowed in the far fields, not far from the Mounties' fort.

Mitch nodded to folks he recognized on the boardwalk, to a ranching neighbor laden with coils of wire exiting the general store, to the jeweler and his wife sitting in the café. He passed his sister's pub—Quigley's Irish Pub—but it was still too early in the day to see signs of life. When they turned the corner at the livery stables—one of three stables in town—Mitch said hello to an old school chum strapping saddlebags to a draft horse.

They approached the factory's narrow building. The smell of dank feathers breezed past his nostrils. It contrasted to the pleasant scent of soap drifting from Diana's bonnet.

He noticed little things about her. The cleanliness of her oval fingernails, the smooth stretch of skin across her high cheekbones and the downy hairs at the back of her neck. He told himself he was a policeman, an inspector, and inspectors *should* notice everything around them.

But he also noticed things about her that made him sentimental. The poorly mended fabric on her bonnet reminded him of his grandma's failing sight when she'd gotten so old she could no longer see to mend properly. Diana's lack of jewelry, too, seemed unusual for a woman her age. Most young women in search of a husband wore earbobs, or a necklace, and often a ring passed down from their mothers. But then again, she was going to work and earbobs would be impractical. The rigid starching of her work tunic reflected the pride she had in her job and made him wonder how early she arose to iron.

Across the street at the stockyards, the banker's daughters cast friendly glances in his direction. Now why couldn't one of them have won him for the day?

He tipped his black leather hat and smiled hello, appreciative of their gentle curves.

"Kind of a shame one of *them* didn't win you, isn't it?" With an amused twinkle in her green eyes, Diana made her way across the pounded grass to the factory's side door.

Caught red-handed. Deciding it best to ignore the comment, he shrugged, opening the door for her to enter. Hot, steamy air billowed from the room. Mitch beamed at her. "Lead the way, princess."

With a flutter, Diana lifted her skirts and squeezed past him, close enough for him to breathe in the soapy fragrance of her skin.

He entered the moist room, cocooned in warmth.

She untied her bonnet and placed it on a hook. "May I ask when it was you last plucked a chicken?"

His mouth curved with humor. They were doing it again. The alphabet thing. K, L, M, where they'd left off at the fair. It made his pulse hum.

"Never have, this'll be my first."

"Oh, please let me be your teacher."

Something about the way she said that made his chest squeeze.

She strode into the clothing racks, already swarming with afternoon workers hanging up their coats and putting on their tunics. Grabbing a full-length canvas apron, she tossed it to him. "Put this on."

It hit him in the ribs and slid down his waist. Grabbing it with a free hand, he inched closer to prop her lunch basket on the shelf above her head. He kept his distance as he struggled to reach the upper shelf since the lower one was full. A worker jammed into his backside, thrusting Mitch into Diana, face-to-face. His hard body collided with her soft one.

"Quite a tight spot, unfortunately, which requires some maneuvering." Proud of himself for managing to work in the letter Q, he slid his arms up over her shoulders as she hastily looked away.

A whistle blasted from the other room. Her face rose to his. Neither moved. Neither spoke.

"Right, let's get moving then," he continued alphabetically, since she wasn't.

"Sam's blowing the whistle," she said, tugging in a breath of air, "telling us we've got five minutes."

"Tell me where you learned this game," he whispered, his mouth inches from hers. She had amazing green eyes.

"Under the direction of my father, the managing editor of Toronto's largest newspaper, and you?"

"Vying for my grandmother's affections when she was teaching me to read."

The whistle blasted again but they didn't move.

"We should get going," she murmured.

"X is the most difficult letter to deal with, don't you find? I used to make lists in my mind in case I ever needed one in an emergency. Xylophone, Xylograph."

She smiled. "Xiphoid process—it's the lowest part of the sternum."

"Yeah? I'll try to remember that one, but it's pretty hard to work into a sentence. Usually I'd get away with made-up names. You know, like, Xenna is knocking on the door, or Xanthamen wants to know if she can play."

Her easy laughter rippled over the sounds of the other workers who grumbled past. Her warm breath at his throat stirred him.

"Zigzag your way behind me." She finally turned, scooted out from beneath his arm and slid her thighs past his.

I'm in trouble, he thought, watching her pretty figure as she walked away, a drizzle of sweat soaking through the cotton along her spine. He'd often seen a man puffing and sweating beneath the strain of shoveling snow or lifting hay in the hot sun, but he'd never seen perspiration bite through the fabric of a woman's clothing. *I'm in trouble.*

Chapter Four

Trying to ignore the hulk behind her, the pounding of her breath and the absurd flash of heat prickling her skin, Diana pushed through the double factory doors. The inspector had been flirting with her and she hadn't known how to extricate herself other than to brush past him.

Scooting around bins of newly plucked feathers stacked in the aisle, she prayed her fellow workers would be kind and ignore her awkward situation—that of bringing her *prize* with her to work. If she could slide into position in the work line, perhaps no one would comment. But judging from the smirks of a dozen men and women as she and Mitch squeezed by, it was obvious that Winnie and Charlotte had already explained his presence. To Diana's discomfort, it seemed everyone had something to say on the matter. And most already knew Mitch.

"Mitch, I bet you never had this in mind when they said a lovely lady might win you!" Samuel Pike, their British foreman, clamped down on his big jaw.

"Watch out for the feathers," said one of the laughing Symthe sisters, her large bosom already covered with clinging white tufts. "They stick to everything!"

"My goodness, one of the Reid brothers about to wear an apron," clucked the other teasing Smythe sister, equally endowed, but six inches shorter than her youthful sister.

"Don't you listen to 'em, Mitch," bellowed a white-haired man with a gold tooth. "Best to get your practice in now for those kitchen chores Miss Oxford will surely have you doin'!"

The crowd chortled as Diana slid into place between Charlotte and Winnie, grateful for the security of her spot. At the mention of Miss Oxford, Diana was reminded that this man belonged to another woman. She sneaked a peek at him. Mitch had left his hat in the cloakroom and was trying to decide how to don his apron with his guns intact.

"You'd best have your guns handy," shouted Mr. Pike, "'cause you never know when one of these birds might ambush!"

Well, didn't that comment send everyone around the bend.

When the laughter simmered, Mitch smiled, turned around in his spot and, like royalty, waved to the crowd. They whistled and waved back. Carefully removing his holster, he placed it beneath the countertop, in the dry upper shelf.

He folded his apron in two and slung it around his hips, tying it around his waist and not using the part that looped over his head. Everyone else wore theirs full-length. Too vain to protect his soft blue shirt, thought Diana. When she glanced across the aisle, she saw the two Smythe sisters smiling at him. He winked back.

"You'll have to guide me through this," he said beside Diana. His body filled every spare inch of space between them.

Flustered at the way he leaned in close, Diana blew

a strand of hair off her moist forehead. It seemed hotter than usual. "Just follow my lead and you'll be fine. I'll show you how to pluck a few and then I'll step out and you can replace me."

"Don't leave me," he groaned.

The deep tenor of his voice and cocky half grin made her pulse flutter. He was a flirt. Everything he said held a hidden innuendo. She could well imagine him saying something similar to one of his women. *Don't leave me,* he'd beg, one long, bare leg peeking out from beneath rumpled bed sheets.

She spun around and scrubbed her work surface with bleach, hoping to hide her blush. "You'll ruin your shirt," she snapped. "You should wear the apron the way it's intended."

"Nah. I'll be careful."

"Suit yourself." She set to work for the next hour, trying to ignore the fact that he was an officer, trying to remember that he was her assistant and ready to do her bidding.

Along the far wall, a massive stone fireplace continually heated ten cauldrons of boiling water. Winnie handed her a new chicken every fifteen minutes. Diana was expected to keep up with the work, and hoped that training Mitch wouldn't slow her down too much. She grabbed the chicken by its spongy feet and plucked from the underbelly.

"Like this," she said, her fingers working over the bird. "Try it with me."

He did as she asked, quietly and quickly, surprising her with his speed. "It's not so bad."

She smiled, knowing that the first few hours were never difficult. It was holding your arms upright for eight hours that had made others quit the line.

The poultry factory was an extraordinary operation; the town's biggest factory. Of the three buildings, she worked inside the preparatory one where poultry was plucked, carved, then boxed into wholes or halves. Contracted meat was shipped by horse and wagon twice a day to the town's seven restaurants, four saloons, the fort and two butcher shops. Every morning on the north and southbound trains, iceboxes were packed with fresh cuts of poultry for neighboring towns.

Diana's brothers and sisters enjoyed a whole chicken on payday, every Thursday. Sometimes she was lucky enough to get a free package of soup bones, although it had happened only twice in her month of being here.

After two hours, close to their break time, Diana noticed Mitch battling fatigue. He rolled his head back and forth from shoulder to shoulder.

"It's not as easy as it seems," he mumbled.

"You're holding up better than I expected."

Clamping a hand over his heart and staggering back, he pretended he was hurt by her words. His shirt was covered with grime, of course, but she pretended not to notice.

Winnie blew a whistle. As the captain of the women, she ensured their schedule. The men had their own captain.

"We'll take a short break," Diana told Mitch, waiting for her turn to wash her hands in the provided buckets. "I'll ask the foreman if you could take my place for two hours while I read."

"Read?" he asked. "Why don't you stay, instead, and ask for additional money for my time?"

She fidgeted. "Money?"

"Payment for my work. You seem like you could use…" His words trailed off as his gaze lowered over her skirt. Was he feeling sorry for her? He diffused the situation by adding with amusement, "Surely, I must be worth something."

"You're not quite as fast as me, half as fast in fact, but…what a brilliant idea." However, the cheap Mr. Pike would never agree.

"Mr. Pike," Mitch called to the foreman.

Her body seized with uncertainty. Speaking up might jeopardize her situation.

Mr. Pike stopped on his chunky heels. "Yeah? How are you holdin' up, sir?"

"Fine."

"We could always use another set of hands 'round here, if you decide to leave the police force."

Passersby snickered.

"You're a bit distractin' to the women," joked Mr. Pike. But the man held Mitch in high esteem, judging by the way he looked him straight in the eye and nodded in respect. "But you'll do. Are you here for the next six hours?"

Mitch nodded. "The first two hours were a trial, I'll admit, but I was wondering how much you'd like to pay Miss Campbell for my services."

"What?" The smile wiped clean.

"Payment for four chickens plucked, so far. Seems like the fair thing to do." Mitch straightened his legs and towered over the shorter man. "Through a policeman's eyes."

Diana cringed at the insinuation of using the law.

The English gent eyed him for what seemed like an eternity, then laughed. "Right then. Since you're half as fast as she is, I'll pay half her salary."

Mitch ran his sleeve over his sweaty face. *Take it,* Diana wanted to shout, mesmerized by the turn of events. *Let's take it!*

Mitch looked at her. "What do you say, Diana?"

"Oh," she blubbered with enthusiasm. "Oh, I think that's terribly fair."

"Right, then," said the forceful officer. "It's a deal. How much is half her salary?"

"Two cents an hour, chap." Mr. Pike strolled away.

"Two cents?" Mitch repeated, incredulous. He recovered and called after Mr. Pike. "A penny a chicken?"

"That's what I'll give you."

"Two cents an hour is a quarter of my salary," said an old gent as he squeezed past. He chuckled. "You're gettin' paid like a woman. But then, the men who work here do have families to support."

Diana lowered her eyes and, reaching a water bucket, scrubbed her hands. She had a family to support, too. "An extra two cents an hour is a godsend," she said to him. "Thank you."

Then because she knew she didn't have much time to look at her library book, she rushed off to the cloakroom, leaving him behind to wash his hands.

"What now?" he asked at her side, a minute later.

Diana had just opened the text to page one hundred and fifty when she looked up to his curious expression. He glanced at the front cover which read, *Anatomy and Physiology of the Eye and Its Diseases.*

"Have a drink of water from the goblets provided, there, or stretch your legs outdoors like the rest of the company. The privies are to the back, past the first building."

She lowered her head and kept reading. On every break for the past three weeks, she had memorized two or three pages. When break time was over, she'd go back to plucking chickens while learning and repeating in her mind what she had read—myopia, farsighted vision, astigmatism, corneal ulcers. She understood the corrective eyeglasses available—the lorgnette with the slender metal handle, pince-nez, monocles, gold or tortoiseshell frames and the benefits of each.

So far, combined with the studying at home, she had read two entire textbooks and one journal from the newly established Optometrists Association. In the one-room library located in the town hall, the librarian was helpful in selecting passages on the topic.

Immersed in her work, Diana barely registered the thud of Mitch's boots as he left her side. Minutes later the shrill blast of Winnie's whistle brought her back from her studies.

Closing the textbook, Diana reentered the factory.

Mitch must have gotten friendlier with the Smythe sisters outdoors, for they accompanied him back into the factory. When it was time to cross the aisle to their stations, he whirled them both in a waltzing spin which brought them to laughter.

Diana tried not to let it bother her, but for some reason the scene made her envious. She wondered if it was because of the inviting way he smiled at them, or the way his hands lingered on their waists.

At least they were enjoying themselves. Diana found herself smiling as Mitch stepped back into place beside her. She daydreamed what it might be like to lose herself in a man's embrace, what it might be like to kiss Mitch full on the lips, or to run away with obsession so uncontrollable it would culminate in making love. Did such things really happen?

The beaming faces of the Smythe sisters told her *yes*.

"Good break, was it?" Mitch's shoulder brushed Diana's, sending a tingle down her arm.

She straightened. "I was admiring your dance skills."

"It comes in handy sometimes." He accepted a fresh chicken from Winnie and began to pull feathers.

As the night progressed, he tried to move faster in his duties. After the second break, his laughter died down to a more perturbed state. His new blue shirt had soaked through with perspiration, feathers and chicken flesh, and he bounced from boot to boot as if his feet were sore.

Once in a while he'd mutter a complaint.

"This job isn't easy."

"How can you hold your arms up for so long?"

"I could use a foot rub," he said after the sixth hour, which caused Winnie, Charlotte and Diana to burst into laughter.

When Mr. Pike blew the whistle at eleven o'clock finishing time, Mitch mumbled, "I don't know how you do it."

Diana glanced up. Mitch was a mess. The black hair at his temples was stuffed with scattered white down, his jawline shadowed with dark stubble, boots covered with drippings, shirt absolutely ruined and the canvas apron askew beneath long, probably aching legs.

Even so, he raced to finish his last chicken.

"Comin' back Monday?" asked the taller Smythe sister. The top button of her blouse had accidentally come undone, Diana noted with sympathy, accentuating hefty cleavage. Diana opened her mouth to discreetly inform the woman when it dawned on her that it was no accident.

Rolling her eyes, Diana walked away, removed her apron and began to wash the pails. Winnie had already asked the foreman if she, Diana and Charlotte could stay for an extra thirty minutes to do the cleanup tonight, thereby making up for the nickel it cost them for the raffle. And the foreman had already agreed. The second

Mitch was through talking with the buxom sisters, Diana would say good-night and release him.

With her back turned, she couldn't help but overhear the conversation between him and the Smythes.

"When's your time over with Diana?"

"Two-fifteen tomorrow."

"Pity you won't be takin' her to your father's barbecue tomorrow night, then. I hear it's quite an event. We're available, though."

"I'm afraid I'm all tied up. I'll keep you ladies in mind for the next one."

With an unexpected smile, Diana scrubbed her arms. Drying them with a thin towel, she turned as Mitch walked toward her with the foreman.

"About my pay." Mitch began to explain to Mr. Pike. "Two chickens per hour for the first two hours, then three chickens an hour for the next six. That's twenty-two chickens I plucked. I believe you owe Miss Campbell twenty-two cents."

Diana felt her pulse skip at the extreme amount.

"What?" asked Mr. Pike. "We didn't agree to that. I said two cents an hour. Eight hours equals sixteen cents."

"No, sir. That's how it began, but in the end you agreed to a penny a chicken."

The older man grumbled. "I won't argue with a Mountie. But if you stay to help them clean, I'm not paying you extra for stayin' late, too."

Diana couldn't believe her ears. That's why Mitch had increased his speed. To make more money for *her.*

Mr. Pike walked away. Mitch swiveled toward her, gazing down into her eyes.

"It's been a long time since someone's…" Touched beyond words, she stuttered with her speech and with her breathing. "Can't believe you'd... twenty-two cents... I'll split it with Charlotte and Winnie. It'll buy us half a chicken each plus a lot of soup bones."

"You're welcome," he said softly, blinking those deep black eyes.

And once again, she felt imprisoned. Her pulse pounded and that absurd flash of heat prickled her skin.

The problem was, as Mitch saw it, he loved women.

That generally was where his troubles began. Close to midnight, beneath a quarter moon and walking along the lit boardwalk beside Diana, he contemplated this revelation. An owl hooted from the whispering cedars behind the mercantile, a donkey brayed inside the livery, and a warm, autumn wind stirred the soft hairs along his wrists.

Take for instance the two Symthe sisters back at the factory, he marveled. One was tall and thin, the other short and plump, yet both attractive and buxom. He found that fact interesting. Most men would.

And take for instance the quiet woman walking beside him. Her brothers might lack moral character and maybe she did, too, but Mitch enjoyed the way Diana's blouse gathered into her waistband, accentuating the tug of buttons along her bosom. And let him be the first to admit, he *had* taken a gander at the shapely silhouette of her legs through her thin skirt when she'd bent over the counter at the factory.

Now walking gracefully beside him, she'd removed her bonnet and her kerchief. Her long, brown hair shone in the moon's caress.

Yes, sir, he loved all women. Admitting this weakness helped. At least now, he knew to avoid them if he wanted to keep focused on his work. He'd be done with Diana soon enough, so her temptations would cease altogether.

Relieved that he had it sorted in his head, he drew in a full breath of night air and listened to the comforting buzz of crickets. His leg muscles still pounded from the ache of standing, and his neck felt as tight as a spring. Charlotte and Winnie lived on the other side of the factory next door to each other, and Pike was walking them home.

Mitch had donned his holster and while he and Diana walked, his boots and her shoes tapped in rhythm along the planks. He gripped the empty lunch basket that contained her library book, bonnet and kerchief. After he walked her home, he'd keep walking to the officers' quarters at the fort to catch some sleep.

Although the streets were deserted, saloon music drifted from the alleyway. And at the fort half a mile away, the town social was still kicking strong for he could hear the hum of music coming from that direction, too.

"I'm sorry to hear about your situation," he offered as kindly as he could, thinking about the difficulties that faced her.

Diana scowled, but warm moonlight filtered across her face and softened its edges. "I'd prefer not to stir your pity, or anyone else's."

"Maybe there's something…*someone* can do to help. There's no reason to get upset with me."

"Quite frankly, I think there is." Carrying her soiled apron in one hand, turned inside out so the stains wouldn't dirty her clean clothes, she pressed the apron to her bosom.

Now why did she go and do that? If a woman pressed something to her bosom, how was a man supposed to avoid looking at her breasts? He tugged the brim of his hat lower over his eyes and looked ahead at the closed storefronts. And the clean condition of her clothing was another thing that irked him. He looked as if he'd been rolling in chicken leftovers, while she simply had a few feathers stuck in her hair.

"It was…wonderful what you did in there for me," she continued, stepping to the street and crossing. "Staying to help clean up, and cornering Mr. Pike like that for extra pay, but that's no reason to be condescending. You've been looking at me for the last hour with such sorrow in your eyes that it's impossible to look back at you. Stop it."

"I'm not trying to be condescending. I'm simply stating that I'm terribly sorry about your situation."

She pulled her lips into a thinner line and walked faster.

"How bad is it?"

Her body stiffened. "That's none of your business."

"You must be worried about your brothers and sisters, and what's going to happen to them."

"That's *enough*."

"All right. I won't say another word. But there's nothing to be ashamed of. All kinds of people have all kinds of problems. Most folks are helpful if you give them a chance. You don't have to be embarrassed because you're inflicted with a horrible eye disease."

She slowed down. "Eye disease?"

"How bad is it?"

Her long hair bounced along a curved shoulder blade. "All this time you've been talking about an eye disease?"

He sighed and motioned around the next turn. "If I were you, I might read all the books I could, too. Quite brave of you, frankly. I saw some of those colorful diagrams, and the size of that red bulging eyeball on page one hundred and fifty was enough to silence me. You don't have *that* disease, do you?" He stopped beneath the lamppost, its golden light flickering, then whirled her by a shoulder and peered into her eyes. Bowing his head, he murmured, "I don't see any redness. Yet."

She smiled slightly. "I thought you weren't going to say another word."

"My God, you can even laugh about it. You're made of iron."

"I don't have an eye disease, Mitch."

He pulled away, confused by her statement, but drawn to the way she said his name. "Are you sure?"

"Quite certain."

"Well…that's a relief."

They turned the corner at the café and made their way along one of the town's poorest quarters. The kerosene lampposts ended at the boardwalk and disappeared altogether on her dirt street. Only the moonlight lit their path. Shanties crowded both sides of the narrow ribbon. He knew the homes were filled with railway laborers, cowboys and drifters who needed temporary lodging, or settlers and families who'd lost everything getting to the North-West Territories.

Mitch glanced down at the library book nestled in the basket. "Why the book?"

"I'd like to work for the town's new optometrist. Dr. Emmit York."

"Ah, that explains it. The young Dr. York. I did see a sign in his window yesterday proclaiming he was looking for an assistant."

That fact seemed to annoy her. "Dr. York made that sign only after I approached him three weeks ago, suggesting how a good assistant working in the office might double the sales of his spectacles, leaving him free to make house calls. He said he wanted a full choice of candidates before making a decision. I suspect he'd prefer to hire a man."

"Is he considering you for the position?"

"He interviewed two other people today, both of them men, but I got him to promise he wouldn't choose until he formally interviewed me. My appointment is at eleven tomorrow morning."

"Good for you." She was full of surprises. "Explain something to me, then. If we weren't talking about eye disease, then what did you think I was being condescending about?"

"I thought…you were thinking I needed every penny…"

"Oh," he said softly. He did think that, but he'd never say it aloud. When he had walked into that poultry factory and seen the crowded conditions and the sweat pouring down her back for a few measly pennies, his chest had ached with sympathy. Some people were born lucky and had everything; some people had to work for every penny scrounged.

"Here we are." Diana stopped in front of her home. Gray boards were splintered from the weather. The windows, not quite leveled, undoubtedly let in rain and snow. Her face was strained. "I see a lantern lit in the kitchen. If my brothers were home, there'd be one lit upstairs, too." Then with a nervous nod, she said, "I'll take my things, now, thank you."

"Would you like me to wait while you check if your brothers are there?" Her brothers were damn undependable, he thought with a grimace.

She shook her head vigorously. "If they're not in, the neighbor from across the street, Mrs. Hillyard, will be sitting in the kitchen waiting for me. Her husband works at the factory and she likes to spend time with my younger sisters…and I've got to get up early tomorrow…six-thirty." She trailed off.

Mitch pushed open the rusty front gate, but Diana didn't follow his lead. He hesitated, getting the distinct impression she didn't want him to go farther. Neither of them moved. The gate squeaked beneath his fingers as he let it close again.

Looping her arm through the basket as she tried to take it from him, she accidentally brushed her wrist against his. The warm contact made him shiver. He heard her brisk intake of breath. He didn't know why, but he didn't release the basket.

So there they stood, arms pressed together in the moonlight, her face tilted upward and gilded by the golden light, full lips drawn, eyes sparkling with life.

He felt a ripple of unexpected want.

"Why didn't you go to the social tonight, Mitch?"

"Because you won me in the raffle. I had to go with you."

"I offered to release you."

"I don't like parties."

"But you're so jovial in a crowd, and the way you were twirling the Smythe sisters…"

It's a mask, he thought, that hid his disappointment with life. It hid his sorrow for the loss of his good friend and even his empathy for women like Diana, who had to walk home alone from a chicken factory at midnight on a beautiful Saturday evening when she should be out dancing.

"I don't like parties," he repeated, wondering why he was being open with her. Maybe because she'd exposed her world to him, in an evening that struck him as one of the most memorable he'd had in the past five years.

She didn't move or speak.

He felt a rising tide of need and connection. The moment prolonged. *Walk away,* he ordered himself. He tingled with a growing urge, looking into her deepening gaze, and instead found himself reaching down to touch her silky face.

Chapter Five

The stays on Diana's undergarments felt suddenly constrictive as she fought to catch her breath. Mitch ran his fingers along her cheekbone and the warm graze ignited every pore of her body.

Objections flashed through her mind. But instead of stepping away, she parted her lips. Her eyes riveted to the firm outline of his cheek, caught in the moon's round perimeter and the golden rays behind him that flickered somewhere between the earth and eternity.

"You're softer than you look," he murmured, winding a blazing path along her jaw and chin. His strong fingers coaxed her tilted face upward. Their stance was incredibly intimate.

Heat radiated from his feathery touch, penetrating deeper to her muscles and then her soul.

"And you're bigger up close," she whispered.

Caught with a man alone. At midnight no less, with no chaperone to raise an objection. She wondered if he'd planned this, touching her as if she were his to touch, wondering if this was how he said good-night to all his ladies.

"Good night," she said weakly, trying to step back from the draw of raw masculinity. The brim of his hat shadowed one side of his face, but not enough to obstruct glistening eyes.

With his arm still entwined against hers at the basket handle, he glided forward to match her step, as if they were waltzing beneath the stars.

"I think you'd better—" she gulped "—let go of my basket."

He peered intently. She stared with crazy longing. How might a kiss feel? Mitch's kiss?

His voice dropped to a lulling rasp. "Maybe I like your basket… Maybe I like the curve of your handle… Maybe I like the way your bottom engages my attention."

Her heart drummed with his suggestive words. He was being racy, and she was drunk with his presence. A warm breeze whispered over her face, stirring her skin, arousing the blood that rushed to her lips and throat. The cool iron railing of the gate imbedded in her behind as her skirts rustled against the chain link. "Then I'll have to…slap your hand."

A light flared in his eyes. With a briskness that shocked her, he reached a muscled arm around her waist, brushing against the cloth, causing her flesh beneath to tense. He tugged at the gate's handle behind her.

It likely hadn't budged, for he rattled it again, while she stood encircled and trapped in his embrace.

"To hell with it," he muttered, then swooped down to her face, crushing her mouth with his own.

She gasped. Her first kiss, and he wasn't even her suitor.

"No," she mumbled, tilting her face away.

"Yes," he insisted, running his mouth along her throat, causing her flesh to rise in heated shivers.

The basket barricaded him from pressing closer, or perhaps he didn't want to stain her clothes with his shirt. Either way, she was grateful for the distance between her powerless response and his insistent one.

When his mouth found hers again, Diana succumbed to a torrent of sensation—his warm, seductive lips, one masculine hand moving up along her arm to her shoulder, the other splayed across her ear and entangling itself in her windblown locks.

It was a kiss worthy of every fantasy she had imagined.

Rich, rippling heat intensified between them. Pressed against the railing, she was trapped from running. How many other women had he trapped like this? How many did they number?

She fought from answering her own questions, lost in a maddening crush for air, longing for the protectiveness of his arms, her insides quelled by arousal. She wanted him. The very air seemed to ignite with unbridled passion as she melded her mouth to his and kissed him just as eagerly.

While they kissed, she felt his exploring fingers reaching from around her ear to the back of her neck beneath her hair, stroking the hollow curve with such intimacy that her limbs were infused with a heavy rush of blood. Her breasts tingled beneath the seam line of her blouse, her thighs weakened.

Gripping the basket handle with both hands, she felt her heart thumping, pounding madly, leaping with excitement.

She felt the quiver surging through his lips, too, sending tremors through them both.

Her muscles felt heavy, yet her breath fluttered in her ears. She never would have thought that such a brute man could have such velvety, pliable lips.

And then he did the most incredible thing. He parted his mouth and hers naturally followed, then he brought his tongue out to gently run it along the seam of her bottom lip.

She gasped, never suspecting her body could come to life beneath a master's hand.

Were all his women this eager and excited? Was Allison Oxford?

Diana broke free, lowering her head as he, in surprise, brushed his lips against her nose before pulling back an inch to catch some air.

"That's enough," she said so quietly her breath strummed. "That's enough. I—I won't be one of your women."

As if he was only now reeling to his senses, he rubbed the back of his hand against his swollen lips, heaving as he watched her.

After these painful last five years, she'd come to the realization that sooner or later, everyone she'd been blind enough to trust had wanted something from her. From the servants who had taken whatever they could carry even before her parents were six feet underground—silver candlesticks and golden brooches and imported leather belts—to her uncle Desmond, only relative and executor of the estate, who'd said selling their home was the only way to support her and her brothers and sisters, but who in the end had absconded with their fortune to Africa.

It had been her fault. As the eldest and the one in charge, she'd been so stupid she'd allowed them to steal everything her brothers and sisters should have had. They should be sleeping on spring mattresses tonight instead of straw.

Diana rubbed her moist palm along her waist. "What is it that you want from me?"

His sharp eyes flickered in the moonlight. "Nothing," he whispered.

"Everyone always wants something. What is it that *you* value? Certainly not my money. A turn in the hay? The twelfth kiss from the twelfth woman this week?"

His mouth twisted. "I want nothing from you."

She trembled in her shoes. "Then it's nothing you shall have." With arteries pounding, she thrust the basket into his gut, causing him to stumble backward. Then in a whirl of faded cotton that slapped against her ankles, she spun around, unhitched the gate with shaking fingers, and flew down the darkened path toward her battered kitchen door.

The kiss had been sensational.

But why on earth Mitch had kissed her in the first place was still a mystery to him.

Sliding his fingers into his pockets and clenching his shoulders to protect against the cooling wind, he watched Diana flee into the house. Within a minute, he saw a candle flickering through the side window. Listening for deep male voices, he heard none. So her brothers weren't with her. When Mitch heard the door open again and another woman speaking softly, he knew that the neighbor had sat with the children.

Diana was safe and it was time for him to leave. He walked away, ensuring that Mrs. Hillyard crossed the street and entered her home securely. Waiting on their porch, her husband had noticed her, too, and met her halfway.

Pivoting on his large boots, Mitch turned the corner and made his way along Macleod Trail toward the fort. Three men exited the main saloon, jumping on their horses and shouting goodbye to each other. Their voices and the sounds of the tinkling piano carried down the lonely street.

What was it about Diana Campbell, thought Mitch, adjusting his hat and pushing forward, that sent his stomach into spirals? Maybe her detached mannerism. Unlike plenty of other women, Diana had barely glanced up from her book or her work to acknowledge him. Not that he sought or particularly cared for attention, but he found it less threatening, less prickly, to enjoy the friendships of many women than only one. She was the singular woman at the factory who refused to return his smile.

Since coming home, he'd given Allison a light kiss on the cheek, a brush on the lips, but no kiss had ever been as thunderous as what he'd experienced with Diana.

She'd put more feeling and sensuality into the touch. She was clenching her basket the whole time, not even running her hands along his body, and he wondered how it might have felt if they'd been freer to press together. He'd sensed the slight hesitation in her lips and her body at the beginning of the kiss, but her hesitation had only fueled him.

He wondered where Diana had learned to kiss like that. Had someone taught her in the city?

Why wasn't she married? Mitch hadn't learned much about the Campbell past, other than what her brothers had told him. Their parents had died in a stagecoach accident, Diana cared for the family, and they'd been in town a month. They'd moved here to sample the freedom, her brothers had said. Diana had seen a poster put out by the Canadian national railroad, showcasing the expansion of the West and opportunities available. As a family, they'd voted to come.

Their father had been an important editor. Too bad,

thought Mitch, that he hadn't thought of looking after his children if tragedy struck, as, unfortunately, it had.

Maybe Mitch's powerful response to Diana's kiss was because he hadn't been kissed with such explosive feeling in well over a year. That's what was missing in his relationship with Allison, and no amount of reasoning or discussion between them could bring it back. And he knew *that* discussion would be coming tomorrow evening.

He shouldn't be kissing Diana when he hadn't yet backed away from Allison. He knew that. He believed that. And yet, he hadn't been able to stop himself from reaching out to her tonight.

He kicked at a stone. It bounced down the boardwalk. He ran down the steps and dashed across the street. It got darker as he left the town limits. He reached the steel bridge, within sight of the massive palisade gates of the fort.

The whole damn reason he was breaking up with Allison was because he wasn't ready to entertain thoughts of settling down.

Diana's brothers were headed for serious trouble. She wasn't willing to see that, let alone stop it from happening. Tonight at the factory, Mitch had seen Diana's strength of character shine through what at first glance appeared to be weakness, so he suspected there was more to her than her troublesome brothers. But she had a ready-built family to provide for.

What man could easily take that burden upon himself?

Certainly not Mitch. Certainly not when he was trying to prove himself as a devoted officer of the North-West Mounted Police. He'd only been in town for a short while and he had no intention of sliding back into his former bad behavior, repeating the mistakes he'd made with women in his past. Sooner or later, they always assumed he wanted a permanent relationship, marriage even, when in the end all he really cared for was the courting.

Diana awoke to the sound of a fist pounding on the front door.

A male voice boomed through the solid pine. "Is anyone awake in there?"

Groggy but startled, she shot up to a sitting position on the old sofa. Cool air blasted her face. Loose hair tickled her neck, weaving soft strands around her long, unbuttoned nightshift. A crack of light filtered through the window curtains. Upstairs, the younger children occupied the two bedrooms, divided between girls and boys, but Diana had more privacy and less constraint upon rising early if she slept permanently in the cramped parlor. But who, in heaven's name, was knocking on their door?

"Is anyone in there?" When the man called again, Diana realized with a jolt that it was Mitch.

Mumbling beneath her breath, she looked at the clock on the knickknack table. It sat amongst two porcelain cups from England, the only decorative things in the house. Seven o'clock. She'd slept in thirty minutes later than she'd intended. The house was quiet. Had the older boys come home last night? She looked to the front door and saw their boots. Yes, they had.

What did Mitch want?

At the memory of his kiss last night, her cheeks flared. It had been an incredible moment.

But why did her first kiss have to be with him? He hadn't even sought her permission, but had simply planted his lips on hers. How bold to think she'd allow it. She *had* allowed it, she realized with a fluster, and had even enjoyed—*adored*—it, but that wasn't the point.

After the kiss, her thoughts were too muddled to tell him he need not appear this morning. True, she had his services till two-fifteen today, but frankly he was too much of a distraction and she had serious matters to accomplish. And land's sake, she was in her nightclothes. He couldn't expect her to come trouncing out like some tart! What sort of women did he normally court?

If she refused to budge, he might suspect she'd gone to the Saturday-morning market. If she never answered the door, then he'd go away.

He continued pounding.

She continued sitting.

He banged with the rusty knocker.

She examined her nails.

His body flashed across the narrow side window. Thoroughly embarrassed by his proximity through the curtains, Diana brought the sheet to her mouth and yelped. He froze for a moment, perhaps listening. She froze, as well, although she swore he could hear her heart beating.

She reminded herself there were no lanterns lit inside and therefore he couldn't see her. But she saw *his* clean-shaven face distinctly. She clamped a hand around her mouth.

"Diana! I brought you something!"

He'd brought her something? What on earth for?

Well, she wasn't biting. He could leave. All she had to do was pretend she wasn't in. As long as none of the children arose, she'd be fine. It was curious that his knocking hadn't awoken the younger ones. Her adolescent brothers loved to sleep late and no amount of pounding would rouse them, but when they all did come racing down the stairs, she'd tell them to be quiet till the inspector left.

It seemed he wouldn't leave easily for he continued calling. Exasperated, she rose to begin her chores. For all she cared, he could stand outside till the neighbor's chickens laid a golden egg.

Last night, she'd prepared her clothes for her interview, but first she had to treat her hair. Slipping into her only shoes, she thumped along the planks to the kitchen and threw another log into the cast-iron stove. She washed her face and teeth, applied her tonics, then added water to the bowl of hair powder that Winnie had given her for the special occasion. A strong smell drifted up from the mixture. Diana draped an old towel around her neck in case things got sticky.

"Open up, Diana! I think you'll like what I brought!"

Lord, he was still there. Was he sitting around the log table outside, waiting for her? What would the neighbors think, a man hollering at her through her door? Didn't he have any sense? And what could he possibly have brought that he thought she'd like? A new wardrobe? A set of matching china?

Perhaps he'd brought her something intimate…silk stockings…or a silver compact of rouge for her lips… Those thoughts brought another rise of heat to her cheeks. How totally improper of her to think it. But it was in keeping with her fantasy of being swept off her feet.

Looking into the scratched mirror resting on the kitchen wall above the counter, Diana used a flat stick to apply the paste to her dark hair. She was already running late and needed to scramble.

"It looks like you're not going to open! Are you still sleeping or ignoring me?"

She cringed, feeling a trifle guilty. But not guilty enough to open the door.

"Then I guess I'd better leave!"

"Yes," she whispered softly so he couldn't hear, "why don't you?"

"I'll leave my gift behind."

"I really wish you wouldn't," she muttered. That would mean she'd have to seek him out to thank him, and fuss over what he'd brought, and pretend that yes, she really did appreciate the hand-me-down broom, or the cotton rags he figured she could use for scrubbing her floors.

When Diana heard stifled giggles coming through the outside door, her heart bolted. Those were children's voices outside!

Oh, no!

But it was too late. She leaped toward the door to check the dead bolt, but the door creaked and little Elizabeth and Margaret, dressed in sloppy play clothes, pushed it open. Pointing a finger at her, they proclaimed to one startled Mountie, "There's our sister! We told you she'd be awake!"

Diana withered. Paste was glued to her hair and face.

Mitch, dressed in a clean white shirt and tight black breeches, so crisp and fresh and…and presentable…stared at her as if she were a creature in a zoo.

Her cheeks flooded with humiliation as his eyes flickered up and down her flimsy shift. Thank the blessed stars her towel was long enough to conceal the outline of her breasts.

He pushed his black leather hat above his forehead. "What on earth is that god-awful stench?"

"It's the henna in her hair," reported the youngest girl. "Miss Winnie warned us it would smell bad."

Diana found her voice. "Elizabeth, that's enough."

Mitch squinted. "And that jelly on your cheeks and nose?"

"Miss Charlotte told her it would even out her freckles," explained the other scalawag.

"Margaret, don't talk about me to strangers."

"Ah," he said with dawning comprehension. "Your interview with Dr. York today. You're trying to look your best."

Diana narrowed her eyes at him.

His mouth turned upward into a slight grin. "Why didn't you open the door when I called?"

She paused. "Perhaps—perhaps I didn't hear you. Did you—did you try knocking?"

The young girls lost their interest and raced from view, shouting at their middle brother. Were all the children up and running? Sometimes when Diana fell into a deep sleep, they sneaked past her and played in the yard till she arose. Their timing this morning, however, was terrible.

Mitch took a step closer, his bulky shoulders looming above her as he leaned against the door frame.

"You're not allowed inside!" yelled Elizabeth from somewhere in the yard.

Mitch jumped back in alarm, falling back onto the front stoop. "I know, I know. You told me enough times. But you never told me why." He turned to Diana for an explanation.

"It's a family secret." She gripped the ends of her towel and tried to close the door. Her pasted hair moved in one united mass, jiggling on top of her head.

He shoved a big boot into the door space, blocking her ability to close it. "I think you did hear me calling. I think you heard me fine. Why were you afraid to open the door?"

"What a ridiculous assumption."

"You must have heard me. I saw a puff of smoke coming from the chimney when you put on another log. That means you were three feet away when I called."

"That doesn't prove anything!"

"Won't answer, huh? Then I'll tell you why."

She huffed and tried to slam the door again, although he wouldn't allow it. The fact that he was using only one powerful hand to hold the door while she heaved with both, vexed her beyond belief. "I'm busy, if you please!"

"You were afraid to answer the door," he argued on the other side of the splintered pine, "because you're scared out of your wits at how you felt when I kissed you."

She sputtered. "You're audacious!"

The movements on the other side of the door ceased. "And you're fussy and difficult to please."

She gasped. The gall.

"Get your behind out here," he grumbled. "Your two oldest brothers are still in bed, I'm told, but the other four can't wait much longer. The gift's for all of you and you won't want to disappoint them. Now, hurry up!"

Chapter Six

Kneeling in the dry grass twenty minutes later, peering at the upside-down unicycle and swarmed by four youngsters, Mitch tried to get the lovely image of Diana in her nightshift out of his mind. He knew it was illogical to feel as strongly as he did about her. The reason—the only reason—he was intrigued by her, somehow confusing his anger with tugs of yearning was because no other woman in town had ever ignored his knock!

To leave him standing here in the yard, in front of pint-size witnesses, would be humiliating for any man. Had his kiss been that awful?

Or that good?

He didn't know what had possessed him to bring a little gift…a good-morning hello. He'd awoken in his quarters with the sunrise streaming in, the bugle tapping reveille, and he couldn't help if he was in a good mood. Brighter than he'd been for many months.

"Can you fix the wheel?" Slender, nine-year-old Robert peered around Mitch's broad back with his eight-year-old sister, Gena. The two younger girls ran by in the trampled grass. He'd gotten to know their names while waiting for Diana to open the door.

"I think so," said Mitch, eliciting a smile from the boy. Earlier, Mitch had tossed aside his cowboy hat and now the morning sun warmed his hair. On the backyard hill in the distance, two empty clotheslines swung in the breeze. "There's nothing actually wrong with the iron wheel. The seat was collapsed. I pulled it up and tightened the screw underneath. There are three spokes missing, but the rusty wheel just needs a dab of oil. That'll get rid of the squeal and make it run smoother."

"Do you have any oil on ya?" asked Robert.

"Well, no…" What household didn't have oil? It cost next to nothing and was a household staple, in Mitch's opinion, for upkeep and maintenance. "I'll try to get some to you later."

"Is this your gift?" asked Diana in a friendly tone behind them. "To fix the unicycle?"

Startled, Mitch dropped his wrench. He jumped to his feet and turned around.

"No," shouted Gena, pointing farther into the yard to the food basket wrapped in the red cloth that Mitch had placed on the log table. "He's brought us something from the bakery."

While Diana swiveled to look at the table, Mitch swiveled to look at her.

He sucked in his breath. She was wearing pants.

He gaped at her figure.

Pants!

He'd never seen a woman in pants and the sight knocked him speechless. They were blue, faded denims, tight as skin around the waist, looped with an oversize, thick black belt. The denims were loose around her hips and thighs, tapering down the knees to her black shoes.

The vision was shocking. Sensual. Blatantly accentuating all parts female.

God, he loved those pants.

His gaze rose above her waist to the brown checkered flannel shirt that draped too far over her shoulders but clung to her ample chest. It struck him that she was wearing someone's hand-me-downs, but the oversize items accentuated rather than concealed her femininity.

She'd washed the dung from her black hair, left it long and loose and wet over her shoulders. The jelly was gone from her cheeks, leaving a healthy sheen of pink skin. Her warm, green eyes roamed over the baked goods he'd brought. The baker had tied a red tablecloth over the basket. Mitch promised to return the basket and cloth later in the day.

He nodded to the children and they unfolded the cloth to reveal fresh scones, butter and jam.

"Oh," Diana whispered, gazing at the sight. She turned toward Mitch. "How lovely." She stepped closer to the table, inhaled deeply and smiled. "It smells like heaven."

Mitch smiled back as he watched the children tear through the basket, eagerly setting out the butter knife and napkins. He was unexpectedly proud that he could provide for them.

"Slow down," said Diana. "Take it with ease. There's a napkin here for each of you. Pull one out. Here, I'll help you cut the scone, Elizabeth, and then you can add some butter and blueberry jam."

Giggling with delight, Diana helped them with the jam, then straightened, licking her fingers, beaming at Mitch. "This was very generous. Thank you."

"Why don't you have some?"

She hesitated. "I'll wait for the older boys. They're always so hungry, there never seems to be…"

"Have a bite of mine," said Elizabeth, leaning forward. Diana bent at the waist, hair swinging, pants swishing, figure mesmerizing, and bit.

"Hmm," she said, closing her eyes.

It was the best compliment Mitch had ever received. She licked her fingers again, and watching her, he pulled in a staggering breath.

"How long do we get ya as a prize?" Robert asked between bites.

"Robert," said Diana. "Be polite. He's not your prize, he's mine."

"But look," said Elizabeth, shoving her dirty porcelain doll in the air. "He fixed my baby's head. It fell off again."

Margaret held out her boot from beneath the table. "And he restrung my laces."

Diana frowned. She looked to Mitch with curiosity.

"There wasn't much to do while I waited for you to decide whether you were going to open the door or not."

Her cheeks tingled at the truth. "But didn't you tell them there was no transfer of prizes?"

"I did indeed. More than once. But then Robert asked if that sign the commander had painted said anything specifically about no transfer of prizes to children." Mitch shrugged his shoulders with amusement. "Couldn't say there was."

Diana's eyes twinkled. "Robert is definitely one to watch. He can smooth-talk anyone out of anything."

"He's smart. A natural-born lawyer."

The comment made her face flicker with sadness. She couldn't afford new shoes, thought Mitch, let alone sending her brother to law school.

"Why did you come by this morning?"

The woman was more direct than any other woman

he'd ever met. Save for his grandmother, but she had been a thousand years old.

He hooked his thumb into his waistband. He'd needed to remove his holsters while fixing the unicycle, and his guns were resting high in the aspen, beyond the reach of tiny hands. "The commander's wife, Mrs. Ridgeway, found me at the fort this morning. She asked how it went with you yesterday and what I was going to do for you today."

"So to save face, you came by to fulfill your obligations."

He walked to the aspen and slung his holsters back on his hips. She followed him. "I came by because I'm a man of my word. Now what can I do for you this morning?"

She peered at the shack, back to the children who were finishing up at the table, then back to the shack.

"The front step is broken. Are you good with a hammer?"

"I am, if you've got one."

She cocked her head, wet hair bouncing around her shoulders. "Well, now, what household doesn't own a hammer?"

He shrugged, running a hand along the side of his bare head. The same household that didn't have oil.

"And the chimney clogged up twice this week." Cupping a hand over her eyes to shield them from the sun's glare, she stretched on tiptoe to peer at the roof. "I think there's an old nest or something in it."

"Have you got a ladder?" *What household didn't own a ladder?* he thought.

"Of course not. Where would I keep a ladder?"

He blinked.

"But the neighbors do." She nodded to the shanty beyond the aspen and past the clotheslines. "They're very nice folks and won't mind if we borrow theirs. I'll send the children."

"Anything else?"

She stared past his shoulders. He turned to see what she was staring at. The privy.

"Ah, the privy," he said. "Let me guess. It's time for lye?"

"If you don't mind."

"Shall I borrow the lye from the neighbors, too?"

"Don't be silly. What household doesn't have lye?"

Frustrated, he planted his boots into the ground.

"But the neighbors across the road borrowed the container last week. You'll need to get it back from them."

This was getting more complicated than necessary. "I feel like I should be taking notes."

A smile eased from her lips. "I'll get the hammer."

She went into the house. He followed her to the front stoop to examine the crooked tread. As he leaned over it, the door suddenly opened, she screeched and then tumbled over him.

They both fell backward into the soft grass.

"Sorry," he said, jumping to his feet and extending a hand. "I should have warned you I was there."

She grasped his hand and rolled to her knees, a bundle of checkered brown cloth and blue denim. "My apologies, I didn't see you."

He tugged her to her feet, liking the feel of her weight balancing in his hand and her smooth fingers clasped in his.

"That was clumsy of me." She swayed in his grasp, entrancing him. Then she dusted off her pants, working from the thighs down, bringing his attention back to her womanly form.

God, he loved those pants.

"I'll help the children clean the table. I'll send the two older ones for the ladder, then I've got to go inside and do a bit of reading before my interview. If you don't mind, I'll leave you to your work."

"Not a problem. I'll get started." Lifting the hammer, he peered up at the cabin's second story. "Will I wake your brothers if I start hammering?"

"Don't worry about them. It's time they got up anyway." With a whirl, she dodged by him and his hammer, scooting toward the table, wiping the jam stains off the girls' faces and declaring they'd better leave some scones for their older brothers.

Mitch bent down to the grass, reaching for the weathered boards, but unable to take his eyes off Diana. He had only one thing on his mind.

How much he loved those pants.

Diana wondered if Mitchell would notice her changed appearance when she stepped out the door. Humming to herself, she took one long, last look in the kitchen mirror. It was ten o'clock. She'd pulled her hair up for the interview, twirled it around the back and pinned it. And then she'd reached into the heirloom cedar chest and removed the box containing her mother's silver earbobs. She turned her head and they glistened from her ears in the reflection.

For the first time in a long while, she had a couple of precious hours to indulge herself, and she had Mitch to thank. She heard him clanging outdoors while she washed up, ironed her best clothes, brushed her hair and trimmed her nails.

More than once, she'd heard one of the youngsters turn the outer door handle, only to be stopped by Mitch who'd holler, "Don't bother your sister with that. She's getting ready for her appointment. Come here and I'll help you."

Each time, it caused Diana to stop whatever she was doing and listen to the resulting silence. She felt as if she and Mitch were somehow partners this morning, balancing the children between them. And he'd unknowingly made the fantasy she'd explained to Winnie and Charlotte yesterday at the fair—three minutes of time to herself—come true.

Upstairs, Wayde and Tom could be heard rolling out of bed. She wondered where they'd been last night. They seemed to be coming home later and later and it troubled her. But she also recognized that their responsibilities weren't easy. They'd be putting in their shift at the livery stable later this afternoon from one to six.

Diana hollered up the stairs. "Time to get up, fellas! I need to leave in thirty minutes!"

"We're comin'!"

With a final pat to her worn gray skirt, Diana took a deep breath and opened the door. She stepped out into warm sunshine, enjoying the tingling on her cheeks. There was no one in sight.

Then she saw her troop coming across the neighbor's yard, following Mitch as if he were the pied piper. They must have just returned the ladder. The two black mutts from next door were chasing them. Mitch, especially, seemed to be taken by the dogs. He patted one while tossing a stick for the other to fetch.

He swooped down to Elizabeth's level and laughed at something she said, then looked up and spotted Diana.

She sensed his demeanor shift. The way he undid the top button of his collar, maybe. The way his dark eyebrows drew together. The way his eyes roved her body as if he were hungry.

When they reached her, the children tore off for the old swing in the aspen tree, but Mitch studied her bare neck. She felt the burning sting of male curiosity.

"You fixed your hair."

"Um-hmm."

"And you changed your clothes."

"Um-hmm."

"Well," he said, with lips twitching, "I think you're going to get that job."

"I do hope you're right." The twinkle in his eye caused her palms to sweat and trapped the air in her rib cage.

Changing the subject, she turned to peer at the yard. Everything was in its place. "How did you get the children to put away their things?"

"I threatened them with jail."

"You didn't."

"I did."

"We knew he was kiddin', though," called Robert from behind the swing, where he was pushing Margaret. "No one can put a kid in jail. How old do you gotta be to go to jail, Mitch?"

"It depends on the crime. Around these parts, as early as sixteen."

Tom's age.

Mitch's eyes flickered in her direction.

Diana felt a slight tremor of warning. She was reminded again of her very different, very unfriendly conversation here on the stoop the day before yesterday with this same demanding man.

He was a stranger. She hadn't *invited* him today, she'd won him. He was police. Hesitating, she took a step back. He frowned at her response.

They were interrupted by the sound of deep voices. Wayde and Tom rumbled out the door. They'd combed their hair but hadn't tucked in their shirts.

She suspected her brothers wouldn't appreciate the sight of a police officer. She couldn't blame them.

Yesterday, Wayde had said he'd found the railway tickets outdoors and there was no harm in reselling something he'd found. Diana hadn't argued with him in front of Mitch, but as soon as he'd left she'd given her brothers a tongue-lashing. She had agreed with the police—Wayde and Tom should have returned the tickets to the ticket counter so the person who'd lost them could reclaim them. But threatening to throw them into the jailhouse was an entire other matter, and she sided with her brothers.

"Good morning," said Diana. Her words were softly spoken, but her posture stiffened in defense.

"Mornin'," they hollered.

Wayde, the eldest of the two and honest-to-God crankiest in the family, glared from the youngsters, who were out of earshot playing around the tree, to Mitch. "What's he doin' here?"

Diana bustled around them. "Don't you remember? I told you yesterday. I won him at the raffle and he's come to help around the house this morning."

Wayde was not impressed. "Don't you think, sister, that you might ask us what we thought before you invited him *here?*"

"I—I should have asked." The family had an agreement about strangers, and she should have at least warned them of the possibility that Mitch might appear.

Her brothers were growing up so fast. Sometimes when she looked at Wayde, she forgot she was more than five years older and noticed only that he was already broader and taller than her father had been. Who was she to boss her brothers around? They helped her in every way they could.

Mitch sauntered to the table and picked up his hat. Fingering the brim, he gestured to the baker's basket. "Scones and jam," he offered her brothers. "Your brother and sisters have already eaten. Help yourselves."

Her brothers looked slowly at each other, then Diana. They were hungry. She could see it in their eyes. Maybe befriending the man would be a better tactic than offending him. She nodded silently, and they approached the table.

Lifting the tablecloth, Tom glanced up at Mitch. "Thanks," he muttered.

"Is this the only reason you're here?" asked Wayde, more cautious. "To help my sister?"

Mitch nodded, pressing his hat to his head. He was a giant when he wore his hat, thought Diana. An obnoxious giant yesterday, but a more humble one today.

Diana leaned over Wayde at the table as he lifted a scone. Passing the butter tray, she whispered to his ear. "What time did you get in last night?"

"Don't know for sure. Didn't want to come over to look at your clock in case we woke you up."

"I was up till one and you still weren't home. Where were you?"

"With some friends from the livery. One of them lives in Cedarville."

Mitch drew himself toward the cottonwood beside the table. "There was a bank robbery in Cedarville last night. Did you boys hear about it?"

Diana's hand on the knife drifted to the table. She felt herself turn pale.

"Which of the two banks? The Imperial Bank or the First National?"

"The Imperial."

"Nope," said Wayde, chewing.

"Nope," added Tom.

But the young men looked at each other with a looming expression of guilt. Diana's heart trembled.

While they continued eating, she wove to Mitch's side and tried to keep her voice low, but couldn't keep her anger from rising. Mitch had come here this morning to question her brothers, and for no other reason. "That's why you've come. To loosen their tongues. You're the same as everyone else I've met in my life."

She'd misread everything they'd enjoyed this morning, the laughter and the teasing. Even the gift of scones.

Mitch remained calm, studying her face. "You can't avoid these questions. If not me, then some other Mountie will come calling."

"Why them? Why my brothers?"

"They were spotted at Coyote Corner at one-thirty last night, riding like they had a ghost on their tails. I find it interesting they were in Cedarville last night. The commander does, too."

"I suppose...I suppose you checked the yard to see where they might have hid the money."

"It's obvious it's not in your yard."

"Maybe it's in the house. Maybe that's why you wanted in."

He rubbed his tight jaw.

Diana scoffed at his gall. Staring at him, she couldn't believe he was standing on her property without giving a fair warning of why he'd come. "You pretended to care about fixing broken dolls and lacing shoes. You didn't mean any bit of that. And you wanted me to wake up and get out of the house only so my brothers would follow."

She wouldn't accept it like a fool this time. No one

would dare walk inside her home and tear apart her life again. She'd never allow it.

"I've got a job to do." Mitch crossed his arms. "I'm not accusing your brothers."

"Look at them. They barely shave. I admit they may have a problem with cards, but they'd never *ever* rob a bank."

Mitch grumbled and went back to the table. "Wayde, you're the oldest so you tell me. You were both seen galloping past Coyote Corner last night at breakneck speed."

"So? We like ridin' fast."

"Give me the names of the people you were visiting."

Tom gave his brother a harrowing look. Wayde answered coolly. "They were casual friends from the livery. Cowpokes we'd met who were driving a herd in from Texas."

"Give me names. I'd like to talk to them."

Wayde grew cagey. "Don't recall specific names. Only nicknames... Let's see... There's Slim. There's Cutter. There's Rider. You can't talk to 'em anyway. They left town this morning drivin' another herd, this one headin' west."

Mitch sighed. "That would be the herd headed for the Russell ranch at the base of the Rockies?"

"Yes, sir."

Tom slanted a look at his brother. Diana knew that look usually meant trouble. She pushed forward. "Officer Reid, tell us about the bank robbers."

Three pairs of eyes settled warily on Mitch.

"They've struck three times in the last three weeks, all within a fifty-mile radius of town. Apparently, there are two of them. No one's ever seen them up close, but by their voices, they're described as youthful. From a distance, they were seen wearing dark hats and clothes, similar to the ones you're wearing. They've got a sense of humor, it seems."

"How so?" asked Diana.

"They never try to hurt anyone. They slide in from the back room and catch the tellers off guard. From their muffled voices, they likely wear bandanas. They're being called the Backdoor Bandits. Every time they steal, they leave a calling card."

"A calling card?"

"A poker card. Always a diamond. On their first robbery, they left an ace. On their second, the two of diamonds. Their third, the three."

Wayde and Tom smirked. Diana could have kicked them. The way these two played cards nonstop, if they ever did rob a bank, they would be daft enough to leave one behind.

"We didn't do it," said Wayde, gulping the last scone, pushing up from the table. "But thanks for breakfast."

Diana watched her brothers walk away toward the other children. They swaggered with foolish pride. Didn't they notice the look of grit and determination chiseled into Mitch's face as he watched them? It made her stomach roll.

"I've got to go to my appointment," she hollered to her family, anxious to end the conversation and be rid of Mitch. If he had any proof that her brothers had committed the crime, he would have said so. Powerfully relieved, she opened her arms for her youngest sisters to come running. They kissed goodbye, then Diana lifted her drawstring purse from the front stoop where she'd left it and hurried around the corner.

She dared a glance at Mitchell, who was following with the empty basket and red cloth. "Goodbye, Officer. This is it. By the time I finish my appointment and get lunch ready for the children, it'll be two-fifteen. So we'll say goodbye now. Thank you for your troubles."

"Wait up," he said, catching up quickly with his long strides. "I'm walking to the bakery anyway to return this basket, and thought I might put in a good word for you with the optometrist."

"You know Dr. York?"

"Not that well, since he moved into town while I was in Regina, but we spoke last week when I was making my rounds."

She didn't need his help. "No, thank you, I'll do this on my own."

"How could a recommendation from a Mountie hurt?"

Her shoulders wound with tension. "Because I'm not sure if you're friend or foe."

His stance softened. "Did it ever occur to you that a policeman might be trying to help by questioning your brothers?"

"How on earth could you be helping?"

His dark eyes shimmered. "Maybe I don't think they're capable of bank robbery any more than you do."

"Oh," she countered, softly, completely taken by surprise.

"I'm not your enemy, Diana."

She watched the way his mouth turned up softly, wondering if she could believe him, wondering what it would take for him to prove those words.

Chapter Seven

Touching her felt somehow natural. With Mitch's broad hand lightly pressing Diana's shoulder blade, he steered her through the noisy Saturday-morning crowd to land her in front of the optometrist's office. Mitch liked the warm feel of her beneath his fingers. A slight expression of alarm crossed her face. He wondered if it was due to his grip, or her nervousness about the interview. He dropped his hand.

They'd already dropped off the baker's basket. Mitch was hers till two-fifteen; he felt obligated to complete his duty. After that, he'd get back to his own serious work.

Diana ran a jittery hand over her waistband. "Here we are."

Around them, a mixture of sounds filled the Calgary streets—vendors selling sacks of apples at the corner, another one selling jars of preserves, horses pulling wagons laden with barrels of beer, cowbells clanging in distant fields.

"Don't be nervous, you'll do fine."

"All of sudden, I don't feel properly dressed. I wish I'd borrowed some clothes from Charlotte. This skirt's so old—"

"He won't be hiring you for your clothes, Diana, but you do look charming just the way you are. He'll be hiring you for your friendly approach and your ability to set customers at ease. That seems to come natural to you."

He'd never accompanied a woman on a job opportunity before and it felt odd. He was reminded of how she looked in the factory with sweat staining the back of her blouse. He hoped for her sake she'd get the new position today.

She ran her hand along her neck, earbobs jangling. "You're right. I should concentrate on my abilities rather than my shortcomings."

The door creaked as they entered the office. They squeezed past half a dozen milling people, most of them men. The air smelled like heavy varnish. Mitch was distracted by the curious sight of dozens of eyeglasses displayed on a wooden peg board near the door. A glass counter at the back of the store contained wooden contraptions labeled microscopes, telescopes, then looking glasses and kaleidoscopes. Several charts on the wall contained rows of alphabet letters in descending size. He wondered why those were necessary.

Dr. York, a cheerful man in his late thirties, was speaking with an elderly lady customer near the back till. Mitch recognized her as Mrs. Beazly and nodded hello. Thin sandy hair brushed the collar of Dr. York's starched white shirt. A satin vest covered his slight torso. He looked up and nodded to Diana, then Mitch.

"I'll be right with you." Dr. York adjusted the gold spectacles on his nose. "I don't know when it got so busy."

"Take your time, sir," Diana responded.

But after ten minutes of waiting, Mitch grew impatient.

"Feel free to leave any time," said Diana, obviously trying to get rid of him.

"It's all right, I'll wait." He wasn't expected back at the fort for another three and a half hours. He'd see this mission through to the end.

Mrs. Beazly, standing at the till, was holding up everyone else. She couldn't seem to decide on a pair of spectacles. As she twirled around, testing several in the mirror in front of her, the large burgundy feather that was stuck in her burgundy hat plucked at the air.

Dr. York took that moment to slide over to Diana and Mitch. "I'm afraid you're a bit late for the job, Miss Campbell. I've all but decided on one of the men I interviewed yesterday."

Diana groaned softly. "But Dr. York, we had an appointment set for eleven."

"Yes, I know, but as you can see I'm very busy. I thought we might save ourselves some time."

"I'll wait. I'll wait here till you're finished. There's no need to rush. Take your time with each customer."

Mitch's first instinct was to tell the man to shove off for wasting Diana's time, for dragging her here and telling her at the last minute he didn't need her. Didn't the man realize how much she'd done to prepare for this meeting?

But Mitch stepped forward with enthusiasm. "Dr. York, it's good to see you again. As a police officer, and with all my years of living here, I accompanied Miss Campbell to give her my highest recommendation. As I understand, she's the one who inspired you to put that Help Wanted sign in your window."

Before Dr. York could respond, another customer entered through the creaking door. Instead of making the man happy, the full office seemed to upset him. And the customer sniffed the air, obviously affected by the unpleasant scent of varnish. The shiny floors looked as if they'd been recently coated.

Mrs. Beazly at the till turned to look for the optometrist. She spotted Diana. "My dear," she called, "would you have a moment, please?"

Diana scrambled to her side. Mitch walked to the peg board to look and wait.

"You're the only other woman in here," Mrs. Beazly said to Diana. "I came for reading glasses. Which do you think look more stylish?"

"Why, you're that lovely lady, Mrs. Beazly," said Diana. "Your husband owns the trinket store."

The woman smiled sadly. "I help him sometimes."

To others, Mrs. Beazly's distress might not have been noticeable, but Mitch knew she'd received bad news yesterday concerning her husband's behavior. Mitch felt for the poor woman. And he was ticked at the person, Quinn Turner, who'd told the elderly Mrs. Beazly that her husband was being seen around town with young widow Foster. Everyone knew—the men, anyway—that Mr. Beazly was having an affair with the widow, but it wasn't Quinn's place to tell Mrs. Beazly.

"Take these," said Diana, pointing to the silver set with the single, ornate silver handle. "Just this week I was reading the *London Times* in our library, and these are what the European ladies are wearing. Lorgnettes. Very smart. And since you only need to use them occasionally for reading, you can just hold them to your face with the handle."

"Thank you, dear."

Mitch watched with growing satisfaction. Dr. York kept an eye on the exchange as he helped another customer.

When Diana finished with Mrs. Beazly, she came forward with another suggestion for Dr. York. "Would you like me to take a sheet of paper and write down the names of the customers in the order they entered?"

"What do you mean?"

"No customer likes to wait too long," she whispered. "There's a café next door. If we created a list in the order the customers arrived, it would allow them to go next door for a spell to wait. Or perhaps run another errand."

"Yes, please." Dr. York peered at her with a fresh interest.

For some reason, his eager look reminded Mitch that the man was single. It was a strange thing to come into his mind.

But he was quickly distracted by helping Diana. They wrote the customers' names and promised to keep their place in line when they returned. The new system received calls of approval.

Twenty minutes later the store had cleared and Dr. York called to Diana. "It's usually quiet around this time. Lunchtime. Let's take five minutes to talk. There are some questions I'd like to ask pertaining to your background. We'll go in the back office and leave the door open. We'll hear when the next customer returns. There are three left on the list."

"I'll wait here and direct them," offered Mitch. "So they don't leave again."

While he waited in the empty store, he heard snatches of their conversation.

Diana answered precisely. "…studied several textbooks on eye disease…. Corneal abrasions are painful…. The only other place folks can buy spectacles are from the catalog at the mercantile, but I'm sure I can convince them it's in their best interest to get them personally fitted here. And not simply for the sale, but because I truly believe in getting a personal fit."

Dr. York responded, "Neither of the male applicants had mentioned any books available at the library." And then, "How did you come to know the anatomy of the human eye?"

Seven minutes later, a customer returned and Dr. York came out to serve the man. Diana followed.

She shrugged at Mitch with nervousness and excitement. He found himself rooting for her.

When the customer left and they were alone again, Diana spoke to the optometrist. "You've got a window on the wall right there beside the mirror, yet it's shut tight. Might I suggest you open it? The smell of varnish in here is…rather overwhelming."

It seemed her instincts were good and she'd read Dr. York correctly. He studied her. "You'd definitely be an asset to me here. How soon could you start working?"

Diana and Mitch smiled privately at each other. Part of him openly admired her.

Dammit, she'd gotten the job.

Her air of self-confidence caused him to take a deeper, second look.

Her freckled face was flushed with wonder, her green eyes brimming hope. A full red mouth tipped upward at the corners. She brushed dark tendrils of hair from her ear.

He'd just helped a single woman land a job. He was torn between pride and shame. Pride in her abilities, shame that she had to work so hard, and was so alone.

Diana clapped her hands. "They'd need a few days notice at the factory, but they won't miss me. Wednesday? How would Wednesday work?"

"That would be fine. Could you come back later this afternoon say around two or three, when things have settled here and we can discuss your salary and hours?"

"Yes, sir."

"Good day, then." Dr. York accompanied them to the

door. When the optometrist placed his hand at the back of Diana's waist, Mitch felt a sharp pang of envy and was again reminded the man was unmarried.

They left the office. When they reached farther along the sun-streaked boardwalk in a private little corner, she twirled around, hands outstretched.

Mitch laughed along with her. "Congratulations."

Her exuberance was contagious. "We did it." She reached up and, surprising them both, kissed him softly on the mouth.

Diana was so thrilled at getting the job that her excitement and gratitude to Mitch had somehow translated into a kiss. Or maybe, she thought, the kiss was a good-bye for the past twenty-four hours spent with him.

Stretching on tiptoe, she stabilized herself with a gentle palm to his solid chest. Mitch slid his hand to the back of her neck beneath the jumble of pinned hair, pressing his thumb against the pounding in her throat, letting his warm fingers glide along her skin.

Her heartbeat raced. He uttered a small groan of approval that sent the blood rushing to her face.

Her second kiss with Mitch was as thrilling as the first. She marveled at her own exhilarating response and wondered if all kisses with all men would feel the same.

The clang of a passing cowbell broke the spell.

Flustered for being so brash, she pulled away. Hot sunshine baked her nose and cheeks and mouth. Fortunately, it seemed no one had seen them. The sounds and smells of Calgary poured upon her. The bakery behind Mitch exuded the scent of fresh-baked bread.

"What was that for?" Beneath the leather brim of his hat, Mitch stared down at her, his mouth tilted in a slight smile. His satiny fingers were still entwined with the small hairs at the back of her neck. She tingled all the way from those fingers down her back, her spine, her thighs.

"I—I meant to say thank you for your recommendation in there."

"That's a mighty fine way of saying thanks."

Diana clutched her purse and stepped across the boardwalk. That disentangled them.

They lingered, as if both found it hard to part. But she really needed to leave, to put an end to her ties with this officer. "It must be past one o'clock. That took longer than expected and the children will be waiting for their lunch."

"Right," he mumbled.

"It's been interesting to have met you," she said. "Thank you for your time at the factory, for fixing up the things at the house and for accompanying me to the optometrist."

He tilted his hat in acknowledgement.

He was a strong, silent man, Diana observed. Mitch never wasted his words, and looked directly at a person when he had something to say.

"I can walk myself home from here. Have a pleasant evening tonight at your barbecue." She turned and walked away briskly. A fly buzzed past her ear.

To her surprise, Mitch appeared at her side, long legs in stride, dark features riveted on her face. "About that barbecue," he began.

She stopped. "Say hello to Miss Oxford for me, and do thank her for allowing me to steal your time."

There. She'd said it. He was courting another woman and they both knew it.

He frowned. "I was thinking that you might like to come to the barbecue tonight."

"But your raffle time is up. You don't have to spend any more time with me."

"The Reids have always welcomed new folks in town. I extend the invitation on behalf of my entire family."

"On behalf of the Reids," she repeated. Not on behalf of Mitch.

"Bring your brothers and sisters. I'll bet when you lived in Toronto, they never saw a steer roasted over a fire. And we've got three for tonight."

A pang of strong desire, almost an ache, tore at her insides. "No, they never have." If she accepted the invitation, their bellies would be full tonight.

"Would you come? Our drivers usually ride to town with two wagons full of hay, so folks can climb aboard for the ride back to the ranch."

"What time?"

"About six-thirty." He motioned across the street. "The wagons will be waiting in front of the mercantile."

"It's lovely of you to ask on behalf of your family."

His hair was a rich, deep black. Noticing how it fell across his ear, she wished—*stupidly*—that the invitation had come simply from him to her.

"I'm sure my family would love to come."

"You have to help me, Charlotte, please." Diana rapped on her friend's door an hour later, after she'd put her laundry, wet sheets, on the clotheslines to dry. "I need something to wear. I've been invited to the Reid barbecue."

"Come on in." Eager to listen to the cheerful news, Charlotte bid her friend welcome.

Diana left her four young siblings outside to play, propping open the door to keep watch as the women usually did when they got together. Charlotte led her into the kitchen where they could still see to the outer door. She was frying the chicken she'd bought last night with her bonus money.

"It smells good in here."

"We're having a late lunch." With her hair in a tight bun, Charlotte patted her crisply ironed apron. It was sky-blue with peach-colored polka dots. Despite her tight budget, she always managed to choose the prettiest fabrics for sewing her clothes. "My folks love fried chicken. It's good for their rheumatism when I mix it with garlic." She flipped the battered pieces. Hot oil crackled. "So Mitchell Reid, the town's most wicked bachelor, has invited you to his barbecue?"

Diana bristled at the wording. "He's invited me and all the children. On behalf of his family."

"A likely story. If you ask me, I think he's after your—"

"Don't be silly!" Diana understood the implication but knew there was more teasing than truth to the comment.

Charlotte removed the chicken from the fire. "Were Wayde and Tom looking forward to going to Miner's Gully today?"

"Miner's Gully? No, they went to work at the livery."

"Yeah, but my brother said he's taking them to his cabin on their way to a Clydesdale delivery in Miner's Gully. They're showin' an interest in panning for gold."

Diana's brothers hadn't mentioned an out-of-town trip. Charlotte's fifty-year-old brother, Jedediah, ran the livery, and Diana and her family had been to his dilapidated cabin once, two weeks ago, on Charlotte's invitation for a drive into the country. It'd taken them nearly all day, and Miner's Gully was nothing more than a ghost town. No gold there, only empty dreams. Why were her brothers withholding things from her? Would they return in time for the barbecue?

"Hello!" Winnie appeared at the door. She called to her three young children in the yard. "No yelling and play fair! I'll be here if you need me." Winnie smiled at Diana. "I saw you passing by my house. Margaret and Elizabeth just told me—what's this about a barbecue?"

Diana felt a wave of curious glances. "If I may, I've come to borrow some clothes. You've always been so kind to offer, Charlotte, and this is a special event. It's the first big social my family's been invited to since we arrived."

"Hmm," said Winnie, circling Diana and fingering the wisps of hair that had fallen loose around her ears.

"Um," said Charlotte, gesturing at Diana's worn-out skirt. "Could use a bit of spit and polish. "Whaddya think, Winnie?"

"I think we've got a lot of clay to work with. You'll let us do what we please?"

Diana nodded enthusiastically. "Yes, I promise. Please give me anything else to wear except my own tired things. And if I could just leave the children here for half an hour first while I go speak to Dr. York—"

"Sure you can leave them here. But I don't know if that leaves us enough time to do a proper job."

"I've got an idea," offered Winnie. "There's one special dress I have in my trunk. Something I wore before I had children and gained all this weight."

"What color is it?" asked Diana.

"Don't worry, he'll love it."

"I'm not doing this for him," Diana insisted. "He's courting another woman, remember?"

"Uh-huh. Right." Winnie winked at Charlotte. Diana felt her face flush with embarrassment and confusion at Winnie's next words. "Men like him don't stop at one woman."

Chapter Eight

Mad as hell at four o'clock that same day, Mitch strode into the fort's jailhouse with two battling prisoners in tow.

Once inside the jailhouse, the guard, a man with long white hair and whiskers who went by the nickname Moses, flew to his feet in alarm. "Mitch, you're bleedin'. You're hurt."

Mitch swiped the left side of his jaw with the back of his sleeve, mopping up the blood and trying not to notice the ache in his right fist. "Not bad as these two. Meet Owen Norris and Paul Irwing. The bastards had the nerve to jump me."

"I'd like to speak to a lawyer," said Owen, the heavier, greasier horse thief. His jacket was torn from their fight and his right eye had already swollen to the size of an egg. His accomplice was no better off.

"You'll get your chance." Mitch unlocked their handcuffs and tossed them into separate cells. The metal locks clanged shut behind them. "Due to the thirty-eight horses you stole, you'll be here awhile."

Moses whistled in awe. "Are these the two we've been searchin' for in regard to the Hogan ranch?"

"Yeah," said Mitch. "They work for Hogan and they've been pilfering his stock for two years."

"How the hell did you figure that out? We've had two inspectors on it since last year."

"A hunch."

"Too bad you're not having the same kind of hunch with those bank robbers."

Mitch groaned. He felt a trickle of blood ooze down his neck and mopped it again with his sleeve.

"You better go see the surgeon," the old man told him. "Your jaw looks like it needs stitches."

Mitch agreed and headed out the door. "I'll be back shortly to fill you in on the details."

"All right, but two things before you go. Mrs. Sherman dropped by. Said she's got somethin' to give you."

Mitch sighed. It was probably something that used to belong to her son, Jack. Something Mitch didn't have the heart to take at the moment. "I'll catch up with her another time." He said it but he didn't believe it. "What's the second thing?"

"The company clerk's lookin' for you." The guard followed Mitch out into the sunshine. "A crate's been delivered in your name. It's over there." Moses nodded to a wagon sitting at the corner, three feet away from the jail.

"Where's it from?"

"England."

Mitch neared the wagon. "If it's what I think it is, it took six months to get here. I ordered it while I was stationed in Regina, as soon as I heard rumors that it existed." Mitch went into the jailhouse and came out with a crowbar.

Moses watched him tear back the wood. "It's long and looks heavy. Looks like a crate of rifles to me."

"More dangerous and powerful than a crate of rifles."

"A keg of dynamite?"

"More powerful than that, even." When the lid pulled apart, a number of items lay nestled in a bed of straw, firmly packed for traveling across the Atlantic and two thousand miles of open country. "Looks like nothing broke."

Mitch lifted another box from inside, one foot wide and equally long and high. He opened it. Inside were tubes of watercolor paints, sheets of paper samples, ink blots, tiny brushes and an examining glass. Left in the crate were rollers, pallets and plaster thumb samples.

"Are you gonna do some painting?"

"Sort of. Aha, here it is." Mitch yanked out a leather-bound book. "This is it. An instruction book."

"That's more powerful than rifles and dynamite?"

"Yes, sir."

"What kind of instructions are in it?"

Mitch wiped at a new drizzle of blood. "Have you ever heard of Charles Darwin?"

"Nope."

"He's a British scientist. He's got a cousin named Francis Galton, who's also a scientist. Last year, Francis Galton wrote this manual." Mitch blew the straw off the rich brown leather. "This powerful book, my friend, is called *Finger Prints*."

"Are you certain it doesn't hurt?" Standing twenty feet away from the group of fiddlers on the Reid ranch, Allison peered at the five stitches on Mitch's jaw and winced.

She ran her hand along his arm. It felt warm sliding up his white shirt, making his string tie sway with the movement.

"I'm fine," Mitch hollered above the fiddle playing. He was more concerned about her and how she'd take his impending news of separation than his minor scrape.

Three old mutts came running at him from the stables. He laughed and patted them while Allison stepped away to avoid getting dirty. It was close to seven and the Reid ranch was packed with a hundred cheerful guests. Although Allison had just arrived with her three closest friends, the other young women had already scattered, wooed away by Mitch's gang of single male friends to enjoy a glass of raspberry punch.

Warm autumn air curled around them, but the sun was beginning to set, already making things cooler. Ranch hands were building three bonfires in a well-cleared area to prepare for the cooler evening and corn roasting later.

Beneath the looming cottonwood at the front of the house, Mitch's family was greeting visitors as they arrived at the barbecue. His folks were smiling broadly and steering people to the food and beverage tables. Beside them stood Mitch's brother Travis accompanied by his new wife, Jessica, and their young twins. Mitch's sister, Shawna, and her husband, Tom, sat in the shade changing their son's diaper cloth.

The dogs ran off to someone else's whistle. Allison moved toward him in her wispy yellow gown. "I missed you this past year. I'm happy you came home to me."

Gripped by sudden guilt, Mitch placed a finger into his tight shirt collar and yanked to loosen it. "You know I didn't expect you to wait."

She tilted her head to look up at him. "I wanted to."

He tried to mask his frustration, but she caught it. "What's wrong? What is it?" she asked.

He had every intention of telling her how he felt

about her—or rather, *didn't* feel—but his plan was to take her home by buggy tonight and tell her when they were alone. Let her enjoy the barbecue, he thought. She'd been talking about it for three weeks.

"Do you like the way I look tonight?" She twirled in her gown, oozing feminine charm.

He didn't know much about women's clothing, but he could tell she'd spent a lot of money. The yellow fabric seemed to float around her shoulders and there were lots of beads attached to the revealing neckline. But something about it, about her, seemed overdone. Her sparkling red hair was pinned up in massive curls and she wore gloss on her lips. He tried to force some feeling into his heart as he looked at her, but it wouldn't come. She was a pleasant distraction, funny when she wanted to be, a great dancer and warm to his friends. But there was no overwhelming passion between them.

"You look lovely." He smiled, trying to ignore the jab of pain radiating along his stitches. The fort's surgeon told him it'd hurt for a couple of days. Mitch didn't like the way his head swam under the influence of laudanum, so he hadn't taken anything for the ache. "Let's get a glass of punch."

"Mitch, what is it?"

"We can have this conversation later tonight, in private."

"Whatever it is, I'd like to hear it now."

Mitch sighed. He wondered if they'd be better off leaving the party now while he took her home and talked to her. But as he pulled her aside, a group of children swarmed him.

The four youngest Campbells.

"Mitch, Mitch! We took the hay wagon all the way here!"

"Look at how Diana did my hair!"

"Diana doesn't want to come over and say hello yet. She says we're interruptin' you. We're not interruptin' you, are we, Mitch? We only wanted to say thank you."

Allison prodded Mitch to follow her to the big cottonwood for privacy, but he felt the need to say hello to the children. He peered over the heads of Elizabeth, Margaret, Gena and Robert to look for Diana. He didn't see her at first, but then on his second sweep realized the beauty standing at the punch table with two of his friends pouring her a drink *was* Diana.

His pulse kicked to attention.

She was wearing what appeared to be a plain, off-the-shoulder country dress, much simpler than Allison's, but the way it fit her wasn't plain at all. The pink-and-white checkered fabric had a shimmer to it, like silk. It was cinched tight at the waist and draped softly over Diana's hips. A ribbon of white lace was sewn into the low square neckline, scooping her breasts, making his eyes go directly to that provocative area.

And those bare, creamy shoulders.

Her long black hair was different, too. She wore it loose but it looked curlier, framing her friendly face. Her lips were colored with a stain of pink and she laughed readily.

The dress reached to her feet, covering her shoes, but he noticed a hint of one spiked boot heel. He adored women in high heels. Almost as much as he did women in pants.

Diana looked different than Mitch was used to seeing her. And apparently, he observed with a cold grimace, he wasn't the only one noticing.

Diana accepted and sipped the raspberry punch offered to her by the two cowboys. Unaccustomed to such attention, she let their conversation about the day's weather drift past her as she turned to look for the children. They'd promised they'd only say hello to Mitch then return to her side.

A low groan rasped from the back of her throat when she spotted Mitch being interrupted by Robert, who pulled at Mitch's sleeve. He and Miss Oxford had been staring into each other's faces as if on the verge of an important *kiss*.

"And as I was saying, the dancing will start as soon as everyone's eaten." Art Lambert, the taller of the two blond men who stood beside Diana, fought for her attention. "I'd be honored if you save the first one for me."

Feeling rather trapped, she smiled and nodded, pulling at the white knitted shawl dangling off her elbows.

"I think we should leave that up to the young lady, when the dancing starts." Carrying an interesting banjo, Quinn Turner, shorter and more muscled than his friend, motioned to the table heaped with food and spoils from harvest. "Shall we go help ourselves to the spread?"

"I really need to help my younger brothers and sisters at the dinner table first, but thank you kindly."

The men moaned their goodbyes with promises of dancing later.

Diana turned and left, but to her embarrassment, ten feet away, she spotted the children pulling Mitch along by his sleeve, followed by Miss Oxford. Mitch didn't seem too bothered by the kids, but she looked sour.

Stepping out to greet them, Diana addressed the adults. "I'm terribly sorry."

"Yes, well," said Miss Oxford, standing in a pretty swirl of yellow taffeta and organza.

"Hello, Diana," drawled Mitch, pointedly gazing at her curly hair and then over her revealing dress, causing her neck to heat. She'd been so happy with Winnie and Charlotte's choices, but now that she was standing in front of Mitch, wondered if she looked as transparent as she felt.

She noticed the stitches on the left side of his dark jaw. "Good grief, what happened?"

She scrutinized the lean face, the dark eyebrows, the intense stance. Everything about him was always stretched to the maximum, including the masculine way he moved.

"He told us a bad guy punched him in the face," said Robert. "But Mitch sent him to jail."

Diana clicked her tongue in sympathy. "Are you all right?"

"I'm fine."

Miss Oxford stared at her. Self-conscious, Diana looked away, her gaze roving over the stylish white shirt that silhouetted his torso, the black denim pants that hugged his lower half. Her nerves fluttered.

Still holding her glass of punch, Diana leaned over to the fresh-scrubbed little faces. Her pink gingham dress billowed at the front. The warm wind touched her shoulders. "Please leave Officer Reid and Miss Oxford to finish their—their discussion."

When she straightened, Mitch's gaze flickered over her neckline. She pushed a hand to her throat, suddenly feeling silly for having asked Winnie and Charlotte to do her up so fancy, and wondering why she'd had the urge. Mitch and Miss Oxford certainly didn't need her company.

But deep in her soul, she knew why. It had been part of her ridiculous fantasy. To be swept off her feet. She realized with a stab of disappointment that the only one doing the sweeping would be her tomorrow morning in her kitchen.

"It certainly is a lovely barbecue." Diana sipped the cool, tangy liquid.

"Glad you could make it," said Mitch.

"The Reids always put on a good harvest celebration," said Miss Oxford, with a pleasant smile this time. She slipped her hand around Mitch's elbow. "This year was particularly good for the ranchers. So, how were the twenty-four hours you two spent together?"

Mitch and Diana shifted with unease, but neither answered. Her guilty thoughts raced to the memory of his kiss.

"You never told me, Mitch," Miss Oxford prodded, "how it went. What did you two find to do during all those hours?"

"He unclogged my chimney," blurted Diana. "And the privy."

Apparently appalled, Miss Oxford gasped. Mitch seemed amused.

With an idiotic moan, Diana regretted her outburst. Surely she could talk about more refined matters.

The youngsters added new dimension to the story, complete with where they got the long ladder and their sightings of raccoons and birds.

While they occupied Miss Oxford, Diana took the private moment to speak to Mitch. "Wayde and Tom are here." She nodded to her immediate right, to the open field where her brothers were tossing a ball back and forth between them. "When they spot you, I've asked—they'll likely want to—come around to thank you for the invitation, too. Sorry for the interruption that's coming."

"It's not a problem."

Her name was suddenly called. "Diana! Catch!"

The ball came shooting at her. She caught it easily

and threw it back to Tom. "Keep the ball to yourselves, please! I'm not exactly dressed for playing!"

When she turned around, Mitch and Miss Oxford were staring at her. His look was intimate, hers judgmental.

"Good aim," said Mitch with a soft smile. It was the same thing he'd said to her when she'd won him at the raffle.

"Good splash," said Diana, recalling the same moment, and, recalling it beneath the watchful eyes of Miss Oxford.

Little Elizabeth yanked at the poor woman's sleeve, trying to finish her story. "And then, Miss Oxford, Officer Mitch borrowed oil from the neighbors to grease my brother's unicycle...."

"Did you get back to the optometrist this afternoon?" Mitch asked, close to Diana's ear.

Her chest tightened at his proximity, and at the disappointing memory of her return visit to Dr. York's. For this evening, she was hoping to forget about her financial problems. "I did, but I'm sorry to say it didn't go as well as the morning meeting."

"What happened?"

"It seems there was an underlying reason he decided to hire a woman."

"What does that mean?"

"Are you coming, Mitch?" Miss Oxford pulled at his arm.

"Do you still have the job?" he persisted. And then with rising urgency, "Do *I* need to talk to him?"

Diana wanted to tell him, she wanted to share her letdown with another person who really seemed to care, but Miss Oxford gave him a hard tug and pulled him away.

Diana was left staring after the handsome couple, a thread of failure winding through her. She knew exactly how she figured into this barbecue. As she always did. Standing at the lonesome periphery, looking in.

Mitch was determined to tell Allison what he thought of her rude behavior. He'd never seen her act this possessive, and it wasn't becoming.

He wanted to know what happened between Diana and Emmit York. So help the lens doctor if he'd laid a hand on her.

But several minutes later as Mitch and Allison loaded their plates with barbecued beef and corn on the cob, he told himself to bridle his temper until he was able to speak to Allison calmly.

The sun had completely faded beyond the distant rim of the Rocky Mountains, leaving the sky a dark, glowing blue. He couldn't see Allison's face distinctly as she sat at the long table surrounded by neighbors and friends, but she was outlined in orange by the bonfires blazing behind her.

They ate in relative silence, although others filled the gaps with anecdotes and laughter. Afterward, the festivities flowed behind them as Mitch took her for a walk past the stables.

He needed to be direct with Allison, for being subtle hadn't worked. But he also wanted to be gentle. "Allison, that was rather abrupt back there with Diana Campbell. We were in the middle of a conversation."

Allison scoffed. She arched her fine brown eyebrows. "She and those children were rude for interrupting *us* in a private conversation. We were talking first, remember?"

"You can't blame the kids," he said softly. "They're excited to be at a real Western barbecue."

"I'm not blaming anyone, I'm frustrated to know there's something you want to tell me but you're holding off."

He slid his fingers into his pants pockets. "Maybe I should have said this as soon as I returned from Regina, but I didn't realize then what you were expecting from me."

A beat passed. Her voice grew cold. "Say it."

He planted his hands on her shoulders and hoped she wouldn't take it too hard. "I'm not interested in marriage."

Turning away to look at the path, she shook her head. Her face, silhouetted in flames, hardened. "You're a damn good pretender, Mitch. Pretending you were interested in matrimony."

His hands dropped to his sides. "I wasn't pretending. I didn't make any promises before I left. As a matter of fact, I wished you luck on that last day—remember, at the train station?"

"What I remember is how you kissed me."

"A small kiss on the cheek as I recall."

"But it held a promise."

"That wasn't my intent." He touched her cheek. "You can tell your friends it's my fault. I apologize in abundance."

"I knew you were deeply hurt when your friend Jack Sherman drowned. And when you lost that dog of yours, too."

Mitch winced. *Digger*. His dog's name had been Digger.

"Let me help you through it. Mrs. Sherman is a lovely woman and she couldn't possibly hold you forever respons—"

"*No*. What's going on between us has nothing to do with that night. I can see where you think our courtship is heading, but it's not heading that way. Let's call it quits while we're still fine friends."

She grimaced. No matter how many times he'd geared up for this conversation, he hadn't seen a way out where Allison wouldn't be hurt.

"I'm sorry," he said. "For disappointing you."

Allison didn't say another word. She covered her mouth with her hand, a sob bursting forth, and stalked off toward the bonfires.

Hell, that was hard. He felt like dirt.

Music diverted his attention. Dancing had started on a rectangular patch of pounded grass between two of the five stables. The fiddlers had transplanted themselves and men and women were square-dancing.

Quinn had brought his banjo and, seeking the attention of several young ladies in the crowd, strummed with enthusiasm. Mitch couldn't stomach watching him. The song reminded Mitch of the awful night of Jack's drowning.

His eyes found the shape of another female figure, surrounded by her six brothers and sisters while they tried to teach themselves the dance steps. They weren't very good and doubled up in laughter.

Enthralled by her simple charm, Mitch compared the two women. Diana worked so much harder than Allison for what she had, yet complained so little. He couldn't picture sweat trickling down Allison's pretty face while she plucked chickens, nor Allison having to make do with hand-me-down shoes.

A hollow ache scraped at his gut. He didn't belong here with anyone. Not with Quinn, not his friends, not Allison, not Diana. Turning to leave and call it a night, Mitch headed for the stables. He'd slip out and return quietly to the barracks.

But there were still more guests arriving. One, in particular, made Mitch stop. The lens doctor hopped out from his buggy and with a nod to Mitch as he passed, headed in Diana's direction.

Mitch's folks had likely invited the good doctor to the harvest celebration and there was no harm in being neighborly. But what did Emmit want from Diana? Mitch was struck by a pang of intrusion. He stiffened, primed for something but unsure of what. Maybe for protecting Diana.

With a curt tug at his collar, he decided to stay a while longer. He hadn't finished his conversation with Diana, he justified, and he was curious what had gone wrong between her and Emmit. But as Mitch stepped closer to the crowd, he wondered why he cared so much.

Chapter Nine

Diana sensed several eyes upon her as she danced with the children, most especially the deep brown ones belonging to Mitch.

Enjoying the wind whispering at her bare shoulders and rustling the hair at her neck, Diana looped her arm through nine-year-old Robert's and whirled in beat to the music. She'd never in her life danced outside in the dark. It felt like freedom and her problems seemed ten thousand miles away.

The announcer called another turn. The fiddles wailed. She wondered if Mitch would ask her to dance.

"This way," said Robert, turning to his right.

"But I thought this way," said Diana. Still feeling blissfully full from the meal, she laughed along with her brother when they turned right instead of left.

Standing beneath a bowed aspen and watching them, Mitch was the object of her curiosity, too. He looked different tonight in his starched white shirt and suede string tie, more subdued than he'd been in the factory when he'd twirled the Smythe sisters back to their place in line. As he stood beneath the gnarled branches, there was a sadness about him that she'd never seen before, a defenseless quality that pulled at her insides and made her want to know what he was thinking.

He was no longer standing with Miss Oxford—she was off with a different group of young ladies and men who were talking around the bonfire. By the way Allison kept glancing over at Mitch, but the way he never glanced back, it seemed to Diana that they'd argued.

It was a shame to waste this special night on arguing.

Diana wondered everything imaginable about the couple—how long they'd been courting, how their attraction had first started, what they laughed about, how they got along with each other's families, and even, heaven strike her for thinking it, if they'd shared anything more intimate than a kiss.

Diana exhaled a long sigh of appreciation. Mitch was a good kisser. Even though he'd overstepped the line of courtesy and decency by kissing her when he was courting another, he was a good kisser. With regrettable honesty, she realized she was much too interested in him than need be.

Her thoughts were interrupted by a tap on her arm.

Dr. York leaned over her, narrow body clothed in a fine gold suit. "May I cut in?"

Diana's brother left immediately to join his other sisters at dancing, while Diana was left in the awkward position of answering. This afternoon she had dropped by his office in between her visits with Charlotte. Diana had been eager to discuss her working hours and salary only to be severely disappointed. But when she'd mentioned that she was going to the Reid barbecue, he said he'd been invited by the senior Mr. Reid.

"May I have this dance, Miss Campbell?" Dr. York repeated.

Diana smiled stiffly and placed her warm hands into his sweaty ones. He was a pleasant man and no doctor had ever been interested in her before. "Certainly."

They began.

"I'm looking forward to having you start on Wednesday. The office seems to run smoother already."

"It'll be a pleasant change for me, too, and I thank you again for the opportunity." Chafing with embarrassment, she'd never admit her money problems to him. She'd deal with them on her own and she already had a solution brewing.

The doctor led her deep into the crowd, blending seamlessly with her steps and attracting the admiration of several other unattached women. For a fleeting moment, Diana wondered what it might be like to kiss him.

She barely had time to think about that when she was caught up in the arms of several other men—the two cowboys she'd met earlier, Art then Quinn—then complete strangers. The whole time, she had her sights geared for seeing Mitch among the dancers, but was indescribably disappointed when he didn't appear.

Her stomach squeezed whenever she'd catch him in various spots around the dancing area—talking to the ranch hands, then a gang of men roughly the same age, then bringing water to the musicians. Several times, she'd caught him staring back at her. She'd catch her breath and feel her heart skip. No other man had ever made her so conscious of her sex.

Mitch wasn't drinking like the other men. He didn't bother dancing with anyone, either. She wondered why.

She felt uplifted by the unexpected attention of all the men who were asking her to be their partner, but couldn't reconcile the undeniable pull between her and Mitch.

Maybe it had something to do with dancing in the

dark, with feeling the gentle stir of hair along her skin, the glow of being swept away in a beautiful dress that wasn't hers, on a moonlit night that didn't belong in her normal world.

Or maybe it had to do with the tough officer who watched her moving, who in the center of bustling activity appeared dark and silent.

Everything in him seemed to strain against confinement—the rich outline of his shoulders against the fabric of his shirt, the long, lean thighs in the denim, and then beyond the physical, even his cool manner strained against the jovial nature of his friends.

The evening flew by before Diana had barely learned the dance steps. Catching her breath, she passed the senior Mr. and Mrs. Reid and stopped to ask the time.

"It's only getting started, my dear," boomed Mr. Reid, after bending closer to cup his ear and ask her to repeat the question. Broad and over six feet tall, he was hard of hearing.

Mrs. Reid, a buxom woman and as gray as her husband, checked her pocket watch. "Nine o'clock."

"Thank you," said Diana, "and for your hospit—"

They spun away to another talkative couple. Diana had noticed earlier that many neighbors swarmed to them for conversation. The Reids were cherished by the community and Diana felt a slight awkwardness at being dismissed. They hadn't meant anything by it, she told herself. Nonetheless, it pronounced how desperately she wanted to fit in.

She ran her hand along the puckered gathers of her waistline and searched for her sisters.

It was nine o'clock, already past the younger children's bedtime, and the time they'd agreed as a family to leave. With an ache of longing, she gathered the children and peered through the swarming faces to say goodbye to Mitch, realizing with inexplicable sadness that her fantasy night was ending.

"Have a drink with us, Mitch." Standing in the dark near the table that held three oak barrels filled with ale, Clay Hayward pushed on the far spout and refilled his mug. He was a thin young man, and true to his nature as the quietest drinker among them, Clay spoke softly, having already retreated to somewhere peaceful in his mind.

"I'll pass." Mitch crossed his arms and leaned against the table. He listened to the lull of bullfrogs croaking behind him in the reeds. "I've got to get up early tomorrow."

"It's only nine o'clock. One drink won't hurt you."

Quinn leaned against the table and lifted a copy of the day's newspaper. Mitch squirmed at the glimpse of the front-page photograph.

"Look at this," said Quinn, passing it around. "The caption reads Officer Mitchell Reid takes a splash, courtesy of Miss Diana Campbell."

His friends gathered around and laughed, but Mitch didn't.

Normally he would have, but there was a mean-spirited tone to Quinn's ribbing tonight. It had been there for over a year, Mitch realized with a sharp thud, ever since that night.

Mitch wondered why he'd never noticed how competitive Quinn was, or maybe it had never much bothered him. Quinn had a real need to always be the fastest rider, the smoothest talker with the ladies, the man who made the most money, or in this case with the photo, the one who got the last laugh. He'd also been the first to inform Mrs. Beazly that her husband was being seen around town with another woman. That, thought Mitch, was unnecessarily heartless.

"Allison told us you argued," Art said to Mitch. He plucked at his bushy mustache. "Why don't you go ask her to dance?"

Mitch grumbled. His friends knew enough not to push him. He didn't feel like dancing with Allison, and if he danced with any of the other women, he would only be hurting Allison more tonight than he had already.

"Surely," he scoffed, "I can miss out on one night of dancing without it affecting the entire town."

"Where's the pretty gal in the checkered dress you were watching? The one in the photo?" Quinn's dark eyes blazed with a challenge. "Maybe I'll ask her to dance again."

In a flash of unexpected anger and trying to diffuse it, Mitch twisted to the table and poured himself a glass of water. Ignoring the comment, he guzzled the drink. It slid down his throat, cool and easy. He poured himself another and turned around.

"How's the investigation going?" Art ran his tobacco-stained fingers along his pocket, then pulled out a pre-rolled cigarette. "Any closer to the bank robbers?"

Mitch was relieved to change the topic. His friends were always interested in hearing about police business. Two of them had talked about joining the force themselves—Art and Quinn—but it had never panned out. Ranch work seemed to be in their blood, and they were damn good at it. "We've got some new information."

"What new information?" asked Quinn.

"Boring stuff," Mitch replied.

Quinn didn't pursue it. "What do you say we men go into the stables, pick out four of your fastest horses and put some money down on who can ride the fastest into town and back?"

"Nah," said Clay. "I'm too drunk."

The rest of them laughed, including Mitch.

Surprising Mitch by coming out of the shadows, Diana and her family stepped around the beer barrels. Wayde and Tom stood tall beside her.

The men heaved to attention. Mitch shot up into his boots and slid his glass of water to the table.

Moonlight poured over Diana's fine shape. "Mitch, we've come to say good-night."

"So soon?"

"Why don't you stay longer, Miss Campbell?" Art stroked his mustache.

"The children need to get to bed. There's a hay wagon leaving in a few minutes."

The youngsters began saying good-night. Mitch walked Diana away from the table and his friends with their sporting curiosity. Diana stood awash in a buttery river of light. The moon dipped across the bridge of her nose, outlined her long dark lashes and melted against her mouth.

"It's a shame we've all got to go home," said Wayde. "Why don't you stay and Tom and I will put everyone to bed?"

Mitch raised an eyebrow. Maybe her brothers weren't as selfish as he'd first thought. "That's generous of your brother. Why don't you take him up on it?"

Diana hesitated. "I don't know."

"Go on," said her other brother. "We put 'em to bed five nights a week. One more won't make any difference. Besides, you should stay and dance some more with Dr. York."

Diana bristled and looked away, stroking the braids

of the littlest girl, avoiding Mitch's hard glare. It seemed her brothers and sisters had taken a shine to the lens doctor.

Something about the man didn't sit right with Mitch. Again, he wondered what the doctor had said or done to Diana this afternoon that had disappointed her. If he were alone with her, he'd ask.

Then the man himself raced along to join them. Panting from dancing hard, he wiped a handkerchief across his forehead. "What's this? You're not leaving already?"

"Nah, she's stayin'," her brothers insisted. "We're goin'."

"All right, I'll stay." Diana smiled. Her teeth sparkled in the darkness. A cloud drifted over the moon, then broke again, and another beam of light caught one side of her body.

"Great," said York. "I can drive you home. I brought my best buggy."

Mitch shot forward. "*I'll* take her home."

Everyone pivoted toward Mitch.

"Why you?" asked York.

"Police protection."

He meant to be humorous, but didn't hear anyone laughing. Solemn, Diana looked from one man to the other. It was crazy, but Mitch craved to be alone with her.

"Police sounds good in this case," said Wayde.

"I'll be fine," she whispered to her brothers. "I'll ride home with Mitch." She said goodbye to her family and they headed to the hay wagon that was quickly filling with other families and young children.

"Now then," said York to Diana. He hitched his hand to the small of her back and led her away. "Let's go for another spin."

They walked away, her skirt kicking up at her slender, high heels and her long hair jostling along the curve of her spine. Mitch watched in withering silence. His disturbing mood didn't get any better as the evening progressed.

Diana laughed in pleasant exhaustion as yet another man called on her. Her eyes sparkled, her hips swayed. Something in her manner entranced Mitch, kept his gaze coming back to her as the night wore on. She seemed aware of her own attraction, perhaps an attraction she wasn't used to commanding. The ensuing flush to her cheeks drove more men to notice her.

Every time she flicked her loose black hair over her bare shoulder, she roused Mitch from his stupor. Whenever the moon came out from beneath the clouds it painted her face with streams of gold.

But getting involved with another woman so soon after leaving Allison would defeat everything he'd set out to do. He wanted to be on his own for a while, to leave his reputation as a womanizer buried with his troublesome past.

It seemed, though, that he was powerless to resist watching Diana. When Quinn asked her to dance and slid his hand to her back, Mitch turned away. Later, as she danced a close waltz with York and he coaxed her to the outer edge of the crowd and in full view of Mitch, he turned away again.

To his great irritation, his moods were swinging as erratically as a summer storm. Taking a deep breath, he peered up at the sky. And judging by the heavy clouds, there was a storm coming sometime tonight.

He tried to distract himself by talking with some of the old-timers about how things used to be when the land was first settled. That distraction, too, didn't last long because Allison joined the dancing. With her gay laughter, strangers would never guess she was bothered in the least about her earlier argument with Mitch.

But a nervous tingle scraped the inside of Mitch's gut. He suspected her of being up to something.

He was right. At eleven o'clock when Diana slid to Mitch's side, smiling and finally asking for that ride home, Allison immediately slid next to him on the other side.

"May I ask you for a ride home now, Mitch?" Allison's mouth puckered into a soft smile. "The friends I came with are going home with their neighbors and I prefer not to take them out of their way."

"Oh," said Diana, wavering. "I didn't mean to interrupt anything. I'll—I'll find another way home."

Allison looked at him with accusation. The news that he had promised to drive Diana home took Allison by surprise.

Diana stepped away to leave, but Mitch pulled her back gently by her arm. He allowed his fingers to linger on her bare flesh, feeling the slow heat travel between them. "I've promised Diana a ride home already."

Allison took note of Diana's bare shoulders. Her cheek twitched. "Well, what a fine gentleman you are. I agree. There's always room for one more." She tossed one edge of her yellow shawl, a perfect match to her yellow taffeta dress, around her throat and walked toward the stables, where stable hands were already hitching extra buggies to horses for the folks who were leaving.

Mitch turned to Diana. His stance softened in silent apology. "Would you mind?"

Her lips parted slightly. "Not at all. Why would I mind? You're a couple and I think it's generous of her to allow me to tag along."

Diana's good-natured spirit was compelling.

There wasn't much he could do to order Allison to

stay behind. How would that look? He was responsible for Allison's safety, at least for this final night. But hell, he was sick of taking responsibility for everyone and everything. After tonight, Allison was responsible for herself.

To everyone else at this moment, they still appeared to be a couple and it would be natural for him to drive her home. And it was, he rationalized, simply a ride home for both women.

But as Diana tilted her mouth upward, he sensed defeat of this simple explanation. He wasn't going to enjoy forty-five minutes alone with Diana, as he'd thought. And although he was determined that Allison could take care of herself after tonight, he liked the thought of being responsible for Diana. He was stuck with the realization that being with her and doing things for her never felt like a burden.

Chapter Ten

"There's a storm coming." Mitch peered up at the darkening sky as the three of them walked toward the stables.

Feeling self-conscious for being in the company of two arguing lovers, Diana did the same but Allison didn't bother. Allison looked straight ahead to the darkened blur of stables as if on a mission to reach the buggy first.

"But the air's so warm." Diana couldn't see much of anything. The clouds had rolled in and covered the moon, weaving the darkness like a cozy blanket around the three of them.

"That's the chinook." Mitch's deep voice rumbled through the air. Five hundred feet behind them and still audible, the fiddles whirred and the crowd hummed. "It's the wind that's been giving us this Indian summer for the past few days, but it won't last forever."

They reached the stables. The double-door opening was blocked by the hay wagon and mounting passengers, so Mitch allowed Allison, then Diana to pass ahead of him. The stables were lit up with a line of lanterns and people swarmed about, petting the horses. Mindful of her step on the dirt floor, Diana was aware there wasn't an extra inch of space between her slender body and Mitch's hard one.

She breathed in the scent of his clothing—a heady mixture of wood fire and shaving cream. She felt his warm breath on her forehead and made the mistake of glancing up at him as she squeezed past. His dark eyes deepened in the light and she detected a warm flush of his lips. Ill at ease, she hiked her shawl to cover bare shoulders. The soft, angora knit stroked her skin and helped anchor her nerves.

They reached a four-seater covered buggy near the back double doors. The doors had been swung open, letting in the breezy night air. Mitch called out his thanks to a stable hand as the man finished harnessing two mares to the buggy, then disappeared to help someone else.

Allison quickly slid up to the front passenger side, which meant Diana was left to sit in the back, behind her. Diana didn't mind. She was relieved to be out of the way. But due to the tight space between her side of the buggy opening and the stall boards, it was difficult to raise her skirts and jump in, as Allison easily had in the clearing.

Mitch was right behind her. "We better take this tarp."

Without a word of warning, he threw the folded tarp into the buggy, then grabbed her by the waist and lifted her. The touch of his hands startled her. He must have felt her flinch. Her pulse raced a thousand times to the stars and back.

She murmured as he set her gently in the back, lifting her as easily as he might a sack of feathers. But her shawl unexpectedly dipped off her back and one bare shoulder was exposed, a breath away from his mouth. He stared at it, blinked, then gently released her.

Seated quietly in the front, Allison hadn't noticed.

Mitch lit a kerosene lantern, adjusted the flame inside the glass and then hung it on a peg at the buggy's front, between the two horses to light their path to town.

And then he did the oddest thing.

He threw another canvas tarp in the front seat, between where he would soon be sitting, and where Allison sat now. It would divide them on the ride home.

Allison clicked her tongue. "Do we really need this?"

"Just in case it rains, to cover your legs."

But there was an acre of space in the back, thought Diana. He could place that tarp on top of the other one and leave the space between himself and Allison clear, in case she wanted to sit closer to him.

Mitch settled his dark gaze on Diana, as if they were both conspirators in the quest to keep Allison away from him.

With haste, Diana rearranged the fabric of her skirts. Her rib cage squeezed. She didn't quite comprehend what was happening in the hushed silence between her and Mitch, what had been happening all evening, but understood that feelings were building, tensions were mounting and questions were being asked and answered without either of them saying a word.

Walking, Mitch grabbed the bridle of one mare and led the team outside. The buggy rolled forward into darkness. Mitch's walk was smooth and graceful, his posture one of restrained control. Hatless, his black hair gleaming in streams of light flashing from the rocking lantern, he peered up at the clouds. "We might still make it to town before the rain hits."

Diana wasn't sure she could bear the ride. Mental images wove through her mind of the kiss they'd shared yesterday, and then again this afternoon on the boardwalk. Images of taking that kiss further, of lying down beside him, of kissing his throat and his chest, of feeling his heart pounding through his flesh and beating against her naked breast.

She closed her lids to erase the thoughts. When she opened her eyes again, they were on their way.

They passed the Reid house and rumbled onto the road. Several people on horseback rode ahead of them. Rolling behind them along the pebbles, the hay wagon creaked. It was filled with chattering guests.

Without the benefit of a visible moon, the prairie night was black as coal dust. After a while, her eyes grew more accustomed. Allison murmured comments to Mitch that Diana couldn't hear, nor did she strain to try. Mitch would nod or murmur something short in reply.

No one spoke to Diana and she relaxed. But to her surprise, Mitch was dropping Allison off first. Her family owned the first cattle ranch heading west out of Calgary. Lanterns lit the house as they drove in.

"I'll be a minute," Mitch said to Diana.

"Take your time. I'm enjoying the fresh air."

Allison mumbled good-night, Diana replied politely and Mitch walked the woman to the side door.

Diana tried not to listen, but their voices rose. She couldn't make out Allison's words, but they were harsh. Mitch folded his arms across his chest. He shook his head softly in disagreement to whatever she was saying, then opened the door to let her in.

He didn't kiss Allison good-night.

Diana tried to tell herself it didn't matter to her.

It didn't matter.

But her feelings, her misgivings about being totally alone with him shot to the surface.

When he reached the buggy, he ran his hand along the leather seat. "You could ride up front."

She hesitated. He stared. She replied, "I suppose it would look rather silly, you sitting in front as if you were my private driver."

She gave a nervous cough as she slid out of the back. "Do you need help?" He started to come at her.

"No! I'm fine. There's—there's much more space here to maneuver than there was in the stables." She dived into the front seat.

Tugging at the fabric beneath her thighs, she felt the buggy jostle forward. "Well, then, here we go again."

Thank heaven there was a canvas tarp between them. It buffered her from his long thighs, from the sensual heat of his body.

But to her dismay, Mitch grabbed the tarp with a muscled arm and tossed it to the back. "I don't think we'll need this. The rain's holding off."

A shock rolled through her. Why had he done that? Simply a coincidence?

Desperately trying to get her feelings under control, she told herself they had another ten minutes. She had to remain coherent and calm for only ten minutes.

She sensed Mitch's disquiet. In the pitch dark, the silence seemed to be an entity unto itself, ripening and deepening between them. With a gulp, she observed that the horses and other guests who'd been ahead and behind them had faded into the distance, nowhere visible.

Diana stared ahead as their buggy reached the town's perimeter. The stores were closed, although piano music and men's loud voices filtered from the saloon. Quigley's Irish Pub on the next block was open, too, but much more subdued.

When Mitch steered the mares down the next street, curving around the livery stable and stopping beneath one of the large cottonwoods, he finally broke the heavy silence.

"Allison and I called it quits this evening."

He couldn't have stunned Diana more if he'd taken one of the leather reins he held in his fist and slapped her legs with it. With their buggy parked beneath a smoldering streetlight, she swallowed hard and watched his Adam's apple rise and fall.

"For good?"

"Yeah. For good."

"She doesn't agree, though. She doesn't want to call it quits."

"Now, how would you know something like that?"

"I didn't hear her words, exactly, but…I could see it in the way she moved."

"She doesn't agree, but it's been a long time coming. I thought I'd made it clear to her a year ago, before I left for Regina, that there was nothing between us."

"A year ago…" That was a long time for Mitch to have called it off. Diana pressed her fingers into her gingham dress. She didn't want to be cheered up at Allison's expense. In fact, Allison must have felt bad this whole evening.

They hadn't been a serious couple for over a year, thought Diana, buoyed by the knowledge, and Mitch *hadn't* been kissing her when his heart was with Allison.

"Why are you telling me this?"

Mitch slid out of his side of the buggy, hitched the horses to the rings that studded the cottonwood and came around her side. They were half a block away from her home, but she gathered that it might be too difficult to turn the large team around in her narrow street.

Better to park it here. She, too, felt like walking rather than riding to her front door.

"I'm not sure exactly." He held out his hand.

She slid her moist fingers into his warm palm, struggling with the uncertainty of where this was leading, trying to curtail the pounding of her heart, the fluttering of her hopes.

"Let's take a walk," he murmured as he slid his other hand along her waist and helped her to her feet.

Mitch was aroused by Diana, by the tilt of her chin, and the stretch of her spine beneath her heavy black hair as she walked beside him on the rutted road. He listened to the hypnotic rustle of her skirts, watched her angora shawl slither up her arms, and wondered when it was that he'd become so hypnotized by Diana.

A sixth sense cautioned him to be honest about what he felt, about what he wanted to say, although he wondered why he had the need to tell her about his breakup with Allison.

"I've only known you for two days, Diana. How is it possible that I feel closer to you than I ever have to Allison?"

Diana's mouth quivered. "I suppose," she whispered as they passed the quiet row houses, "because you spent time with me yesterday. There was no pretense between us at the factory, or in my yard when you fixed things for us. And then at the optometrist's."

"Ah, the optometrist."

A dog barked in someone's backyard as they passed along the front street.

Mitch reached up over his head and slapped a passing branch. "Is Dr. York a good dancer?"

She nodded and smiled gently, and Mitch regretted

asking. It was crazy, but he wished she'd show such enthusiasm for him.

"Why were you disappointed this afternoon when you went back to his office to discuss work schedules and salary?"

She pulled at her shawl. Her drawstring purse shimmered on her wrist. "I shouldn't trouble you further with my problems."

"I'd like to know. It's been on my mind all evening."

He listened to her restless movements.

"I was disappointed because I thought by getting this job, I would be earning a larger wage than at the factory."

"You'll be making *less* money than you're earning now?"

She nodded awkwardly in agreement.

"But how is this possible? You've educated yourself in eye diseases and—and the job entails skills in bookkeeping and balancing ledgers, whereas the poultry factory requires only labor."

She braced herself, tugging a naked arm through her shawl. "Dr. York said that in hiring a woman, at least he doesn't have to pay as much as hiring a man."

Mitch groaned. "It's the excuse that most men have families to support, so women don't need to earn as much."

She stood in a patch of moonlight, one hand pressed to her ivory throat. "It's the same at the factory."

He jumped off the path and around a water trough. "But you aren't most women, are you? You *too* have a large family to support."

She nodded, weaving the other way around the trough, dipping her shapely figure in the dark.

"What will you do?"

"I'm keeping both jobs."

"Both?"

"I'll work for the optometrist Tuesday to Saturday. On Mondays I'll work at the factory, and sometimes on Sunday evenings, if need be. That'll give me fifty cents more per week."

He stopped at the walkway in front of her gate and toyed with the metal latch. Somewhere miles away, wolves howled. "You had such high hopes for this new job."

"And still do." She stood there imploring him, her face raised. "Don't tell Dr. York, but I've got another plan forming in mind. Of increasing the amount of eyeglasses we sell in the store, if I could work on getting a commission on top of my salary."

She smelled of night warmth and femininity, a scent of barbecued beef woven in her hair. Mitch smiled at how quickly her mind worked. She'd been knocked a blow and was already standing upright.

"Our secret," he promised.

She rubbed her fingers along her temple. "Anyway, it's not as bad as I've made it out to be. Dr. York is a fine man and he's given me lots to think about this evening."

Edgy, Mitch lifted and released the gate latch. "What sort of things?"

Her lips turned upward. "Maybe this is getting too personal."

"Maybe you're right." He backed off, unhooked the gate and held it open for her.

She studied his expression. He wondered if she sensed his wounded pride at being rebuffed.

"Well, the thing is," she offered timidly, lifting her hemline and weaving through the gate, "Dr. York's invited me next Saturday evening to another dance."

Startled, Mitch turned to follow her in the darkness. The doctor was paying her a fraction of what he would pay a man, knowing Diana needed to support her family, and now he was trying to charm her, as well.

"I'd watch out for him if I were you."

Twisting at the back door, she frowned. "Now why would you say that?"

She whispered the words as if her brothers and sisters could hear. But the windows were shut tight and the lights were out. The neighbors' houses were darkened, too. "So far, it's been a perfectly wonderful evening."

His voice rippled in the warm chinook. "I guess I can't help being a policeman. I'm cautious about everyone."

He heard a soft ping echoing off metal, coming from somewhere behind them. He peered past the privy to the shed in the distance. "What's that sound?"

She turned toward the back field and listened. "The sheets are still up on the clothesline. Do you see them? It sounds like one peg got loose and is hitting the post."

He made out a blur of whitish rectangles flopping in the breeze.

"I forgot about taking the laundry down before I left, and the children obviously hadn't noticed. But it might rain tonight. I'll take them down before I go in. We should say good—"

"I'll help you."

She hesitated at his offer, but then didn't resist. Setting her purse down on the wooden table where they'd shared scones this morning, she lifted a wooden laundry hamper from beneath it and carried it fifty feet to the two lines. Folks kept the laundry at a healthy distance from their privies—and their gardens, where they often spread manure in the spring and fall.

Mitch felt a tide of emotion as he followed her. The air rolled still and black.

Diana reached the laundry first. There were two

clotheslines and as she moved between them, a dozen bedsheets stirred in the wind, curling around her calves. She turned to face him. The breeze lifted her skirt and pressed it against her thighs, outlining the lovely curve of her legs. The same wind whipped at her hair and flung it high, as if taunting him to tame it.

His pulse beat to a steady drum.

"Why did you break it off with Allison?" she whispered.

He felt the soft hairs on his neck rise with her gentle voice.

"It didn't feel right." He moved closer.

"Umm," Diana answered. She stepped backward, breathless from the walk, he noticed, or perhaps breathless with alarm at what she was feeling. What he was feeling.

No one could see them even if they looked. Even if they looked out of every window possible in the neighborhood, they couldn't see him and Diana, protected from view by a dozen worn-out and faded cotton sheets.

"We're invisible," he whispered.

She fought the tremble in her voice. "I know."

The thought of complete privacy to do and say as they pleased brought a rush of excitement. She seemed to sense it, too, and kept walking backward, deeper and longer into the grass, weaving beyond the sheets billowing on the laundry lines.

"There was never any of this between Allison and me."

"Any of what?" Her voice was raw and affected.

"This. What's happening between us. This uncontrollable, relentless urge that's been chasing us all evening."

"I don't know what you mean."

"Yes, you do." He finally made it to stand in front of her, beneath the moon.

With a powerful grip, he roped his fingers through her wild hair.

"Mitch, why didn't you ask me to dance tonight?"

He could barely breathe. "I wanted to."

"Why didn't you?"

Reaching out to her with his other hand, he ran his fingers along her skirt, tracing the lacy pocket at the swell of her hip, moving up to the intake of her waist, and watching with delight as gooseflesh formed on her naked shoulders. He wondered what she'd look like if he tugged down on her lacy neckline, if he slid the fabric below her breasts.

"Because I knew if I touched you," he whispered, "I'd be afraid of my own reaction."

Chapter Eleven

The moon was playing hide-and-seek. Its creamy shape slid in and out of the dark clouds, first illuminating Mitch so Diana could see the soft planes of his face and the five stitches on his jaw, then obscuring his body in a sea of midnight black.

She was chilled by his presence. As they stood a foot apart connected by his hand on her hip, as he explained in such a lovely manner why he hadn't danced with her, she felt her angora shawl slide off her elbow. It fell against her leg and slapped gently against her thigh in the warm, stirring wind.

"I was afraid," he murmured, "if we danced and I was forced to hold you, I wouldn't be able to stop from doing this."

His long fingers kept tracing up along her waist, up along the princess seam of her bodice, up the bottom curve of her breast, wringing such aching splendor from her body that she half closed her eyes and let her mind swim.

It was a drill in self-discipline, standing completely still and allowing Mitch to trace the intimate curves of her breast without running for safety, without covering her body with shame.

She tried to inhale his scent, smiling when she caught the wisp of wood fire and the minty tang of shaving lotion.

His fingers grazed over the square opening of her neckline, flicking in and over the lacy eyelet trim, fluttering over her bare skin. The heat from his touch, combined with the pressing wind, made her quiver to her shoes. He was lightly, gently, exploring the hollow of her throat.

When his thumb traced the flesh upward, she swore he might feel the pulse throbbing there, swore he might see how he was affecting her, how quickly he'd made her skin pound and her lips dry.

Then both his hands were around her throat, gliding beneath her dampened hair to the outer rim of her shoulders. He cupped her shoulders gently, pressing the silky muscles, smiling lazily down upon her as if he were lost in his own world.

"I've wanted to do this all evening." He lowered his lips to her shoulder and kissed it. And again. He showered her with a hundred kisses, trailing a steamy path around the base of her throat and then across to the other shoulder.

"Diana," he whispered, sounding tortured. "Diana. You've got the most gorgeous shoulders. It should be against the law to have such hypnotic curves."

His tantalizing words raised the flesh along her arms and made her chest rise and fall quickly. If ever there was a moment where she knew she was reaching the point of no return, this was it. She needed to turn back now if she was to be left intact, body, heart and soul.

But she couldn't turn back. Didn't want to. Didn't have the strength to fight her need, her urge, her sex.

And so she raised her arms up behind his back, gripping her shawl and winding her hands around him, testing the sensation of his warm, bumpy spine beneath her touch.

He groaned and pressed himself against her. She felt the tension in his solid muscles, the hovering sensations in her stomach as she wondered what he'd do to her. What she craved for him to do.

"Touch me," she breathed, straining to be heard above the pinging of the clothes-peg on metal. She parted her lips and raised her face, unsure of where to begin, only knowing that the kiss he'd given her last night had made her body ache for more.

"Don't ask me…don't ask me because I couldn't stop…." He buried his face in her hair and pressed his hips against her belly.

Even fully clothed, she felt how much she'd aroused him. He was rigid. With her ear pressed to his chest, his heart beat wildly.

Timid, unsure of how to begin but knowing she didn't want this fantasy with Mitch to end, she offered her lips.

He moaned and roped his hand into her hair, then kissed her fully on the mouth.

It was even better than before and she gasped with the pleasure. "I like this so much," she said against his lips.

He seemed lost in the rhythm of a sensual world, lost in the offering of her body. His tongue dipped against hers. Her fist caught in the tangle of his thick, black hair, her fingers delving into the hollow spot at the back of his neck that made her heart leap against her ribs.

His mouth slanted against hers, demanding a response and she was eager to give it. Her soft breasts strained against his firm chest, her nipples growing hard, her skin effusing heat. When he cinched his arms across her waist, she shuddered with his power, feeling a drizzle of warmth somewhere deep in her core.

It was a kiss that evoked emotion, sensuality, everything erotic her mind could imagine. When her shawl slipped from one hand, the wind caught it from behind and whipped it against her body, enveloping the two of them in their black, midnight sea.

The wind must have tugged harder, for the flannel sheet that was one peg loose slid off the line completely, whipped against her back and engulfed them in a soft, shimmering sail.

Mitch lowered her to the grass, entwined himself on top of her in warm, tufted cotton. She sank into the ground. The fuzz was soft and splendid, the long grass cushiony against her bottom.

"Diana, I've got to know…" He pressed his silky lips at her throat and she knew what he was asking.

Her hands fell still around his neck. "You'd be the first."

"Then I'm not sure…"

"Please…"

"Why me, Diana?"

"Because you're part of a dream that I thought I'd lost forever."

He swallowed hard. "I'm not sure I know what that means." His fingers traced her jaw, causing new sensations to ripple beneath her skin. He pressed his forehead against hers and moaned soft words beneath his breath.

She didn't want the tender night to end. She'd never go back to being that naive young woman in Toronto who no one wanted. "Make love to me, Mitch. Show me how it's done."

"…I'd be taking advantage."

"Not if I give myself to you willingly. If I tell you I

want you to lift my dress, slide off my stockings and…and make love to me."

"You are torture itself," he moaned.

The moon slid out from the clouds again and bathed the side of his face with gold. His eyes glistened the color of charcoal, and thick black eyebrows framed their depths. The sweet yearning in her body melted all resistance she might have had for this moment.

Taking her jaw with one large palm, he tilted her face and kissed her temple. He seared her skin as he brushed his mouth against her ear. He kissed her earlobe, her neck, her collarbone, and then bracing himself up on his elbows, he hoisted his body lower so he could run his tongue along her neckline.

He made her tremble beneath his soft, moist touch. His tongue lapped the contour of her bosom through the fabric, made her nipple tingle, then he found the warm clay of her cleavage and buried his mouth there.

"Is that how it's done?" she asked with a tremor to her words.

"That's how I dreamed of doing it when I saw you tonight." He smiled and bit down on the lace of her neckline.

Raising her legs on either side of his chest, she planted the soles of her high-heeled boots firmly into the grass beside his narrow hips.

He captured one rounded calf and moaned, running his hand up from the top of her ankle-high boots over her stockings to her knees, and then upward past the lace top to the bareness of her thigh. "Nice boots."

"They're Charlotte's."

His breathing snagged when he met with the naked flesh of her upper legs.

She smiled at how pleased he was and then almost as

if suddenly awakening from her own bliss, she noticed that his leather string tie was dragging along her waist, tickling her belly beneath the soft, pink gingham cloth.

With eager fingers, she undid the buttons of his collar. The tie fell forward as she continued to unbutton lower.

He helped her by tilting so she could get at the shirt. When she yanked it out of his pants with a firm grasp, he laughed in delight, sending another wave of pleasure through her.

She made him slip out of his shirt altogether, tossing it aside in the wispy dry grass as she studied the lines and cut of his brown torso.

"No wonder you're such a danger to the women in town," she murmured.

"I am? It's you I find dangerous."

"Why?" She ran her hand along his smooth shoulders, the wisp of black hair along his upper chest, remembering that she'd first seen him like this yesterday as he'd sat perched above the water during the Mountie raffle.

"Because I never know what you're thinking."

It pleased her that he said so. She wanted to remain mysterious and sensual. She didn't want to be another woman in his nest. Maybe it was wrong of her to do this when she was unmarried, but Mitch was so persuasive.

He grabbed her by the hips and swung her completely over so that she was lying on top of him. The flannel was wide enough that his bare back was resting on cloth beneath him.

Her hair arced over them like a blanket. She pressed it back behind her shoulders. He tugged on the soft puffs of her sleeves, sliding her entire bodice down to her waist and exposing the top of her corset.

Her corset was a hand-me-down, as well, but frilly,

white, strapless and pretty. The whalebone along her ribs pushed up her bosom and created two golden spheres for Mitch's approval.

"That's nice," he whispered, stilling beneath her.

She was sitting on his lap. "Your belt buckle is pressing up against me in a strategic place."

"Oh, I'm sorry." The smile that formed on his lips was dreamy. "I can replace that buckle with something more effective."

"I'll bet you can." She wiggled down and kissed him on the mouth as he fought with the buttons at the back of her dress. He only needed to undo three before the gown slid off her hips and to the ground.

"Let me look at you," he gasped.

His fingers roved over her skin. Sitting above him, she was dressed in her corset, short white pantaloons, then thigh-high blue stockings that clung to her ivory legs.

Uttering pleas of joy, he rolled her to her side on the sheet and then lowered himself to remove her one black boot, then the other.

Slowly, he splayed his fingers along one stocking, rolling it down her leg, over her knee, her calf, then her slender toes. She loved the warm feel of his hand and the burning desire she saw in his eyes.

The other stocking followed, then her pantaloons, till she was simply encased in a corset from her breasts to her waist.

He rolled her to sit on top of him again.

The warm wind stirred the hairs on her body, whispering through the private area that no man, no lover, had seen before.

"I'll always remember you in this position." Gently, he slid her corset lower till it was covering only her ribs and waist. Her breasts popped up, pointed and pink.

They felt heavy and swollen. And ready to burst, aching for his touch.

"What a beautiful shape," he murmured as he raised his face and kissed one point.

She eased the breast into his mouth. So eager for him to taste it, eager to feel his breath on her skin.

He raised his hands and filled his palms with her generous curves. Stroking his thumb against one nipple, he licked the other, the pressure of his lips as light as fluttering bird's wings. Her skin tingled with anticipation, with the steamy feel of his mouth and the soft caress of his masterful hands.

He chuckled softly as her nipples grew hard beneath his tongue. She hadn't realized such pleasure existed.

As he coaxed her body, rolling her flat to the ground, she tried not to think of tomorrow, of what she thought of herself right now, only how right it felt with Mitch.

"Take off your pants," she begged as he towered over her, his tanned chest silhouetted in a strand of disappearing moonlight.

"Help me," he urged in a hoarse whisper.

She unbuckled his belt and slid the buttons of his fly undone. His hard shaft strained beneath the black denim. She wondered what he felt like, and reaching out, rubbed her thumb along the fabric swell.

He sighed in blissful pleasure.

Rolling to his rump, he removed his boots and socks then slid off his pants, revealing muscled legs.

Feeling playful, she reached into the blades of grass and pulled out his leather tie. Flicking it behind his neck, she pulled him down to kiss her.

He kissed her everywhere, beginning with her mouth, working over the rise and fall of her chest, the slight curve of her belly, then her inner thigh.

He wouldn't kiss her there, would he?

Oh, he did. He splayed her legs, parted her and suckled the feminine tip. She'd never felt such a rush of ecstasy. Heat flooded the area and she twisted, raising her bottom toward his mouth for more.

He laughed at her reaction and was soon teasing her with his fingers. He slid them over the fleshy folds, drenched in the wetness he was responsible for creating.

"I'd love to be inside you now, when you're wet and throbbing," he said, watching her face.

"Yes."

"But we'll wait till you're ready."

"I'm ready now."

"No, not yet." He teased her, nibbling on her arm. "Not yet." He kissed her breast. She rolled to her side, still with his fingers trapped between her legs, and allowed her breast to flop into his mouth.

His lips raced over her body, his hand pressing up and down and urging her to an unknown brink. Her muscles clenched, she pushed hard on his fingers and rode the tide by instinct. They climbed together till her body exploded in a cascade of exquisite spasm.

When the air had stilled, when her body had calmed, she laughed softly and kissed the bridge of his nose. His hand slackened between her thighs. He slid his palm over her legs, leaving a trail of wetness as he gripped her buttocks.

"I want more," he said, rising on his knees in the soft grass, placing himself between her legs.

He was a shadowy form of hardened muscles and tanned skin and he looked good between her legs.

His erection, satiny smooth in her grip, was as rigid as a post.

"Now," he said.

"Mitch…" She held him and led him gently to her opening. She knew it would hurt, expected it to hurt, yet wanted to feel him fully inside of her.

He rubbed the head of his shaft along her wetness, along the tingling of her fleshy tip, making her quiver with longing.

Slowly, he pushed himself into her body, stretching her skin until she groaned in pain.

"Keep going," she urged. He pushed deeper and she whimpered at the flash of agony that seemed to cut her body in two.

But it subsided as Mitch held his course steady, not moving but for a fraction until her tense muscles loosened around his erection.

He began a slight shift in his movements, an easing in and out of her body. Their tempo increased, the wetness tripled and soon she relaxed and enjoyed the sensation of being totally filled by Mitch.

His hands moved beneath her buttocks, sliding along her hips and encompassing her waist. He slid his fingers up around each breast and moaned as he dug into her in a steady, rhythmic beat. He pressed her stomach, whispered her name against her throat and closed his eyes to the heavens above.

She watched, sensuous and wholly aroused, sleek and wet and moist for Mitch. He seemed to lose all sense of restraint as his beat grew bolder, deeper and more urgent.

He was near his climax and she adored watching him lose control. It crept softly into his features, a twitch of his eyebrow, a flicker of his closed lids, the clenching of his lips. And then it burst forth like a massive storm, unstoppable if he tried, his thighs clenching, his stomach gripped with the power, his broad chest heaving above her.

"Now I know," she whispered into the crux of his elbow, kissing softly. "I know what it's like."

And nothing else at this timeless, magical moment, mattered to Diana.

With his muscles feeling drained with exhausted pleasure, Mitch rolled to his back on the flannel cloth next to Diana, their bare shoulders grazing. Spent from lovemaking, they were both naked in the darkness. He loved the sight of her beside him.

He stared up at the dark clouds billowing across the moon. "I've never seen nature as beautiful and mysterious as when I stare into the depths of a black sky."

She murmured in agreement.

He cupped his hand over hers, weaving their fingers together and knotting them in spirit.

"Hey," he said, squeezing her fingers.

"Hey," she responded with gentle laughter.

"Are you cold?"

"A little."

He reached over her chest and tugged the sheet over the other edge of her, covering one shoulder and arm. Kissing her softly on the lips, he again felt the warmth and comfort of being with this extraordinary woman.

A sheen of guilt crept over him. He'd been with several women in his lifetime, but he'd never given much thought to what came the day after a night like this.

With Diana, it was different. He hadn't expected to make love to her, was astounded at how great they were together, and yearned for more of her company.

She had been a virgin and had given herself to him, and the sentimentality of that alone touched his heart in a tender spot he'd never felt before.

The night must have meant a lot to her. *He* must

mean a lot to her. That thought both scared and delighted him. It made him scared of where that meant he was headed, scared that she might be too much for him to handle, scared that he might lose her just when he'd met her.

Yesterday his main concern had been telling Allison they weren't suitable. He hadn't even properly met Diana till yesterday. And now his blood pumped with such strength and passion for her, he wasn't sure what was happening to him. Or how he'd feel tomorrow.

How she'd feel.

Yes, he would devote himself to his police duties and they would be his first priority for a while, but how could he walk away from Diana?

Meeting her was unexpected. Falling for her unbelievable.

He rolled onto his side and propped his head on his hand. He traced her skin beneath the swell of her breast, loving the shape and feel of her. "You know I don't take this lightly."

She smiled up at the moon. "I know."

"What just happened between us, Diana?"

"Something lovely. Something private."

She wouldn't look at him, though, and it concerned him. "Will you be able to look at me tomorrow?"

Biting the inside of her mouth, she slid her gaze toward him. "Yes, Mitch, I'll be able to look at you tomorrow."

"I'll be here bright and early. I want to talk about this in the light of day. I want to show you I'm not the kind of man… Well, you've likely heard the rumors about the kind of man… I'll be here in the morning, Diana. I'll look you in the eye and I'll tell you that I still feel what I feel tonight."

She smiled, but her mouth quivered lightly and her eyes shone so defensively that his heart squeezed with a thousand silent misgivings.

Chapter Twelve

It was after one o'clock when they finally rose to dress. Diana tried not to think about the guilty pleasures of the last hour. Lying with Mitch in the grass, she had pretended they were far from civilization and the rules of society and that she was free to explore her sexuality in any manner she chose.

She had, and it had been the most incredible fantasy.

But it was now early Sunday morning. A day when maybe she should fall to her knees and say her prayers and ask for forgiveness for allowing her body to come between good judgment and decency in going to bed with a man.

She had small children to think about, and their care and well-being mattered more to her than her own. When she thought of Allison, and how betrayed the woman would feel if she knew about this, Diana lowered her gaze to the long blades of grass.

"Let me dress you," said Mitch with his dark, charming grin, rising to stand beside her.

"You're teasing." She slapped his backside with her

stocking. Her feelings for Mitch intensified every time she looked at him.

"It'll be a first for me, to put a woman's clothes back on her." He grabbed the stocking from her hand.

She slipped her foot into it but her smile waned. She knew he was joking, but his comment illuminated their differences. How many women had he disrobed?

Was she another one in his numbers?

With clarity, Diana recognized that Mitch had been loving and kind this evening, thinking of her feelings, ensuring she was safe and warm and well looked after while they'd made love.

Still, sadness permeated her bubble as Mitch helped her fold the remaining clean sheets off the lines and then bundled her to the shanty's back door.

With his long arm pressed against the door frame and his tie slung over his shoulder like a prize he'd caught in hunting, he kissed her lightly on the lips.

"Good night," he said softly. "Remember now. I'll see you in the morning."

Although she fought it, she felt that melancholy ache squeeze inside of her again.

She nodded and pressed her mouth to his bristled cheek. He still smelled wonderful. The scent of dry, wild grass had been added to his skin. She kissed his cheek and stepped back. It had been a night of splendor, entangled in the arms of this caring man, a respected Mountie officer who had done nothing but make her laugh and had shown her the pleasures of the universe. No matter what happened from here, she would never be the same.

Optimism ruled Mitch's heart. At six o'clock that morning, four hours after he'd gone to bed, he awoke in the barracks to the bugler's wail of reveille. Sunshine streamed into his private quarters, onto his bed and into his opening eyes. The rays warmed his jaw and gently urged him to rise, for this morning, he had a woman to see.

Sundays usually entailed light duties for the Mounties, but Mitch had worked last Sunday, so today was his day of rest.

Whistling through breakfast in the officer's dining hall, Mitch struggled to understand what had happened to him. Yesterday he wanted nothing to do with women, today he couldn't down his food quickly enough to see Diana.

It wasn't serious, he told himself. How many other times had he fallen for a woman, only to see himself grow distracted? And he had plenty of duties in his criminal investigations to occupy his mind—it shouldn't be occupied by a young woman in a pink checkered dress who had legs that went from here to heaven.

But the hum in his voice as he strode to the stables to get his mare belied the quiet, calm exterior he tried to evoke. He felt good, dammit. Better than he'd felt in a long while.

The commander's wife, Annabelle Ridgeway, was turning her buggy around to head home again after dropping off the commander when Mitch stepped in front of the stables.

"Fine morning, Mrs. Ridgeway." He pressed his fingers to the brim of his black leather hat.

She pressed her plump fingers to her reins. "Good morning to you, Mitch. Thank you for your contribution in the bachelor raffle. How did you fare with Miss Campbell yesterday?"

A smile entertained his lips as he thought of last night with Diana. "Better than I expected."

Her green satin bonnet blazed in the sunshine, framing her clear, wide face. "So you're satisfied that you participated?"

"Yes, ma'am."

"Did she get her money's worth?"

He was sure Mrs. Ridgeway would spot a mischievous twinkle in his eye. "And then some."

"Pleased to hear it. I congratulate you on a job finely done."

With a friendly wave goodbye, Mrs. Ridgeway left. Her one-horse buggy kicked up a gust of dirt.

Entering the stables with a cheerful whistle, Mitch saddled his mare and headed toward the Campbell residence. It was roughly seven-thirty when he found Diana and the children outside. The youngest ones, Elizabeth and Margaret, showed no hesitation in running to his side and welcoming him. The middle children continued taking turns on their unicycle.

In the distance on the grassy hill they'd shared last night, Diana was hanging fresh laundry. She hadn't noticed Mitch's arrival.

"Did you sleep well?" he asked the children, sliding off his horse and hitching it to the post outside the front gate.

"Very well. Diana says it's because of all that dancin'."

"She's likely right." He doffed his hat and banged it across his wide thigh. "Did she—did she say how *she* slept?"

"Diana's a bit quiet this morning," said Elizabeth as she squinted up at him, "so we didn't ask."

"She's makin' us go to church," replied the other girl, skipping to the gate to open it for him. "So we gotta go change into our best clothes."

As the girls ran off, Mitch cautiously regarded Diana for a moment. Unsmiling, she bent down to her hamper, hair tied behind her neck with a faded red ribbon, then strung up a pair of socks. Her movements lacked her usual sparkle.

Was she simply tired from the short sleep?

"Hello, Miss Campbell!" His deep voice boomed across the way and startled her. Closing the distance between them with long, limber strides, Mitch offered a warm smile.

He'd put on his best blue shirt for the occasion.

"Lovely day for hanging a line of bedsheets, isn't it?" He peered over the clothesline at her as she pegged a corner of the flannel he recognized from last night. It certainly had needed rewashing.

A dotted brown apron, tied around her waist, accentuated the jutting of her breasts and he was reminded of how he'd held those breasts last night. Lucky man.

Her cheeks flooded with color, but the smile he was hoping for came out like a sunrise. "Hello, Mitch."

And just as strong as last night, the tingling returned to his skin. "Hello, yourself. It's good to see you. Standing up, I mean," he added with humour.

Whatever was going through her mind, she laughed and tossed a soft, wet cloth at his face. It slid down his nose.

He recovered quickly and slung it over the thin cord of the clothesline. "Why are you rewashing so many sheets?"

Her hands slid across the flannel as she smoothed the wrinkles. She whispered, "Washing only one sheet seemed suspicious. Saying six needed rewashing because they'd fallen off the line seemed easier to explain."

Mitch squinted beneath the brim of his hat. "How are you?"

"Fine," she said with a dip of hesitation. Lifting the basket to her hip, she walked away then set it down again, ten feet beyond him. There was a firmness to her this morning that hadn't been there last night.

Instantly uncertain of where he stood with her, he rubbed his palm along his waist. He bridged the distance, still on the other side of the line. "I mean, Diana, how are you?" This time as she pegged another sheet to the cord, he anchored his hand on top of hers to keep her there.

Her mouth thinned into a straight line. "I'll be fine."

His tone softened. "I came like I said I would. I'd like you to know how much last night meant to me."

Her green eyes flashed. Pivoting quietly, she slid her fingers out from beneath his and bent down to pick up more wet laundry.

An ominous weight sank to the bottom of his gut. "I get the feeling you don't want me here."

She didn't leap to answer. She took her time, carefully sifting through her words, which made the silence more painful.

"You're always welcome to drop by. Elizabeth and Margaret are always happy to see you."

"Why aren't you?"

Her fingers moved over the sheets. "Of course I'm pleased to see you."

He wasn't convinced. "What happened to the woman I held in my arms last night?"

Peering down at her hamper, she exhaled in a long, thin breath. "She woke up and looked around."

"What does that mean?"

Diana squinted in the beam of sunshine. Even the bright light couldn't penetrate their dark conversation. "You want the truth?"

"Of course."

"I've got two adolescent boys in there still sleeping,

but when they awaken they'll be hungry. They won't tell me how much their stomachs ache. They never do. I only know it because I feel the ache myself. There are four other children to feed here. Do you know what I have in the house to make breakfast with, for seven hungry people? Two eggs and a quarter loaf of bread."

He swallowed at the depth of her poverty and the tremble he saw in her eyes. It must be frightening to live so close to the edge of survival. He felt shamed for not having seen it. "I'll buy you more eggs. I'll buy you more bread."

"Sure you will." Her cheek dimpled with a smile, but there was no laughter in her voice. "And shall I sleep with you again tonight so you'll buy me more eggs next week?"

A sob broke from her throat. With gritty determination, she slammed more pegs onto the flannel. The clothesline between them suddenly felt like a cruel fence.

She focused on her task. "I've got to look after my family, Mitch. Dr. York…Dr. York has land of his own and a thriving business. He's interested in me, I felt it at the barbecue. He said he'd like to court me." She wiped her hand on her apron, then ran her shaking fingers across her forehead. "It's so different in Alberta than it was in Toronto. No one was interested in me there…and I've got to make a choice." She lifted her eyes to his face. He saw sorrow buried there. "I told myself all night and all morning that I owed it to you to speak the truth. This is the truth."

"You didn't mention York last night."

"Last night was a dream. I won you in a raffle. Our relationship didn't come naturally and I'm not sure what it's based on. I've got to think of my family."

His throat felt thick, difficult to open. "But you're sacrificing yourself and maybe what *you* want out of life."

"I have responsibilities toward the children."

Agonized by her decision, he couldn't argue.

He'd only known Diana for two days. What was he to do? Commit to her on the spot? He didn't own any property. He lived at the barracks and his account at the bank totaled twenty dollars. And what the hell had Mitch ever committed to in his life?

He needed time to think.

"Dr. York is a decent man," she said quietly.

Mitch couldn't debate that point. He'd been envious of York's attention to Diana, and perhaps because of that had found some minor flaws, but overall, York was decent.

Mitch murmured, "But last night with me meant something to you, didn't it?" There was more to Mitch and Diana's relationship than comparing his wealth to Dr. York's.

"That's why this is so difficult."

Every wrong he'd ever done to any woman flashed through his mind. This is how it must have felt when he walked away from them, when he didn't bother to drop by and say hello for days after spending an evening with them, when he at times didn't even explain why he wasn't coming back.

Interrupting them, Margaret hollered from the back stoop. "Diana! My good dress needs to be ironed!"

"I didn't mean to hurt your feelings," Diana said in a coarse whisper.

He winced. He'd said those words several times himself in the past decade. But he'd never been on the receiving end of them. They didn't ease the hurt at all.

Margaret yelled again. "Shall I set the iron in the coals to heat?"

"Don't touch anything, fire is dangerous! I'll be right

there!" With a flash of regret at Mitch, Diana lifted the empty hamper and scuttled beneath the clothesline.

Crushed by her rebuff, Mitch was left standing in a sea of flapping sheets on top of the lone hill, the glorious spot where they'd made love last night. He'd never completely had Diana, yet wondered how he'd lost her.

Three days later, Diana still remained at the back of his mind while Mitch worked, ate and slept. He verged on the edge of exhaustion, thinking about her. Standing in the jailhouse, Mitch removed items from his fingerprinting kit and lined them on the desk. The old guard watched him along with the two horse thieves behind bars, equally wary. Mitch walked to the door and propped it open. Late September sunshine lit his work. When he sat down, he adjusted the glass magnifier over the sample fingerprint he'd taken from Owen Norris, wondering if he'd ever see her again.

Today was her first day at the optometrist's office.

He didn't blame her for looking out for herself and doing what was best for her family. In the past he'd done it, too. He'd pushed aside other people—*women*—in his own bid to do what was right for himself. But the shameful thing, the selfish thing and what grated most, he admitted as he looked at the ink spirals and whorls, was that no one had ever pushed *him* aside.

"Whaddya see, sir?" Standing by the rifle case, Moses scratched his white beard.

Mitch fine-tuned the microscope and peered at the sample. "I believe we have a match."

"Matchin' up our fingers to the smudges we left on a dinner plate don't prove nothin'." Behind bars, Owen rubbed his hands. Remnants of India ink used an hour ago stained his fingers.

His partner, Paul, muttered protests.

"Correct, Owen, it doesn't prove anything in your trial. I'm testing your prints as an example to prove Galton's theory of identification."

"You keep talkin' about that scientist like he was standin' in the next room. He lives across an ocean so his opinion doesn't have anything to do with anything."

"Let me see the microscope," said Moses, coming closer. Mitch stepped aside and let the old-timer look. "I don't see how you can make sense of all the squiggles."

"If you look at this chart, the way Galton's classified all ten fingers, you can see this single furrow bifurcating—"

"Black magic," whispered Moses, withdrawing from the room. He stepped outside. Mitch heard him speaking to two men outdoors. "Yup, he says he's done it."

As requested, the commander walked in, puffing on a strong cigar and followed by his clerk. "All right, Inspector, let's see what you've cooked up."

"With all due respect, sir," said Mitch, adjusting the focus as the commander peered through the lens, "I didn't concoct it. I'm following the directions."

"So you said. But what makes Galton an expert? How does he know that fingerprints don't change over time?"

"He submits an interesting piece of evidence. Fingerprints from another fellow who took samples of his own two fingers, one made in 1860, the other in 1888. Over this interval of twenty-eight years, the fingerprints didn't change, sir."

The commander sat back and exhaled cigar smoke, filling the small room with the pleasant, strong scent of tobacco.

Moses and the company clerk whispered to each

other. To his irritation, Mitch heard one of them pro-
claim, "Bullshit."

The commander took his time. "But you told me according to your papers that Galton also says he can tell
two other things simply by looking at fingerprints. What
race a man belongs to, and how smart he is."

Mitch squirmed. He didn't agree with that part of the
theory. It seemed wrong to judge a man and his intelli-
gence by a physical part of his body—namely fingerprints. And he had his doubts about proving a fellow's
race. "Sir...he admits he doesn't have evidence on those
theories. But the claims on fingerprint identification
seem valid. Particularly useful in matching criminals to
the scene of a crime."

In the cell, the prisoners chortled. "Can ya tell by
lookin' at my prints, Inspector, that I've got to use the
privy?"

Mitch cringed as the guard and the clerk laughed
along with the prisoners. Dammit, whose side were the
Mounties on?

The commander delivered the most critical blow. "If
we can't trust Galton on one claim, we can't trust him
on the other. We'll go by hard evidence like we always
have. Not a scholar's idea of how to handle police work.
Get rid of this stuff, Inspector. I don't want you using it."

Diana's first day of work brought a sense of confusion
she hadn't expected. Wednesday morning passed quickly
but the afternoon dragged. Outwardly, she displayed a
great deal of energy dealing with several customers and
Dr. York, but inwardly her thoughts stole to Mitch.

While she explained to a farmer's wife to stand behind the line drawn on the hardwood floor and read from
the eye chart, Diana fought the hold Mitch had over her.

The evening of intimacy she'd spent with him had been beyond what she'd imagined could happen between them. She had knowledge about the physical acts of reproduction, but she'd never realized how her heart would thump with a simple glance from Mitch's dark, brooding eyes.

That was likely how she'd feel with Emmit. If he might only brush his arm against her as he cranked the grindstone, or glance longer in her direction when he demonstrated how to bend the rims of spectacles to fit the customers' ears, or perhaps if he even kissed her as Mitch had, she might compare the two. She *wanted* to prove Emmit could hold her fantasies just as well as Mitch.

They were both young attractive men. Although Emmit didn't seem as physically fit, he was an accomplished fencer, swift on his feet and quick to lunge with his sword, as he'd demonstrated to Diana in the back room. He went on tournaments, he said, and enjoyed a physical challenge. His office was successful, too, and he hadn't criticized her brothers.

Thinking of Wayde and Tom, she tried to shake off her arguments of the last three mornings. Why wouldn't they explain to her where they'd been the nights before?

It seemed the more she prodded, the more deceptive they became. As young men fighting for independence, they needed their freedom, but were still too young to support themselves despite their jobs. Their lame excuses had Diana convinced there were young women involved.

Did the whole world revolve around love?

Because her brothers' secrecy seemed to stem from matters of the heart, Diana didn't push too hard for answers. Their romantic life wasn't a sister's business.

But in her imagination, she could picture how Mitch's mouth would pucker with disapproval at the mention of trouble with her brothers. It was another vexing factor about Mitch.

According to the town, Mitch was a carefree solitary man with a taste for splashy women and drinking with his gang of friends. Diana hadn't witnessed the drinking, but she certainly felt the ramifications of being targeted as an easy woman.

She chastised herself for falling so quickly for his charm and wondered, with a rising tide of humiliation, how Mitch likely compared her sexual performance to Allison's.

For he and Allison, Diana conjured, had certainly been intimate.

Watching Emmit, tall and innocent as he spoke to his customers, shamed Diana. If he should ever discover what she'd done with Mitch… She was no longer a virgin, and might have to explain that to some man, some day, if and when she married, but for now she tried to bury her sense of embarrassment.

At five o'clock, the cuckoo bird in the wall clock jumped out and chirped five times. Diana flinched. The silly thing surprised her every hour on the hour.

"Time to go," said Emmit. "You did a fine job today."

Diana smiled at the compliment. *Move closer,* she silently begged, *that I might feel your touch and compare it to Mitch's.*

He locked the front door, then led the way down the hall and to the cloakroom. Helping her with her cape, Emmit slid his hands along her shoulders. Facing away from him, she closed her eyes and tried to drown herself in the feeling, testing her reaction to Emmit's touch.

A little flutter in her stomach, she was sure of it. But then, it was five o'clock and she hadn't eaten since noon. Her stomach had been growling for the last hour.

Turning around, she allowed herself to linger inches away from him. His shiny vest caught the light glowing off the kerosene lantern. He darted to the side wall and turned it off.

When they were bathed in darkness, Diana was pleased. Perhaps now he'd attempt something.

"Shall we leave?" He cleared his throat and placed one hand directly on her back. *Directly.* She waited for the rush of body heat.

There was a tingle. But perhaps that came from the scratching of her corset where his palm rested on her spine.

He took a step toward the hall, maybe expecting her to follow, but instead, she stood rooted. Now his face was inches from hers.

Kiss me, she hoped.

"I have a sudden urge to kiss you," he whispered.

"Fancy that," she croaked.

"May I?"

How splendid of him to ask rather than take. "Please do."

His movements came so quickly, he stole her breath. And that was definitely good. He gave her a light peck on the cheek. He smelled nice, she thought, like baked beans.

Hmm. Maybe she was truly hungry.

She didn't allow him to recover from the peck on the cheek when she reached up and pressed her mouth lightly against his.

This time he gasped. It was a nice effect to have on a man. Definitely a strong reaction in his favor.

"Oh, my goodness. Yes, well, let's see. That was pleasant, Miss Campbell." He coughed. "Diana."

Her palms slid together. They were sweaty, she noticed with glee. Yes, indeed. It was warm beneath the wool cape and her palms were sweaty.

It was a definite sign. She and Emmit were a fit. Sailing from the room with her cape flying behind her, she silently offered good luck to Officer Mitchell Reid in his quest for another easy target.

Chapter Thirteen

Even the lively sounds of the children while Diana washed their hair in the kitchen on Friday evening wasn't enough to sway her gloom.

A fire crackled in the stove. Heat steamed the room. Dressed in her cozy night robe, Diana lifted the mason jar of dried rose petals from the counter and sniffed. Again today Emmit had kissed her soundly after her day had ended, but she hadn't reacted. Not a stomach growl or sweaty palm within an inch of the man. But at the office this morning, he had brought her these rose petals, asked about her family and promised to pick her up at seven tomorrow evening for the community dance.

Concentrating on his positive attributes and warning herself not to measure him against Mitch, Diana set down the rose petals and turned to her present task. Dressed in cozy nightclothes, four youngsters sat on the bench, propped on their knees with heads lowered over a tin bathtub and towels tucked behind their necks.

Diana lifted the heavy pail of water and glanced at the upturned faces. "Everybody ready?"

"Yeah," they mumbled.

She started with five-and-a-half-year-old Elizabeth, pouring water over her soapy hair. Each child scrubbed their scalp as Diana passed. Tonight if it wasn't too late when Wayde and Tom got in, she'd asked them to carry the tub outdoors to drain it.

She was combing knots from Elizabeth's hair when a loud knock on the side door made the little girl jump.

Diana gave her an extralong tickle beneath her chin. "Let's see who that is."

With a glowing lantern swinging from her hand, a mob of chirping children behind her, Diana went to the door. "Who is it?"

"Mitchell Reid."

With a startle, she clenched her robe around her throat and opened the door.

Mitch stood there in his handsome red uniform with another policeman standing behind him.

The sight of Mitch's dark features and the hard lines of his body tensing beneath the red wool made her pulse instantly blaze. He, in turn, pressed his hand to his holster and shifted his gaze over her robe. The muscles along his jaw tightened.

Conscious of his trailing eyes, the lateness of the evening and the chill of the autumn draft, Diana gripped the robe tighter to conceal her torn flannel gown. When she raised the lantern, light sparkled over his black hair.

"Mitch, what is it?"

"Good evening, Diana." Glancing past her shoulder, he smiled briefly at the children. "Are Wayde and Tom home?"

An instant panic clamped her throat. "They're not in. What is it?"

He was careful not to give himself away. He stood there like an officer on duty, cool and detached, which threw her emotions in the opposite direction. He made her body flash with fear and her mind race with urgency. She knew he hadn't come to tell her Wayde and Tom were hurt, otherwise he wouldn't be asking if they were in, because he'd know. Which meant her brothers were embroiled in some sort of trouble.

Mitch tempered his voice to an even keel. "May we talk with you a moment?"

"What is it? Please don't make me ask again."

He blinked and looked down at the children woven around her legs and Diana instantly understood he didn't want to speak in front of them. She silently agreed.

She lifted the lantern above their heads. "Children, it's bedtime."

"Aw, do we have to?"

"Yes, you do." Diana shooed them from the door. Their socked feet thumped up the pine stairs. Her own feet, encased in woolen stockings, felt suddenly cold.

When she turned back to Mitch, he was talking to the Mountie behind him. "Wait here, Corporal. We don't want to scare the children. I'll go in alone." Turning to Diana, he asked gently, "Is it all right if I come inside for a few minutes?"

No strangers allowed inside our home. Now what was she to do? This was official police business, she was dressed in a thin night robe, and it was too cold to talk outside.

Then faster than she could snap her fingers, he was walking in.

Struck by dismay as he passed, she stood breathless, clenching the lantern with trembling fingers, knowing she was breaking an important promise to her brothers and sisters.

For all intents, the Toronto police had done nothing

to protect them. She recalled their useless questions. *Do you have proof your things were stolen? We asked the butler but he denies it. And how do we know, miss, as he suggests, that you had a sterling silver candelabra to begin with? And your uncle…did he not use your money to buy food for you at the market and to pay the servants' wages?*

And on and on, they'd suffered in humiliation. They were children who'd been robbed by adults more cunning and relentless than she'd known possible.

Her father used to tell her while she was growing up, "Every school costs money." He wasn't referring to formal education but everyday lessons, and she'd received an education that would last her a lifetime.

These next few moments with Mitch might cost her dearly, too. Her heart had gotten involved with a man who threatened the stability of everything she knew and held dear about herself.

They approached the kitchen. He squeezed his large body through the small hallway and ran his hand through his hair. She indicated a chair but he shook his head. The man preferred to stand.

Diana placed the lantern on the counter beside her mason jar of rose petals. Emmit flashed through her mind. He seemed so safe compared to Mitch.

"There's been another bank robbery in Cedarville," he said.

"Again?"

"There are two banks there, and this time it was the First National. They got away with five thousand dollars."

Her lips went numb. "Did—did my brothers witness it? Is that why you're here?"

He strained to say the words. "I'm afraid they've been accused of the crime."

Her gaze froze on his sober face. "By whom?"

"An eyewitness. The managing banker himself."

"I don't believe it."

"Harvey Franklin describes a red-haired young man."

She paused. "Is that all?"

"They left an entire deck of cards this time, ones with blue-and-white striped patterns on the back—"

"So?" Reeling with mental images, Diana knew Mitch had seen her brothers playing with a similar deck on the day of the harvest fair when she'd won Mitch in the raffle and they'd met her family by the carousel. "They sell those cards for a nickel at the Beazly's trinket store. Half the town likely has the same deck."

He listened carefully and nodded. "True enough. But I need to speak to them. Where are they?"

"What time are we talking about? When did this robbery occur?"

"Late this afternoon."

Anger told hold of her. "And you couldn't wait to come to my door and accuse them. It would be an easy solution, wouldn't it?"

"That's not how I run my investigations."

She yanked hard on the ties of her robe. They squeezed her rib cage. "You'll have to look deeper than inside my home. I know my brothers. They didn't do this." Fear chilled the room. "Go away and please don't come back."

He winced. "There were a lot of different ways to approach this tonight. I fought for the right to put everything on the table in front of you."

Her mouth thinned. "And who fought for the opposite?"

"The commander thought it would be best if I bypassed you and spoke only to your brothers."

"Well...should you be commended then? Thank you for being an accuser right to my face."

"Give me a minute's break to listen to what I have to say."

But her terror held the upper hand. She wanted him to leave this instant. Her world was tipping out of control again with the same horror she'd felt when she was told her uncle had sold their home right from underneath them. "My brothers aren't here and I have no idea where they are. What else do you need to know?"

She was leaving Calgary, she vowed. She would begin packing the instant Mitch left through that door. They would leave this horrible town.

Mitch didn't flinch at her icy glare. With a heavy sigh, he strode toward the door. "I'm going to wait outside for them to arrive, however long it takes. I'll send my men in other directions. You're not to leave the house."

She looked directly into his calculating face. "You don't want me to leave in case I run to warn them."

His jaw was set firm, but an artery pulsed at his temple, indicating this wasn't easy for him. "You know, there were more determined men who wanted to head this investigation. Mounties who'd never let you talk to them like this."

Despite her fear and need to retaliate, she bit back her reply.

"But I insisted on leading it. I thought it might be easier on you."

Her fingers trembled on her robe.

Then deep voices resonated behind the door. The knob turned and her brothers walked in, as casual as ever.

"Wayde. Tom." Diana stepped calmly to their side.

They were wearing denim pants and flannel shirts, looking a bit windswept but well-groomed and tidy.

"What's goin' on?" Wayde looked from his sister to Mitch.

Mitch stepped forward. "Where were you both today?"

"Workin' at the livery, as usual."

"Your boss said you left at two o'clock."

The brothers looked at each other.

Mitch persevered. "Where were you at six o'clock this evening?"

"Reckon that's no one's concern except ours."

"There was a bank robbery in Cedarville."

Wayde flinched. Tom gaped.

"Which one?" Wayde asked.

"The First National," Mitch said slowly. "And an eyewitness describes one of the men as you."

They stepped back in confusion. Tom's face hardened. Wayde's gaze flew to Diana's. She shivered.

"I'll repeat my question. Where were you at six o'clock?"

No answer.

Diana broke in, trying to bring words of comfort. "I'll get a lawyer." God only knew how they'd pay for one.

Mitch removed the handcuffs from the back of his uniform and called to the corporal outside for assistance.

"No," Diana begged.

Mitch ignored her. "You're both under arrest, by order of Commander Ridgeway. For bank robbery and attempted *murder*."

"Attempted murder?"

"There's a man in a coma with a bullet lodged in his spine. Arthur Billings. He's a teller who tried to apprehend the robbers. If he wakes up and says you didn't do it, you'll be lucky. If he dies, you'll be tried for murder."

Wayde turned white and shaky. "Was anyone else…hurt?"

"No," said the corporal. He led her brothers outside but Mitch stayed behind. It had happened so fast, Diana's breath was still racing. Mitch leaned the door against the frame so they couldn't be heard by the men outside.

"It's obvious by Wayde's questions that they weren't there. Can't you see that?" Frantic, Diana pleaded. "Mitch…a week ago…up on that hill…we…" She battled the lump in her throat and sting in her eyes. "It doesn't make any difference, does it, what you and I did?"

"It does," he whispered, stepping closer, towering over her like a giant spruce.

She felt her eyes nearly spilling. "How?"

"Because I've been with your family. It's a testament to your bond that your brothers, two fully grown young men, remain at your side and live here. They choose to protect you and the younger children rather than run on their own." The hard edge to his dark features faded. "There's strength and honor in that… I think Wayde and Tom… I'm not so sure of their guilt… I'm not so convinced…."

Stunned, she slumped against the wall behind her. His words caused a wedge in her throat. There was hope.

He leaned away from her, gripping the door handle, exploring it with his rough fingers as if he'd never seen it before. "But I've got to prove it with facts and hard evidence. I've got to do that regardless of how I might feel about you." His deep tone grew raspy. "And what's more, Diana, for the commander to take my work on this investigation as unhampered by my feelings for you, we can't see each other again. Not privately. Not alone."

* * *

Mitch knew he was risking everything by going against the commander's orders. Working in the eerie darkness of twelve o'clock midnight, several hours after putting Wayde and Tom Campbell in jail, Mitch carried his lantern through the First National Bank in Cedarville. He placed the light and his fingerprinting kit on the wooden counter behind the metal till.

Just as Mitch had suspected, the bank was set to resume regular business in the morning, so he knew he had to collect undisturbed evidence from the robbery tonight.

"I'll be outside on duty if you need me." The bank guard, who'd had a gun jammed into his back the entire time of the robbery and hadn't witnessed much, left Mitch to his work.

"Thanks, I'll have a final look around."

Mitch hadn't told him he'd be collecting fingerprints, only residual evidence. Twenty minutes ago, the banker's wife, Mrs. Franklin, and her butler had appeared, she rumpled and upset and begging her husband to retire to bed. Mr. Franklin had left with his wife. Mitch was through questioning him and the guard. He'd return tomorrow at a decent hour to further question the tellers.

The wooden lid of the kit creaked as Mitch lifted it. He removed two colors of dust powder—one black, one white. Since the till drawer was made of silver metal, Mitch would use black powder which would give him the biggest contrast in lifting the prints. He poured the black powder onto a piece of stiff cardboard, a palette of sorts, then dipped the ostrich feather into the powder and stroked it across the metal drawer. Two prints appeared. Using his rubber lifter, he gently lifted the prints and pressed them onto a fresh sheet of paper.

Then he took his quill, dipped it in India ink, wrote the date, time and location of print.

Methodically, he went about the bank and lifted several more. It would be impossible to lift everything due to the high volume of customers they'd had for several days, according to the manager, but Mitch lifted several sets near the spots where the robbers had entered and exited.

When he had the sheets labeled, he took out a small brush and varnished the prints to seal them. He had devised a system of wires and clothespins to hang the damp pages inside the box and be transportable to Calgary overnight.

He let them set for half an hour as he collected different samples from the room—a strand of red hair on the floor beside the till, minute particles of brown broken glass near the back door, chipped red paint near the wicket counter, a tiny trace of soil on the carpet by the door. And most importantly, what he'd discovered from his interviews was that two shots—not one—had been fired at Mr. Billings as he'd attempted to apprehend the robbers. One was lodged in the man's spine, the other in the plastered wall behind the desks. With a sharp pocketknife, Mitch gouged the wall and removed a half-inch diameter of plaster and wood in which the bullet lay imbedded.

He removed his sketch pad and very carefully drew the pattern of footprints he saw leading to and from the back door. Some imprints had been left in dry dirt, others in moist grass, some were just lines scuffed in gravel. With his expandable wooden ruler, he measured boot sizes and heel depths.

When he was finished, he said goodbye to the guard. Striding to his mare, Mitch tilted his cowboy hat. "See you tomorrow. I'll be back to take a look in the daylight."

"I'll be here. Good night, sir."

With his blood pumping with the day's events, Mitch slid the fingerprinting kit into his saddlebag. Galloping into the darkness, he hoped like hell the prints would amount to something, and that he hadn't just jeopardized his future for unreadable ink smudges. Sometime down the road, he'd figure out when and how to present the fingerprints to the commander.

And as for Diana Campbell, he thought with a tremble, she'd have to wait blindly and hope like hell the prints amounted to something, too.

Chapter Fourteen

Diana knew Mitch wouldn't like her approaching him after his warning to keep away, but she was on a mission to speak with him. She had no choice.

With trepidation, Diana walked through the fort gates and spoke with the guards. They gave her permission to head to the jailhouse. Behind her in the drafty morning, roosters crowed from the fenced chicken coop. The sunrise slanted above the horizon. Uncontrollable events of the past two days whipped around her as if she was in a tornado—her brothers imprisoned, her younger brother and sisters at home frantic and crying for hours on end, and Diana desperately trying to hold everyone together while somehow acquiring counsel for Wayde and Tom. And those two culprits, other than repeating that they were innocent, refused to answer police questions. That infuriated her most. They could at least talk to *her.*

Mitch had told her he was on her side, but she had yet to see how he could help. He hadn't produced any evidence so far in her brothers' favor.

It was up to her. In the end, it was always up to her.

Moving to the prairies had been her mistake. Compounded with the way Emmit had reacted to the situation by looking at her as if she was a criminal, she was more determined to help her brothers, and then flee this unforgiving town.

"Diana," said Mitch, rising from the front office as she opened the jailhouse door and swirled in with her cape whipping around her skirt. "I wasn't expecting you. It's early."

The older guard was there, too, sitting at the main desk beside the cells. He sipped his coffee and nodded hello.

"I—I wanted to catch you before your day got started." She glanced to the cells where Wayde and Tom shifted from their beds to their booted feet. Setting her basket of sparse food on the main desk, she smiled tentatively at them. They didn't smile back. Her brothers were caged and the sight made her sick to her stomach.

By not cooperating with the police, they were protecting someone. She felt it in her bones and it was the only explanation that made sense to her as she laid away last night. The sooner they got a lawyer, the better off they'd be. Who were they protecting?

"Mitch—Officer Reid—may I have a word with you, privately?"

Mitch's expression deepened. His black eyebrows drew together and his mouth twitched with disapproval. Looming above his desk with the confidence and command of an investigator twice his age, he studied her.

Then with a nod of command to the old guard, Mitch gestured to her to enter the side office where he'd been working.

He closed the door behind her and offered her a chair. "I prefer to stand."

He didn't bother with sitting, either. He stood with

his wide shoulders pressed against the pine panel. "I recall telling you we shouldn't see each other privately."

Defensive, she lowered her head, her bonnet's ribbon digging into her chin where it was tied. She swept her gaze absently over the journals and ink bottles on his desk. Flinching at his nearness and the memory of a night that now seemed as if it'd happened years ago, she reminded herself that on the very day her brothers might be found guilty in court, Mitch could walk back to his quarters and sit down at his supper table as if nothing personal had happened to him.

"It's best for your brothers, Diana. How would it seem to a judge and jury if the chief investigating officer was caught up with the prisoners' sister?"

Understanding that it was best for the logical procession of the case, Diana felt duly reprimanded. "It's not easy for me to stay out of this. I brought my brothers to this town. I recommended Calgary to my family and got them so excited they talked about it for weeks before we arrived. I promised we'd get a fresh start and live lives of adventure."

"Try to disengage your feelings."

"Like you have?"

The abruptness of her tone startled him. He sank back onto the door.

She fingered the ties of her drawstring purse. "Has Mr. Billings recovered from his coma?"

"He's still unconscious."

"But is his condition improving?" Her brothers were convinced that once the man could speak, he would clear their name.

"It's worsened. He's not responding to voices anymore."

She quivered with sympathy. Although she wanted

to visit Mr. Billings at the fort's small hospital, his family would likely disapprove and her intentions would seem suspect.

"Your brothers won't talk to me. Do you have any idea why?"

Because maybe they didn't trust Mitch.

Because maybe after all they'd been through, she still couldn't put her brothers' lives in his hands, either.

But Mitch was the sole person in this town who, at least on the surface, said he wanted to believe them. That amounted to something in her heart.

"I think their disappearance, the reason they were gone many evenings from home has to do with a young woman. Or two."

"They were seeing someone?"

"I think so."

"Then why won't they say?"

"I don't know."

"How do you know women are involved?"

"The way they paid attention to the way they combed their hair."

"Go on."

"That's all I have to my explanation." It sounded feeble. "It's silly, isn't it? I tell myself every hour that it's silly to use that as a clue, but it's all I have and I *know* it as the truth."

"Diana, I've talked to almost everybody in this town who knows your brothers. There's no mention of any women. Wouldn't someone have seen them if they were courting?"

Frustrated, Diana shook her head. With her soft movements, her dark hair ruffled at her throat.

"Talk to them, Diana. Tell them how important it is that we get their version of events."

She lowered her voice in a confidential whisper. "They keep telling me they were out riding, alone. That they don't have witnesses to prove it. They keep saying you need to prove that they did the crime, not that they didn't."

"It's not enough to wait for proof to be shown against them," said Mitch. "They have to fight the charges."

"They won't speak to you until they have a lawyer. And I can't blame them." She drew her shoulders tighter with resolve, determined to forge ahead. "The reason I'm here... I've exhausted my possibilities. Initially, I thought Emmit might help me provide one."

"He won't?"

"He says he's unable to lend me that much cash in advance, since he's uncertain of the outcome." Feeling her cheeks sting with embarrassment, Diana couldn't bear to have Mitch watch her. It was bad enough that she'd chosen Emmit as the man to woo her heart even though she hadn't felt near the physical attraction to him as to Mitch, but Emmit's cold refusal—however understandable—to help her family caused a breach of trust that would be difficult, if not impossible, to heal.

But Mitch was already two steps ahead in his thinking. "As the investigating officer, I can't give you the money for getting a lawyer. That would truly be a conflict of position. The commander would see me off this case."

"I don't expect that. But what I need to do right now is speak to the commander. That's why I've come."

Mitch seemed to come to a conclusion. He reopened the door and spoke to the white-haired guard. "Moses, could you tell Superintendent Ridgeway that we need to see him?"

"That's all right," said Diana, walking by Mitch into the jailhouse. "I can go to him."

"No," Mitch ordered the guard, causing a rumble of apprehension to flitter up her spine. "Tell the commander there are pressing things I need to show him here. Pieces of evidence I'd like to bring to his attention—and Miss Campbell's—here on my desk. This can't wait any longer."

"The Crown will provide your brothers with legal counsel, Miss Campbell," said Superintendent Ridgeway, seated across from Mitch in the office thirty minutes later. "But the fella who's available, Mr. Walter, is working somewhere between here and the northern fort in Edmonton. He's due back within a day or two. No longer than a week."

Mitch watched Diana, sitting opposite the desk, as she closed her eyes with relief. The morning breeze from the open window beside his head stirred the hair at his temples, rousing his senses. He'd never been more aware that Diana was alone in her family troubles. She had no older folks to discuss her decisions, or to lean on for strength.

Puffing on his cigar, the commander frowned at Mitch. "Why was it necessary to bring me here to ask about providing a lawyer? The judge is sentencing Owen Norris and Paul Irwing this morning and I need to be in court."

Mitch felt the man's cold blast of irritation. "Sir, that's not all."

"What then?"

"I wanted to demonstrate something I was shown at the officer's academy." He pushed the microscope toward the man. "There's a bullet under the glass. Take a look at the grooves. Then I'd like Miss Campbell to have a look."

The commander exhaled a cloud of smoke, bit down on the cigar and peered through the microscope. "I see lines. Scratches on the bullet."

"Right. You have a look now, Diana."

The commander noticed the casual use of her first name and while she peered into the eyepiece, he studied Mitch. Mitch wished he'd caught himself before he'd said it.

"Those grooves are called rifling marks. I went over it with the fort's gunsmith yesterday. The barrels of some guns have tiny grooves in them to help with the trajectory and aim."

"They showed you that in Regina?"

"Yes, sir."

"What's it mean?"

"It means that every bullet released from a gun that has rifling will have those identical grooves traced onto its shell. So we can match the bullet to the precise firearm."

"Is that a fact?"

"The bullet you're looking at is one I found imbedded in the Cedarville bank. It's got rifling marks."

"Your point?"

"Sir, Wayde and Tom Campbell own simple guns, nothing fancy or expensive. There's no rifling on their barrels."

"Maybe they used different guns to rob the bank."

Mitch met with Diana's nervous glare. "Maybe."

The commander opened the door to leave.

Mitch rose from his chair. "Sir, when I looked at the thick red hair I found at the scene and compared it beneath the microscope to one of Wayde Campbell's, it doesn't match in thickness."

"Microscope? Both hairs are red, aren't they?"

Desperate to be heard, Mitch asked another question. "Sir, what color was the cup you drank your coffee from this morning?"

"What kind of question is that?"

"It's to demonstrate another point."

"Goddammit. Something you read from that Galton book?"

Mitch plowed ahead, determined to prove his point. "Both you and the clerk ate breakfast at the table by the window in your outer office. You sat in the chair facing the picture of Queen Victoria. You drank coffee from a blue tin cup, sir, and had eggs and bacon from a gray one. The clerk ate from crockery. Then you washed your hands on the porcelain bowl resting on the counter twenty feet away from the clerk's desk. At some point, you adjusted the mirror on the wall to comb your hair. You used the tortoiseshell comb in the top right drawer."

"What the hell? Were you spyin' on me?" The commander turned to Diana, who looked just as confused.

"No, sir. Late last night, I went into your outer office and wiped the area clean with a moist cloth. At six o'clock this morning, I returned and dusted the same area for fingerprints."

"You've got a helluva lot of nerve. Did my clerk go along with this?"

"I phrased it as an order, linked to my investigation and let him believe you were aware of it. I...I apologize sir." Mitch pointed to an empty glass on the desk. "Remember when I came to you last night in the officers' dining hall to inform you of Mr. Billings's condition? Well, I borrowed this glass, the one you were using to drink your whisky."

"So that's where it went. Why'd you take it?"

"I used the fingerprints that I knew to be yours from

the whisky glass as a base of comparison to this morning's prints. Look for yourself."

Diana kept her eyes averted. She focused on the microscope and the tiny details on his desk. The breeze from the window behind Mitch flapped the curtain. Fresh air mixed with the scent of the commander's cigar and curled around his stubborn face.

Cornering the superintendent this way wasn't pleasant and it bordered on insubordination, but Mitch countered that by telling himself this was an unusual situation. No Mountie had ever attempted to use fingerprinting to solve a crime. And the commander, as gruff and intimidating as he was, was also known for being fair.

The commander leaned forward and peered through the microscope.

With relief, Mitch explained. "There are twelve identical points of comparison between each set of prints in the office and the one on your glass from last night. In the scientific world, that means they're a match. I thought if I showed you these, you'd see how valuable they are as police tools."

"And I suppose you're here to tell me something about the Campbell fingerprints."

Mitch turned his attention to Diana. "I've asked, but they won't allow me to take their prints for a baseline. I was hoping my demonstration might persuade Miss Campbell to convince them."

Diana hesitated as she peered from one man to the other. She looked small and fragile sitting next to the bulky commander, but Mitch knew she was tougher than iron.

"Superintendent," said Mitch, "the identification of these fingerprints is as valuable and scientific as the bullet is with its rifling. Will you allow me to use fin-gerprinting in this case?"

"I don't approve of your means of convincing me, and don't ever try something like that on me again." The commander chomped on his cigar. "But...it's a mighty persuasive demonstration. All right, I'll allow you to sample the fingerprints in this case. But before you tell anyone the conclusions you come to, you'll discuss them with me and I'll decide with the judge if they're admissible."

"Yes, sir." With great care, Mitch lifted the micro-scope and set it back in front of him on the desk.

"Miss Campbell," said Mitch. Their eyes met. A surge of possibility raced through him. She tipped her face and he was cheered at the strength he witnessed there. "I would recommend you convince your broth-ers to cooperate."

Chapter Fifteen

It seemed to Mitch that everyone had an opinion on the fingerprints he'd recovered from the Cedarville Bank. The commander had only given his permission yesterday morning, but an article had come out in today's paper about the breakthrough. By one o'clock, while Mitch was taking lunch at the Cedarville Diner, the bootmaker, preacher, even the saloon barkeep dropped by his table to marvel at the process.

"Just by pressin' my finger on a piece of paper, you can tell it's me?" asked the banker, Mr. Franklin, later in the afternoon.

"I've got two sisters and one of them is a twin," said Mrs. Patty Upwood, one of three female tellers Mitch had also taken sample fingerprints from. She was young and pretty and caught the attention of several men. Her little finger was broken, which she said she'd caught in the till during the commotion of the robbery. There was an underlying nervousness to all the staff. Likely, they were upset at Mr. Billings's condition, since he was still in a coma. "Wouldn't me and my twin have the same fingerprints?"

"No," replied Mitch. "Even twins have recognizable differences."

"Is that a fact," said Superintendent Ridgeway at six o'clock that evening when Mitch returned to Fort Calgary. "Even twins?"

It took several hours for Mitch to put it together in his jailhouse office. He had twelve sets of fingerprints from the crime scene to match up with his baseline of Cedarville characters. Within hours, he had matched six of those prints to Mr. Billings, Mrs. Upwood, two other female tellers, the banker and the guard. That left six unaccounted for and hopefully two of those would match the robbers' prints.

And yet Wayde and Tom Campbell didn't seem excited by the matching game. The following day, word had spread from Cedarville to Calgary that six remaining sets of fingerprints from the crime scene had no owners. The reporter, David Fitzgibbon, had somehow gotten it into the paper.

Diana walked into the jailhouse at noon the next day, Tuesday, taking a break from the optometrist's office to deliver her brothers each a slice of pumpkin pie.

Her loose hair flowed in a stream behind her shoulders and her mouth was set in determination. Mitch felt a tug on his composure. Whatever had gone on between them had to remain in the past. Even if this business was settled tomorrow with her brothers and the investigation miraculously over, she had chosen Emmit York. Diana had made her choice.

"You know," she said to her brothers sitting in the cell, "if your fingerprints don't match any of the ones Mitch took from the Cedarville bank, a lawyer could argue you were never there."

Mitch was more direct. "Can I take your samples?"

"Is our lawyer here yet?" Wayde asked in reply.

"Not yet."

"We'll wait till he is."

Mitch stepped away. "Fair enough."

But Diana looked perturbed. She wasn't getting anywhere with her brothers. She dusted off her hands with aggravation and left for York's office with barely a nod goodbye.

It wasn't Mitch's place to convince Wayde and Tom of anything. But something caught him strange. The more Mitch wanted to prove they weren't at the crime scene, the more they distanced themselves from him, although they kept proclaiming their innocence.

Was it possible Mitch's instinct about the men was wrong? Were they involved, directly or indirectly, with the robbery?

Mitch had discovered in his questions of Cedarville residents and the livery owner that Wayde and Tom had visited Cedarville several times a week, delivering horses and livestock from one town to another. They often stayed late and played cards—gambled—with other stable hands. Despite Mitch's inquiries, he couldn't trace their visits to any young women, so maybe Diana's suspicions were off target, as well.

Late Tuesday afternoon as the sun drifted behind the Rocky Mountains, casting long shadows in the dirt, Mitch retrieved his horse from the fort stables. He needed to ride into town to speak to the livery owner again. A question was nagging at him, one that no one had addressed yet, when two of his old friends rode into the barracks. Art and Quinn.

"Hey, Mitch," yelled Art from atop his straining mare. His horses always worked hard beneath the heavy weight they had to carry. "We've come to bring you to the saloon to join us for a drink. Clay's meetin' us there and bringin' his brothers."

"No, thanks. I've got work to do." He pulled himself into his saddle. The fringes on his worn suede jacket swayed beneath his arms.

"It could be a good time," said Quinn. "I might pick up the banjo and play the ladies a song. Come on, I'll race you to the saloon." Quinn pressed his shoulders into the wind, about to take flight, competitive as ever.

Mitch shifted in his saddle. "Have an ale for me."

Quinn and Art looked at each other. One yanked nervously at his leather gloves, the other on his cowboy hat.

"Where are you headed?" asked Art.

"To the livery."

"Business?"

"Yeah."

"Is it true," asked Quinn with an insulting grin, "that you're catching criminals these days with an ink pad and paper?"

Mitch gritted his teeth. "You might say that."

The two men snickered. "Doesn't that beat all," said Art.

"It doesn't seem natural," said Quinn.

"Natural?" Mitch peered at his friend. "That's an odd thing to say." What did Quinn know about the natural course of police work? The conversation had started out friendly, but was heading toward trouble.

"It's not the natural way of doing police work. Usually when you've got a crime, you find the weapon and the motive and eyewitnesses, just like the one who saw Wayde Campbell."

"The banker didn't see Wayde Campbell. He saw a young man with red hair."

"Same thing," said Quinn firmly.

"If it was your head in the noose, you might think otherwise."

Quinn's face flashed fury.

Art quietly glanced from one man to the other, as if trying to detect the reason for the outrage between them. Mitch tried to temper his racing breath, knowing Art would never guess.

They rode in silence, passing several riders. Sunlight was fading fast behind the row of stores.

"You know where we'll be when you're done at the livery." Art tipped his hat and galloped off toward the saloon, kicking up a volume of dust.

But Quinn lagged behind. He lashed out, "What's gotten into you since your return from Regina?"

Mitch was sick of pretending he could tolerate Quinn. "What the hell do you mean?"

"I mean you're not the same."

"People change. A man's got to choose his own path."

"Right." Quinn spat on the road in disgust. "You're an officer now, aren't you?"

Losing control, Mitch reined in his horse and came to a full stop. "Would you like a fist in that mouth?"

Quinn's eyes sparked. "I don't see the sense of chasing fingerprints when you've got the two guilty men locked up in jail. And they won't even cooperate with you, I hear. It shows what they think of your fingerprints."

"What do you know about it?"

"People are laughing at you. You walk down the road thinking they're being cooperative, but they're laughing. I thought as your friend, I should tell you."

Mitch's pulse careened. His fists clenched on the reins, ready for battle. "You call yourself my friend? Where were you the night Jack drowned? Why were you sitting on the edge of the riverbank screaming for help? You're an excellent swimmer! Why the hell didn't you dive in?"

Quinn's face hardened in the cold shadows. For a moment, both men inched forward in their saddles, as if debating whether to dive off their horses to fight. Mitch would have welcomed it.

But with a pulsing of his jaw, Quinn tugged on his reins and galloped away to the saloon.

Breathless with rage, Mitch stopped his mare beneath the cottonwood tree in front of the livery stables. Sliding from his mount, he pressed his forehead against the warm saddle and rocked forward on his boots, tortured by the memory of that awful night. He cursed himself for finally saying what he'd been thinking for months, what he'd been praying he'd never say.

Reeling for stability, Mitch tried to think of something—anything—to calm himself with before he lost it completely, before he chased after Quinn and pummeled the shit out of him.

Breathing loudly, aching for the silent comfort of someone who might understand his inner torment, Mitch thought of Diana.

He wanted to be with her tonight.

"These spectacles fit best and they look lovely with your blue eyes, Mrs. Sherman." Diana tilted the mirror toward the elderly woman. They were alone in the store, save for Emmit, who was working in his private office. Light from the setting sun hit the front window and warmed Diana's face.

Mrs. Sherman flicked her white hair off her forehead and peered more closely at her reflection, her thin body slightly hunched from old age. She smiled. "I can see better with these than my old ones. Can I wear 'em home?"

"Absolutely. Let me put your old ones in a case."

Diana took the case to the till and Mrs. Sherman followed. "Say, would you be the woman related to those two Campbell boys the Mounties have in jail?"

Diana shuffled on her feet. After three days, she still wasn't accustomed to the customers' stares and the direct questions than she was on Monday when she'd gone to work at the factory. Here, Emmit didn't appreciate the customers referring to it at all, and Diana wondered with embarrassment if he was listening. But she was grateful that he understood her need to continue working through this catastrophe. Someone still had to feed the family and to keep their spirits up while they prayed for an acquittal. Fortunately, the neighbor across the street was available for watching the children before and after their schooling.

"Wayde and Tom are my brothers," Diana whispered. "They didn't do it. They'll be cleared as soon as their attorney arrives in Calgary."

"They seem like a wild pair. Is it true your folks are gone?"

"Yes, ma'am."

Mrs. Sherman patted Diana's hand. "It's tough to keep 'em under your rule, isn't it? I mean, as the young men grow."

The older woman's touch melted Diana's resistance. "Oh, Mrs. Sherman, it was so much easier when they were younger."

"I know." The older woman slid her wrinkled fingers along the frame of the new glasses sitting on her nose. "It was the same with my Jack."

"You've got a son named Jack?"

"Used to. He passed on last year."

Diana shivered. How sad. She was curious as to how it'd happened, but didn't want to pry. "I'm sorry."

Mrs. Sherman braced her umbrella. She carried an umbrella although there wasn't a cloud in the sky. "You know, Mitch and Jack were the best of friends."

"Officer Mitchell Reid?"

"That's right, the officer investigating your brothers. You won't win, you know," she said calmly. "Not against Mitch."

The warning rippled up Diana's skin. The old woman was just gossiping, she reminded herself.

There was a lonesome cast to Mrs. Sherman's clear blue eyes. "How is Mitch doin'?"

Diana frowned. "You haven't kept in touch?"

"Not Mitch. Haven't seen him since he left for Regina."

It was a shame, thought Diana, to have lost a son and then contact with his best friend. "I think he's doing fine."

"Well, then," said Mrs. Sherman, fingering the leather case with trembling hands.

There was nothing left to say, so they said goodbye. Diana tidied for closing time. Three minutes later at six o'clock, she turned the Closed sign to the window and drew the shade. Lighting the lantern, she made her way to the cloakroom.

Emmit followed her down the hall. His presence almost felt intrusive to her thoughts. He hadn't come near her, physically, since her brothers were arrested six days ago.

Blast him anyway. She was leaving town when this was over.

"How are you holding up, Diana?"

She nodded. "The work helps. It takes my mind off my own problems when I serve the customers."

They reached the dark cloakroom. She sat the flickering lantern on the shelf and removed her cape from the wall peg.

Behind her, she felt the heat of Emmit's body. He pressed her shoulder blade with a tentative hand. "You've been working hard these last two days."

"I'm grateful you understand my need to continue working." She couldn't lose either job while her brothers were in jail. Secretly, she and her siblings had already discussed what items they would sell and how much money they'd need to move on to the next town. Until then, she would act grateful to Emmit for allowing her to stay working, knowing other shop owners wouldn't be so lenient if faced with such a scandal.

But sometimes when she returned Emmit's suspicious gaze, all she felt was burning anger. His hand moving along her back felt odd, as if it didn't belong there. She tried to explore her reaction, concentrating on the smooth, warm feel of his palm and wondering why she felt hollow.

A heavy knock on the side door interrupted them.

Emmit's hand stopped moving along her spine. "We're closed," he whispered, turning her around and tugging her against his body. His size overpowered her. "They'll see the sign and come back tomorrow."

How grateful did she have to act? If he kissed her, did she have to respond? She couldn't. She just couldn't. The knocking continued. Emmit pressed his face into the hollow of her throat and kissed it lightly.

She tugged away. "I didn't lock the side door. I'll go see who it is. If it's something I can help them with quickly, I will. Otherwise I'll take an appointment for the morning."

She tried to scramble from his hold, but he

wouldn't release her. They stumbled into the hallway toward the side door. Nausea trembled up her throat. She couldn't lose this job, but this moment didn't feel right. Emmit was being pushy. "Please, let me see who it is—"

"They'll go away." The more she fought, the tighter he embraced her. Who would have thought such a mild man could be so relentless? In the past, she had flirted outrageously with him, but it had only been to compare his kiss to Mitch's. She didn't want *this*.

She pressed her palms against his chest and heaved with all her might. "Stop—"

"Let go of her, York!"

Mitch's familiar voice boomed into the room. She and Emmit pivoted toward him. His deep dark eyes were fixed on Emmit, glinting as if he'd like to rip his throat out.

"Mitch, it's all right."

"I said get your damn hands off her, or I'll break them."

To her surprise, Emmit tossed her aside and stepped closer to Mitch. "Who the hell are you to barge into my office?"

The men were of equal height, but Mitch was heavier and tougher, and would no doubt win any physical contest. A contest between these two men would only result in devastation for everyone involved, especially her and her already tenuous position of employment.

"And who the hell are you to make your employee beg for her own safety?"

Mitch seemed as if he was already angry at someone or something before he'd even come here. She was furious with Emmit, too, and wanted to smack him, but she controlled herself. "Mitch, don't—"

It was too late. Emmit came barreling toward Mitch, motioning as if he had an imaginary sword in his hand, arms thrusting. Caught by surprise, Mitch was flung back against the side door. He gasped as the wind was knocked out of him. The door flew open and the men tumbled into the alley. Emmit looked dismayed that the door had fallen through.

"Stop it!" Diana raced into the dark alley, begging them as they rolled.

But Emmit had the upper hand since Mitch still hadn't caught his breath. She whimpered as Emmit slapped Mitch in the face. Right on the cut where the five stitches used to be, tearing the scar open again. What a brute, she thought.

"Mind your own business," Emmit yelled at Mitch as he rose from the ground.

"Get off him!" Diana yelled, horrified that Mitch still hadn't regained his breath and Emmit was taking advantage.

Folks passing by on the boardwalk twenty feet away noticed the ruckus and raced closer. "You all right, miss? What's going on?" someone asked.

"Yes, it's just a difference of opinion."

"Good grief," said another passerby. "What are they fighting over?" They stared at Diana as if she were to blame.

Emmit growled, rising. Mitch struggled to a sitting position, gasping.

"This man barged into my office and threatened me." Emmit dusted off his hands, as if completing the job. "Now we'll be on our way."

Diana fell to her knees beside Mitch. Removing her hanky from inside her sleeve, she dabbed at the trickling blood.

But Mitch suddenly got his breath back and jumped to his feet. She watched with alarm as he yanked Emmit back by his shoulder. With one hefty punch to the gut, Mitch knocked Emmit to the ground.

"You deserved that, you son of a bitch."

"Mitch," she pleaded, "you're bigger. Leave him alone." She knew he was used to fighting and could protect himself, but doubted Emmit had any idea at the rage he'd just unleashed in the other man. Mitch could crush him with a single hand.

Rubbing his jaw, Mitch wiped at the fresh blood oozing from his scar. He panted, his breathing out of control.

From the shadow, he glared at Diana. "I told myself I wouldn't come here. I told myself to stay away from you."

She trembled at the sight of him, hurt and disheveled and fighting on behalf of her safety. She abhorred violence, but no one had ever fought for her like this.

She looked from one fiery face to the other. She needed Emmit to continue paying her salary, but she needed Mitch to free her brothers. Everything she believed in always seemed to be in jeopardy around Mitch.

The crowd's eyes were upon her. She was keenly aware that news of this fight would be all over town before the clock moved another hour. Looking at Emmit and thinking how he'd slapped Mitch when he'd had the wind knocked out of him filled her with disgust. She'd never have anything to do with Emmit again. And looking at Mitch clenching his fists while itching to take another swing filled her with horror. How would this night affect her brothers' situation?

Vowing she'd never be caught with Emmit alone again in the cloakroom, or anywhere else, she said what she had to in order to protect her job, to provide food for her younger siblings.

She locked eyes with Mitch. "You shouldn't have come. I'd like you to leave."

Panting for air, Mitch clamped his bleeding jaw. She could still remember the warm grip of his arms around her waist, the flutter of his lips on her breast, the eager look of hope when he'd promised to return the morning after their night together.

But she ignored him, and bending down on one knee, tended to Emmit. Behind her, after a moment, she heard the crunch of dirt beneath Mitch's boots as he parted the murmuring crowd and walked away.

Chapter Sixteen

It was hours later when Diana spoke to him again.

"Mitch?"

The quiet voice took him by surprise as he was crossing the fort's courtyard from the jail to the barracks. It was close to midnight. The sting and the bleeding from his scar had stopped, but the ache inside hurt more. Diana's betrayal hurt most.

At the unexpected sound of her voice and the sight of an unknown figure bursting from the shadows beside the forge, he drew his gun and pointed it at her. She gasped at his weapon. The gentle wind stirred her cape and ruffled her loose, dark hair. Moonlight shifted across her cheeks.

She was alone. He lowered his gun and shoved it into leather. "What are you doing here?"

In the distant fields beyond the fort walls, an owl hooted. Wolves called.

"We need to talk. Is there a place?" She glanced around his broad shoulders.

Even the warm sound of her voice affected him.

"Over here." He led her to the side of the stables.

Sandwiched between two buildings, the stables and the forge, Mitch knew there'd be no windows or doors in the vicinity, so any men still awake and doing chores wouldn't overhear.

"How'd you get past the two guards?"

"They've seen me before, visiting my brothers. I told them I needed to see you and they told me you were in the jailhouse. I waited till I saw you leave. I don't want my brothers to know I'm here this time."

"But it's late. You shouldn't be out alone."

"That's what one of the guards said. He insists on walking me home when I'm finished."

The image of York's pasty white hands on her flesh turned his stomach. Mitch's fury at Quinn after their argument had primed him for a fight with York, but the image of York with his hands on Diana had tipped him over the edge.

Unnerved by her sudden appearance, Mitch pulled her toward a wooden wall, his callused hand clasped over her smooth one. The simple contact stirred the hairs at the back of his neck.

She let his fingers entwine with hers for a second then broke free. It struck him how cold he felt then, standing with the cool breeze blowing between them as if they were strangers and had never been lovers.

"Are you all right? Did York touch you again?"

"No, I haven't seen him."

He stiffened, remembering the last words she'd said to him. "Then what? Are you here to put me in my place again?"

"You should have known better than to punch Emmit."

"Why do you take his side?"

"You're experienced at fighting. It's in your line of

duty. But you also know how people react and you should have controlled yourself."

"Like you control yourself?"

"What does that mean?"

"The way you hold everything in."

The air between them charged. She was passionate in her views, he in his. The collar of her cape fluttered against her slender throat. He watched the moonlight dance across her skin.

Her eyes lifted up toward him, but he could barely see their focus in the dim light. Her lips quivered. "There's something to be said for that. You could use a lesson or two in holding things in."

"I should have known you'd stand by his side. You chose him over me once before."

"I don't like it when you talk like that."

Her defiance pushed him further. "Is he as good a lover?"

She withdrew, her cape lashing against her knees. "It was a mistake to come."

"Maybe you like it rough."

Her upper lip stiffened. "Stop it."

"Maybe you like it when he acts like a beast and handles you without permission. Maybe that's where I went wrong."

This time when she turned her head away, her eyes flashed in the moonlight. "You're the beast, and I'm leaving."

His arm shot out and yanked her by the wrist, easily containing her. "No, you're not. You came to me, remember? What is it you want? Are you playing me like you're playing York? Coming in the middle of the night so no one might guess what you really feel?"

She tried to wrench free. "You're talking nonsense."

He clamped her cheek. "You feel something for me every time you see me and you don't like it."

"You're the one who said we can't see each other while you're leading the investigation." She snapped his arm but he held firm. "My brothers are in jail and I'm fighting for their release. So what do you want from me?"

He let her go. "I don't know. Maybe I want you to admit what you feel for me is natural and exciting and you want it just as much as I do."

"It gets in the way." Her voice trembled. "Feelings always get in the way."

"Welcome to the human race."

"You're not making this easy."

"It might be easier if you admit how you feel about me and what you *don't* feel for York."

"You're telling me to admit my feelings? Well, I saw Mrs. Sherman today. She came into the office. If you're so willing to face your feelings, why do you run from her and from talking about Jack?"

Mitch stumbled backward. It felt as if she'd dumped a bucket of ice water over his head. "That's none of your damn business."

"Welcome to the human race. It hurts, doesn't it?"

Moonlight caught the curve of her jaw, the round plumpness of her neck. Taking a step forward, he pulled her toward him until his arms had encircled her lower back and he was looking down into her face. Breathless, she stared up at him, her lips slightly parted, her eyes wide and disbelieving, her expression so sensual and deep he wanted to kiss her.

"I didn't come for this."

"You're going to get it anyway."

He lowered his mouth to her lips. His pulse dipped, his heart thumped, his senses soared.

His hands raced up her back and into her thick hair; he twirled it between his fingers. He gripped her cheek and crushed her mouth with his own, urgent for her response, needing her to kiss him back as hard as he was giving.

Timid at first, she hesitated beneath his hold then with a soft catch at the base of her throat, slid her arms up his back and slowly opened her mouth. They pressed their lips wider, hungry for each other, tongues meeting. The touch of her moist flesh against his own drew him to sensational heights. When her tongue became bolder, he groaned softly and pulled her body tighter against him.

Cocooned in her soft woolen cape, her sculpted curves molded against his muscles. When he recalled the image of her naked body in the laundered flannel sheets, his heart drummed beneath his ribs. His mouth slid across hers, more demanding, intensifying the heat between them.

She pressed her body willingly against his, entwining her fingers through his hair and playing with the soft tendrils behind his ear. A soft, slow yearning in his limbs rushed through him. He wondered if she could feel how hard he was for her.

"I want you," he murmured.

Her hands fell still, one at his back, one at his throat. He tried to bury his face in her neck, but it was already too late. He'd lost her. She wrenched free of his hold, standing a foot away, panting heavily in the moon's glow, fighting for control of her body and her words.

"No," she said hoarsely. "I—I don't want this."

The inches between them might as well have been an ocean. "That's not how it felt to me."

She tilted her head and a strand of hair fell across her

cheek. "Sometimes…sometimes you have to put other people in front of your own needs, people who depend on you. Sometimes no matter how hard you try or what you want in life, you know you'll never get it."

"But it's worth trying for."

"I came tonight not to share this…but to tell you…to ask what you know about the remaining fingerprints. Have you discovered who the other six are?"

He scoffed. "You came here to control the damage you thought you might have done in taking Emmit's side tonight. You came to use me."

"Maybe I did." She paused. "Are you going to tell me about the prints?"

He ran a hand through his hair and leaned back against the wallboards of the forge. There'd be no harm in spreading the news of his latest find. If he told her, she'd tell others. At times it was handy to let the criminals out there know that the noose was tightening, that the Mounties were getting closer.

"I matched another two sets. Both belong to bank customers—one customer who came in the day of the bank robbery, and one from the previous afternoon. I've got four sets of prints left to identify."

"You'll keep going, won't you?"

"Sure, but there are only so many people I can take samples from. I'm running out of people who visited the bank."

"If your techniques are truly valid, they'll prove my brothers innocent."

He rubbed his jaw. "There's something strange about one of the unidentified samples."

"What?"

"The fingertips are blurred slightly, as if the fingers were swollen. Or possibly suffered a burn. Do either of your brothers smoke?"

"On occasion. When they have spare pocket change. But that doesn't happen very often," she added quickly, obviously wanting to disengage her brothers from the crime.

He squinted at her in the darkness. "What else did you come to tell me?"

"Nothing else."

"You came to tell me something more."

Turning away, she began to walk toward the gate.

"Wait," he whispered. "What did you come to say?"

"If I tell you, you might say I'm trying to use you."

"Tell me anyway."

She spoke so softly he could barely hear her words. "I came to tell you…I believe in you, Mitch."

His blood rushed.

Diana swallowed hard and tried to brush past him, but he reached out with a long arm and trapped her. "Don't make any decisions about being with the doctor," he pleaded softly, "until this case with your brothers is over."

Both of them were looking to the dirt, side-by-side but facing in opposite directions and connected only by his long arm. He loved the feel of her breasts beneath his forearm.

"But it may take weeks."

"If it goes to trial, it may take months. You've sacrificed a lot for your family, Diana. When your parents died, you put your brothers' and sisters' lives before your own. I know it's another huge sacrifice, but I want you to promise. *Wait for me.*"

He'd never felt this way about another woman. He wasn't sure how to label it or how long it would last.

She answered tenderly, sliding from his reach, walking away and crushing him. "I can't make that promise."

* * *

How ironic, Diana observed, that Mitch thought he was competing against Emmit, when neither man controlled her.

The day after her midnight meeting with Mitch and just finishing for the day at the optometrist's, Diana locked the office door and stepped out into the cool wind that grazed the boardwalk. From now on, she'd be careful to bring her cape out into the main part of the store half an hour beforehand, so she could scoot out quickly and avoid being alone with Emmit.

Since his fight with Mitch, Emmit had grown surly. He'd backed away from touching her, which pleased her, but they hadn't spoken in eight hours. It was just as well that this job seemed to be slipping from her fingers. She wouldn't bother to ask for a sales commission on top of her salary, for she knew the answer would be no. She longed for something she'd lost in this town but knew she'd never regain it, for she'd be leaving as soon as humanly possible.

Losing herself in the evening crowd, Diana noticed the signs going up in front of the main livery stables for the livestock auction tomorrow. She didn't see the elderly woman approaching until Mrs. Sherman had reached her side.

"Miss Campbell, I was hoping to catch you before you left the store."

"Are you having problems with your new spectacles?" Diana peered at the oval rims on the bridge of Mrs. Sherman's nose.

"No, no. They're fine, thank you. I was wondering…" Mrs. Sherman, spry on her feet, walked quickly with Diana along the boardwalk. They took the stairs and crossed the street. "I was wondering if you'd like to have tea with me."

"Oh," said Diana, surprised by the invitation.

"To talk about your brothers. I've been through difficult times myself. Jack wasn't my only son. I have two older boys, but they've since grown and now live in the southern part of the territory. Jack was my youngest, and I reckon that's why I miss him so much. Sometimes it helps to unburden your problems when you speak your thoughts aloud."

Diana had an urge to say yes, that she'd love to visit with Mrs. Sherman. They could stop by Diana's home and ask the sitter, Winnie, to stay another hour. Diana would make it up to her another evening, when she'd offer to sit with Winnie's small children. But Diana also realized she was perilously close to stepping onto Mitch's territory. He might not like her visiting with the elderly woman.

Maybe the things between Mitch and Jack and Mrs. Sherman were private things that she had no business exploring.

But something drew her to the gentle face and kind expression of the woman peering up through a bundle of dark clothing with clear blue eyes.

This was the first time since Wayde and Tom were arrested that anyone had extended Diana a gesture of friendliness. "I'd like that very much."

The evening flew and before Diana knew it, the children were in bed and she was stacking dried supper dishes in their rightful places in the cupboard. Humming to herself, she replayed the lovely visit she'd had with Mrs. Sherman.

When someone knocked on the door, Diana bustled to it with a rag in her hand. "Who is it?"

"Police, Diana. It's Mitch."

Instant fear sprang in her throat. She unbolted the door and flung it open. The same corporal who'd come once before stood behind Mitch in the darkness. Dressed in uniform, Mitch loomed above her on the front step.

Her heart pounded a thousand beats per minute. "What is it?"

He fingered the hat he held in his large hands. "The lawyer finally made it into town. I—*we*—thought you'd like to know."

Relieved, she sagged against the door frame. "Thank you, I thought it was something awful you'd come to tell me. Mr. Walter's arrival is good news. It's late now, but I'll speak with him tomorrow morning before my day begins at the office."

Mitch had a strange expression. How had they gotten to be so distant toward each other? This wasn't the man Mrs. Sherman had described to her earlier. It bounded out of Diana before he could continue with whatever else he came to say. "Mitch, I had tea with Mrs. Sherman today. We talked so much about you and Jack—"

"You went to her after knowing how I felt?" The dark eyes were quick to judge.

She dried her hands on the kitchen rag she clutched, wishing she could persuade him to think differently. "I didn't really know how you felt, and neither did Mrs. Sherman. Until I explained how very sorry you must be on the passing of her son."

Gasping lightly, he rubbed his neck. "You spoke on my behalf?"

"I told her what a quiet man you are, and she told me that you never used to be that way, and we decided—"

"*That's enough.*" The corners of his red uniform stiffened at his shoulders. "You have no business interfering in this part of my life, to explain or apologize to Mrs. Sherman about something you don't know anything about."

She had overstepped her bounds. "I may not know anything about you, but Mrs. Sherman knows a lot," Diana said gently. "She's suffering and she adores you, if only you'd visit. She said she's been saving something—"

He raised a palm in the air, silently indicating he'd heard enough, then stepped off the stoop.

She thought she'd helped the situation, but she'd wounded him. Mrs. Sherman hadn't told her the entire story of what had happened the night of the drowning, only what she'd been told, but it was obvious Mitch hadn't gotten over his grief.

When he turned to Diana, his eyes glistened. "Arthur Billings died tonight."

Thunderstruck, she dropped the rag.

"Mr. Billings never regained consciousness. He wasn't able to clear your brothers. They're being charged with murder now as well as robbery."

The night sky spun around her, a thousand points of light spinning like one of the kaleidoscopes in Emmit's store. Mitch's face became a blur.

He faded into the darkness and the two Mounties disappeared, the sound of their heavy boots thudding against the ground and mimicking the beat of her heart. Stumbling to the parlor, Diana fell to her knees on the carpet.

Murder.

Chapter Seventeen

"Who did this to you, Moses?" At sunrise the next morning, Mitch kneeled on the jailhouse floor beside the old guard who sat tied to the cell. Outraged at the turn of events, Mitch tugged at the bandana stuffed in the man's mouth.

The jail cells stood empty. The prisoners had fled.

Moses spat fibers from his mouth. "The Campbells."

Mitch swore. He clawed at the ropes that bound the guard's hands behind his back. A cell door clanged against metal, echoing through the morning chill.

After helping Moses to his feet and ensuring he was fine, Mitch hollered out the door to the nearest passing constables. "Get the night guards and bring them here! Notify the commander! There's been an escape!"

With his fingers pressed against his temples, Mitch raced back to Moses who was sitting in a chair and rubbing his mouth.

"Tell me what happened."

"I was foolish…it was the middle of the night. I took one of the brothers out to the privy. The other one, the bigger one, Wayde, grabbed me and took my keys then threatened to break my wrist."

Looking down at the bruised hand, Mitch cursed again. His white shirt billowed beneath his suspenders and his black breeches stretched across his thighs. "So they got out alone. No accomplices?"

"That's right."

"How long ago?"

"I've been watchin' the wall clock. It was exactly two-ten. Four hours ago."

Other Mounties burst into the jailhouse, including the day guards who'd recently arrived for gate duty. Through the opened door, Mitch saw a dozen Mounties running across the grounds in different directions. The word was out.

Inside, there were a lot of questions and swearing, while outside, Mitch knew horses were being saddled for a chase.

"Sir," mumbled Moses. "Sir, I'm sorry."

"It was just damn bad luck that they chose to escape on your time."

Moses was older than the town itself, a retired Mountie who wasn't fast enough to ride anymore on official duty, but his mind was swift and keen and he was a hell of a good guard.

The Campbell brothers were digging their own graves. Mitch wondered if Diana knew about or was involved in the escape. She was hit hard last night by the news of the murder charge. He expected her to arrive any minute, as she usually did before her day began at work. *If* she was still in town and hadn't fled with her brothers. Their newly appointed lawyer, Mr. Walter, had said last night he'd be back to visit the brothers first thing this morning.

Did this escape mean the brothers were guilty, or scared?

The commander burst through the door with the two young night guards. The guards' shifts had ended at five-thirty reveille. By their swollen eyes, it looked as though they'd just gotten to bed when they were ordered here.

"What the hell happened?" Mitch asked them. "How did two prisoners get by your watch?"

They looked nervously to each other. "No one passed by us, sir."

"They must have."

"No, sir," said the other one. "Not a soul since midnight when the blacksmith went home."

"Were you sleeping?"

One of the men turned crimson. "No, sir."

While the commander asked more questions, Mitch took another approach. "If they didn't go out the gates, they still got out somehow. Search the perimeter of the fort," he told the day guards. "Look for any loose timber they might have slid through. Look for shovels and holes in case they dug their way out. Look for ropes and ladders in case they climbed."

He turned to the night guards. "Did you hear any horses galloping away last night?"

While the men thought about the question, Mitch said to another constable, "Check the stables for any missing horses."

"We didn't hear any galloping," the guards decided.

It was a common sound that might be easily overlooked during the day, but it couldn't be missed on a quiet night.

"Then they're on foot," said Mitch. "Unless they had accomplices waiting in town with horses." He barked out more orders. "Pawson, go to the main livery stables where they worked. Duke, find the owner and speak to him. McKenzie, go to the Campbell residence."

As the men rushed out to fulfill their duties, Mitch felt he was missing something obvious. But what?

The commander was busy questioning Moses. Mitch raced into the side office to see if any fingerprint evidence was gone, but everything looked intact.

Diana arrived. She slid through the door with Mr. Walter beside her. Carrying a basket of food, she seemed taken aback by the commotion.

Quickly looking to the cells, she turned pale and then pivoted to Mitch. The blank expression on her face told him her brothers' disappearance was news to her. Or, she was a mighty fine actress.

Her voice shook. "Where are they? Where'd you take them?"

"I was hoping you might tell me."

Mr. Walter, sporting a bushy gray mustache and a shiny checkered suit, stepped forward. "What's the meaning of this? Where are my clients?"

"They tied up the guard and escaped."

"When?"

"Two o'clock this morning."

"Did they harm the man?"

"Roughed him up." Mitch gestured to Moses, still sitting quietly in the chair.

Diana didn't speak. Blood drained from her face. Gripping the basket handle so hard that the skin on her knuckles went taut, she stood and listened to every one of the five conversations going on.

Mr. Walter asked more questions and Mitch got caught up for thirty seconds. The next time he looked, Diana's food basket was sitting on the desk, but she'd disappeared.

Her lawyer went to speak to Moses while Mitch strode to the door and looked out. Diana was running across the grounds toward the gate, skirt and cape flowing behind her, one length of braided hair bobbing along her back.

He watched her for a minute. She looked determined, as if she knew where she was headed.

"Inspector," one of the day guards called, panting as he raced up to Mitch. "No sign of shovels or digging out of the fort. No loose boards, either. We're still checking for ropes along the top perimeter."

"You won't find any," said Mitch calmly with his eye on Diana. "There aren't any horses missing from the stables, either."

"How do you know, sir?"

Because dammit, he just figured out how they'd escaped. It hit him like a sharp arrow to a target. "They haven't gotten far. They got away on foot and are likely still in town. Hopefully we'll get to them before they find horses. Take ten men and scour the streets. Report all your findings to the commander till I get back."

"Yes, sir."

Mitch strode into his office, donned his cowboy hat and pulled his suede jacket off the wall peg. After consulting the commander, quietly explaining where he was going, Mitch packed fingerprinting supplies into a weathered saddlebag, then quietly followed behind Diana.

"Diana!"

Diana stopped and spun around when she heard Mitch calling. Horses and Mounties raced past the open fields beside them. While Mitch loomed closer, Diana tried to calm her reeling pulse, tried to solidify her stance in the cool, morning breeze that pulled at her braided hair and nipped at her loose hem, threatening to unravel her inner composure as well as her appearance.

Lord, she wished it were anyone but Mitch. Nothing seemed to escape his scrutiny.

"Where are you off to? Can I walk you there?"

"I—I thought I'd let Dr. York know what's happened, that I can't come in to work this morning. I have to be with my family."

Soaring above her, Mitch studied her. She'd never be able to budge him, his body nor his opinion. Was he still on her brothers' side? Even after they'd attacked a Mountie guard?

She understood the fear that must have gripped Wayde and Tom when they'd heard the murder charge. The same fear that trapped her now, speechless as she stared up at one of the accusers, her blood pounding in her throat, her breath cold in her lungs.

She couldn't allow Mitch to read her fear and so locked her gaze with his, trying to manipulate her confidence.

"Do you know where they are, Diana?"

She flinched. Ever so minute, but a flinch that she saw registered in Mitch's eyes. She wasn't certain where her brothers were, but she had a good idea.

Was Mitch friend or foe?

"Listen, if it helps, I know you had nothing to do with their escape."

She lifted her chin a fraction of an inch. "How can you be so sure?"

The suede fringes of his coat clapped together in the breeze. Early-morning sunrise hit the side of his dark, sculpted face. "They didn't escape at two o'clock. They escaped later this morning." He watched her as she felt her expression shift to one of amazement. "They waited behind one of the buildings until I arrived. I called both sets of guards into the jailhouse and while everyone ran around trying to figure out how your brothers had escaped, they were still waiting inside the walls. I fell for the bloody trick. During the time when the gate was unmanned, ninety minutes ago, that's when they likely fled."

"Ninety minutes…"

"Where do you think they went?"

Bitterness seeped into her voice. "As far away from here as possible."

"Your lawyer had told me last night that he would approve my taking their fingerprints this morning, if you all agree. Why the hell did they pick now to leave?"

"Because of the insane new charges! They're scared and no one's done anything to help them!"

She turned on her heel and walked toward the arched metal bridge that would connect them to the main part of town. She walked over it in fuming silence. Shop owners were arriving to open their doors. Curiosity tied them to the streets as they stared at a dozen passing Mounties on horseback.

Mitch kept up with her choppy pace. "Breaking out of jail won't sit well with the judge. Most folks in town are beginning to think they're guilty."

"Are you one of them?"

"I'm trying to keep an open mind."

She wanted to believe him more than any hope she'd ever placed in another human being, but what if they were both wrong? What if Wayde and Tom had some minor role in the robbery that they weren't admitting?

"My brothers aren't bank thieves. If they were stealing money, why on earth would they continue living in poverty with me?"

This case went way beyond politeness and Mitch spoke his mind point-blank. "That's my thought, too."

She wheeled around to scrutinize him, squinting in the sun's rising rays.

"Take me to them," he commanded.

Her mouth went jittery. "I don't know where they are." Huffing, she turned and tried to run.

But he lashed out and gripped her arm, anchoring his hand around the flesh beneath the cape. "By God, you do."

"Do you think I'm sorry they escaped?" She wrenched free of his hold. "I'm glad! I hope they run like hell and never come back!"

"Even if it means you'll never see them again?"

"Yes," she groaned.

"Even if it means their names will never be cleared and they'll never have peace as long as they live?"

Her voice rippled. "Yes."

Mitch rubbed his dark cheek. "Why do you care so much about them?"

"They're my *brothers*."

"I know, but they're also a pain in the ass. What have they ever done to deserve such loyalty from you?"

Faltering, she drew her cape around her. "They were eleven and twelve when our parents died." She squinted at the sunrise. "The rest of us bawled our eyes out continually for weeks, but they never did. Sometimes I'd hear one of them sobbing at night, when they thought I couldn't hear…. Every penny they earned at their jobs since then, they handed over to me. That's how loyal *they* are. But they'd never cry in front of me. They're crying now, and I want to help them."

Gulping, she clutched at her swirling cape. Mitch's absence from their lives was what she wanted, but also what she dreaded. What other investigator would listen to her like this?

Recovering quickly, she dashed along the boardwalk.

But he kept following, his boots pounding the planks. Looking ahead, she noticed a crowd forming around the main livery stables. They were surrounded by oxen and horses, donkeys and cows, by cages of hens and ducks. She recognized a few of the faces. Men were raising fists in the air.

"What's going on there?"

"The livestock auction. It happens every Saturday during harvest."

"Right." She'd seen the sign going up yesterday. In a rush, she asked, "If by chance I knew where my brothers were, and if I…led you there, what would you do to them?"

His gait slowed. Stopping altogether, he leaned against the boardwalk railing. It struck her how forceful he was, how relentless in his pursuit. She held her breath while waiting for him to answer.

"I've got my fingerprinting kit." He patted his saddlebag. "If they're innocent, it's the only way to clear them."

"If." She shook her head, contemplating her choices. "What advice do you think Mr. Walter would give me, if he thought I knew their whereabouts?"

"Your lawyer? He'd likely advise you to go by the proper procedures. That, if you know anything, you should disclose it to him, the judge and my commander."

"Why don't *you* go through proper procedures? Why don't you tell me—force me—to go before the judge and commander?"

"Because if it came down to that, I don't think you'd talk. You might want to, but you wouldn't. Because," he continued softly, reaching out and lifting her chin to point her face to his, "I don't think you trust anyone in this town. You never did. Except maybe…*maybe*…me."

Shaking beneath his touch, Diana pulled back. Two

men shoved past them and ran to the livery stables, muttering something about a posse.

Explosive fear gripped Diana. She glanced to Mitch, who seemed equally stunned, then they both ran across the street.

"I say we help the Mounties and bring 'em back to jail!" someone shouted within the crowd.

Mitch spoke up immediately, lunging forward to the center of the crowd. "We don't need your help! We want you all to remain calm and keep your businesses going. We'll find the Campbell brothers and bring them back to a fair trial."

One of the men stared at Diana. She shuddered with the hatred she saw in his eyes. "The Backroom Bandits might have thought they were playing games, but a man has died. I knew Arthur Billings, as did many of you! His daughter just gave birth to his first grandson."

Diana withdrew from the man's glare.

"It'll all be settled," hollered Mitch. "Calm and orderly. Go back to your auction."

Some of the men grumbled and didn't move, but others brushed past them, leading their animals into the stable.

Four of Mitch's friends stepped out of the crowd. Diana recognized them from the Reid barbecue. One of them was Clay Hayward, the other Quinn Turner, the heavyset man whose name she recalled only as Art and the heavy smoker, Vic Wood.

"Do you need our help to chase them down, Mitch?" asked Art, breathless from exertion.

Diana reeled. *Everyone stay put,* she wanted to scream. *Leave my brothers alone.*

Mitch fingered the gun in his holster. "We don't need any posses."

"It's not a posse," Quinn insisted. There seemed to be an underlying tone of anger beneath Quinn's words. He stepped up to Mitch, nose to nose, running his hands along his own guns, reminding Diana of the possibility of violence.

When Quinn turned to her and tipped his hat cordially, almost mocking Mitch, she flushed with the realization that perhaps they were competing for her attention, as well, as they had the night of the Reid barbecue. Were they after her as a prize, or trying to see who'd find her brothers first?

"We'd bring them back alive," Quinn said coldly. A silent look of agreement passed between him and his other friend, Clay. Diana shuddered as Quinn continued speaking. "We know that posses are illegal. I wouldn't call it a posse, just extra riders out to help the Mounties. We've all got a stake in the Calgary Bank and Loan. Hell, my father owns it, and if the Campbells strike there next, none of us want our money gone."

Mitch ground the words from his mouth. "Go back to your work."

With her head lowered, Diana heard the mumbling as more men shuffled by her with their cattle. "...they're a threat to the town. I heard they beat up on poor Moses this morning, too. We don't need bank robbers causin' any more trouble."

Mitch's friends stood where they were, some watching nervously, others openly defiant at Mitch's refusal of their help.

"Quinn told us what you accused him of, Mitch." Art shook his head. "I reckon if you blame him, you blame us all for what happened that night a year ago with Jack. We were all there and watching. And that's why you don't want to drink with us anymore. Why you don't want our help now."

Diana wondered what they were talking about. Weren't they friends? And even in this moment of fear, she didn't mind stretching out the conversation. It would give Wayde and Tom more time to run.

"Do you want to go over it again, minute by minute, and see who was to blame for what?" Art continued. "Shall we?"

"I've got more pressing things to do." With loud authority, Mitch dispersed the crowd.

She heard the auctioneer hollering calls from inside the stables, oblivious to the rising tensions outside. The loud bidding helped draw some of the argumentative men in, the ones who had cattle and horses to sell or buy.

Silent but pale, Mitch led her away by the elbow. She felt the heated gaze of a dozen eyes upon her shoulder blades as they left the area.

"You better take me to your brothers," Mitch warned, escalating her pounding pulse, "and fast. These men aren't going to stop. A posse's being formed as we speak."

Chapter Eighteen

"It's only a hunch," Diana whispered beside Mitch, minutes later. They crossed the street and stepped onto the boardwalk. Her breath stirred the hairs at his temple, making him conscious of her vulnerability and the extraordinary amount of trust they were placing in each other. "I don't know for sure where Wayde and Tom went. It would take us two hours to ride there and might be a waste of time."

Mitch peered down into wide, green eyes. The wind swept her cape against her body.

"You know your brothers better than anyone else. I'd place my bet on your hunch every time."

Sunshine hit the rooftop of the Calgary Bank and Loan far across the street and bounced onto them. It heated his skin and the morning air around them. Blue skies enveloped the town.

Peering one last time into the stables, Mitch caught sight of Quinn leading a prize stallion inside. He crossed a hundred feet in front of the Bank and Loan's two windows with their black metal bars. A whisper of strange recognition pulled at Mitch. He stared at the sandstone building. Why had Calgary's bank never been robbed by the Backroom Bandits? Because of its proximity to Fort Calgary and ninety policemen?

"Do you have anyone who can watch the children while you're gone?"

"My neighbor, Mrs. Hillyard."

"Good. Turn around and walk slowly back to your home. Don't run or you'll raise suspicion."

"What should I tell her about my absence?"

He removed his black leather hat and banged it along his breeches. "Steer her in a different direction. Tell her that I'm taking you to Cedarville to go over the crime scene."

"And my job, I should tell Emmit—"

"I'll take care of him. Meet me at the corner of Front Street, behind the diner in half an hour."

"We'll need horses."

Mitch peered down the street at two constables trotting through town, peering up and down the side streets looking for the escaped prisoners as they rode by. Sunshine hit the muscled horses, making their coats glisten an earthy brown. "I know where to get them. Just meet me in half an hour."

Thirty-five minutes later with two chestnut horses by his side, Mitch waited calmly at their agreed spot. From the narrow alley, he had a good view of the sunny street and the steady stream of pedestrians and riders. He'd spoken briefly to York, telling him Diana needed to be at home with her family for a couple of days. York didn't seem to like it, but after their last meeting—or rather, fistfight—didn't openly protest. Mitch had a disconcerting feeling that Diana's return to work wouldn't be easy.

For a brief moment Mitch wished he could take her

away from all of this. He wished he had the means and the capability to tell York to go to hell. To get another assistant, that Diana would be staying at home from now on to care for her younger sisters and brothers.

Diana careened around the corner. With a smile of relief at the sight of Mitch, she tossed him a small leather bag. He tied it to his horse on the other side of his saddle to counterbalance the bag containing his fingerprinting kit.

Helping her mount the quieter mare, Mitch noticed Diana wore riding clothes beneath her long skirt. Denim jeans hugged her ankles.

"We're riding east along the river," she said, and gently urged her mare down the alley. "To the town of Miner's Gully."

"What's there?"

"A cabin Charlotte's brother owns. My brothers love it there. It's secluded and…and the only place I can think of that they know in these parts. A place to hide out till it's clear to run farther."

Twenty minutes later with the sun in their faces and the town behind them, Mitch urged his horse into a gallop. Surrounded by whistling prairie grass eight feet high, Diana had her mare follow his lead.

"How did it go with Mrs. Hillyard?"

"She didn't ask a lot of questions." Diana let the wind lift her cape around her arms, exposing her long-sleeved blouse and slender hands holding firmly to leather reins. "But Mitch, I should tell you that as I passed the livery stables to meet you just now, your friends were coming out of the front doors."

"Which friends?"

"Quinn and Art."

"Did either of them see you?"

"I ducked around the corner to avoid them, but I can't be sure."

Dammit. If they'd caught wind of the direction Diana and Mitch were headed, then the posse might be following.

Apprehension took hold of him. He struggled against it but it rooted. How had his life reached the point where he was sorry to see his childhood friends?

He contemplated the situation. In return for their fury, was he angry with all of them, or just a couple? Or just one? Just Quinn Turner?

With a firm grip on his lines, Mitch ignored the churning that ripped through his insides. "Tell me exactly where this cabin is."

Almost two hours later and close to noon, Diana looked over her left shoulder. She grew uneasy again. "You keep looking back, Mitch! What do you see?"

The easiest way to get to the cabin was to follow the railroad tracks. For the first time since their journey began, a train was barreling up behind them, chugging across the autumn plains. The landscape blurred in her vision—a rolling sea of yellow grass, gold-leafed cottonwoods and geese flying low in V formation. The birds squawked above their heads in a cloudless sky of blue as they flew south to escape impending winter.

"A flicker of something on the horizon behind us! Must be another train!"

If it wasn't another train, what then? A posse of angry men? Diana didn't voice her fears. She leaned forward into her saddle and pressed her legs against the mare's straining muscles. She'd changed hours ago, removing her constraining skirt while leaving her comfortable pants on.

Once in a while, she'd catch Mitch watching her, his eyes shifting over her legs. She pretended they weren't alone chasing through the wind, pretended that what she felt for him was secondary to everything else breaking into chaos around them.

The prairie locomotive gained speed, releasing white smoke as it passed. The conductor waved and pulled on the horn in greeting, releasing a loud blast that frightened Diana's horse.

Regaining control, Diana veered to the left and stopped beneath a splatter of dry pines. Painted signs appeared in a fork in the road.

"Miner's Gully," Mitch read, looking left to where the road turned sharply and dipped past a ditch. "Regina, straight ahead for almost five hundred miles." He tilted back his hat. Diana watched a trickle of sweat weave down his temple. The scab on his jaw was healing nicely.

"We'll take Miner's Gully." Diana clicked her tongue and touched her heels to the mare. "We're not far!"

Cabins rose before their eyes. Several stood in a cluster around the meandering river, built twenty years ago when folks had panned through the river silt to search for gold. Nothing major had been found, only a trickle to keep the optimists from leaving, but the cabins remained. There was a general store and a small telegraph office that connected to the rail line two miles south.

"Which one?" hollered Mitch as they rode through the village.

"It's on the other side of town, sitting on its own."

They found it a mile out, planted beside a trickling gully in a rim of pine trees. She prayed that she and Mitch hadn't traveled for nothing.

Mitch tugged hard on his reins, stopping his horse.

Diana followed in kind. Panting through the pines with the sun beating down on her, Diana stared at two horses tethered beside the cabin. When she recognized them, a wave of excitement gripped her.

"Is it them?" Mitch asked.

"I think so. Those are the horses they often use when on duty at the stables." But this time, they likely hadn't asked permission to use them.

Sliding off her saddle, she walked alongside Mitch to the back door. Mitch removed his gun from his holster, to her look of harsh dismay. When they turned the corner, her brothers were standing with their guns raised and pointed at the intruders.

Her smaller brother, Tom, gasped in stunned surprise at Diana's sudden appearance. The next events happened so quickly she didn't have a moment to object.

Mitch dived for Wayde's legs. Wayde slammed to the ground. Mitch knocked the gun out of his hands and quickly turned his own to Wayde's head.

"Don't shoot him!" Tom roared from behind Mitch. "Goddammit, don't shoot my brother!"

The fear clamping Diana's throat tightened hard. "Mitch, what are you doing?"

Mitch ignored her, gripping Wayde by the shirt and shoving him to his feet. The shirt tore. "I'm sick and tired of playing school tag with you boys. Now dammit, you're going to do as I say. I've almost reached my limit and don't rightly care if you don't want to help yourselves. But your sister… Goddammit…your sister…. Look at her!"

Wayde cursed at Mitch.

"You son of a bitch," added Tom.

"Drop your gun at my feet," Mitch ordered her younger brother. "Right goddamn now!"

Tom hesitated. Mitch cocked the hammer of his gun at Wayde. Wayde paled. Diana closed her eyes. Her blood stopped pumping.

"This was not why I brought you," Diana whispered.

"You brought me to help. And if these two slugs would stop for a minute and look around, they might notice that I'm the only lawman here *to* help!"

Tom slowly came around and slipped his gun to Mitch's feet where it bounced off his boot.

Mitch heaved with all his might and flung Wayde into the air. Wayde knocked against a crooked apple tree, downing half a dozen yellow apples before falling into the dirt on his behind.

The men stared at each other.

"Now, I'm going to take my papers out." Mitch's voice shook the air. "I'm going to stick your fingers into my pad of ink, press them onto separate sheets, look at them under the microscope for however long that takes and you two—" his face darkened with splotches of red "—you two are going to sit there and smile and say thank you very much. *You got that?*"

No one argued. Tom and Wayde looked to each other, then to Diana.

Leaving himself open to their trust, Mitch lowered his gun, turned his back and went to his horse to get his things.

The fact that he was trusting them when his back was turned riveted Diana speechless.

"I'm not sure about this," Tom said weakly.

"Let's see what he comes up with," Wayde replied.

Sliding down to sit on a log, Diana finally exhaled the pressure that had been building inside of her. She lifted shaking fingers to sweep the loosened hair off her forehead and tried to calm her jangling nerves.

For the moment she was still too upset to talk, to ask her brothers how they'd gotten here and what other laws they'd broken. They came to sit beside her, and despite the chilled silence between the three of them, she was comforted by their presence.

Mitch worked quickly. Within half an hour, he'd taken ten prints from both young men. He varnished the prints to seal them, he said, then said they needed to dry. He kept glancing to the sun, checking the time she supposed, stopping everything every time he heard a horse and rider gallop past. On his command, Wayde and Tom brought all the horses to the rear of the cabin.

The silence loosened as the afternoon wore on. Wayde and Tom admitted they'd "borrowed" the horses and guns from their boss at the stables, and he hadn't known they were taken. When her brothers asked how their escape had been received by the Mounties and the town, Diana answered truthfully about the posse. Mitch listened and said very little.

She noticed regret in the manner her brothers looked at her, but fear when she mentioned the posse.

"When this is all over," she promised, "we're leaving town like we planned."

Within two hours from the time he began, Mitch was peering into the microscope, comparing Tom's prints to someone else's.

Mitch suddenly lifted his dark face toward them with a pang of alarm.

"What is it, Mitch?" Her stomach tightened with a new unease.

Mitch stared at her brothers. A flash of color heightened his jawline. "What the hell do you think you're doing?"

In a second he was on his feet, hovering over her brothers, who were seated next to her on the log.

Quaking, the three of them jumped to their feet.

"We're just sittin' here," Wayde growled. "Waitin'."

"Do you think I'm a fool? Do you think I'd waste my time on this method if I thought it didn't work?"

"You might," scoffed Wayde.

"You could have saved me a lot of time and aggravation by just telling me what happened the night of the robbery. You lied to me and you're still lying to me."

Moving to within an inch of Wayde, Mitch peered down at the young man. His menacing voice brought the same shiver to Diana as she'd felt on their first meeting, when Mitch had brought Wayde home from the railway station after accusing him of theft.

Mitch hurled his accusations. "Did you think I wouldn't discover that your prints are a perfect match? You were *there,* goddammit. You were both in the goddamn bank!"

Gulls screeched in the overhead sky as Mitch waited for the culprits to answer. Late-afternoon light dipped across the bridge of Wayde's wide nose and cheeks, deepening the color throbbing in his defiant dark eyes. What Mitch wanted to do, what his fists urged him to do, was beat the living tar out of both brothers till they told him the truth.

"Start talking," said Mitch. "And don't stop until I say."

Diana drew herself together and glared at her brothers. "So help you both, it better be the full truth this time. Did you—you rob the bank?"

Wayde straightened his collar. "No."

Tom paced the ground. "We didn't rob anyone."

Mitch saw Diana's shoulders droop with relief. He flexed his bicep and rubbed his bristly jaw. "Your prints match the ones I lifted on the brass doorknob of the front door. When were you in the bank?"

"We were there the day before."

"Doing what?"

Wayde sighed.

"You better tell him the truth, Wayde," Tom said. "We were visiting with Mrs. Patty Upwood."

Wayde kicked dirt at his brother's feet. "There's no need to get into that."

"I interviewed her," said Mitch. "She's the young bank teller with the silver earrings shaped like horseshoes, and a broken little finger on her right hand. She seemed nervous when I spoke to her, but insisted it was due to the terror of being robbed. Is there more to it?"

Before the brothers could answer, he confronted them with another question. "What were you doing with a married woman?"

Wayde lowered his gaze to the ground. "Agreeing on a time when she and her youngest sister would meet us for lunch."

"A *married* woman?" Diana's tone sent a visible shudder through Wayde. "Is her sister married, too?"

"Abbie's not married. Not yet. She's only fifteen," said Tom, making it clear how he felt about Abbie.

"A married woman. How could you get involved?"

There was only one explanation in Mitch's mind. Wayde wasn't the first to fool around with a married woman.

The guilty brother kept his mouth shut, but his thunderous face couldn't mask his rising temper.

Tom, more talkative than his brother, peered at Mitch, crossing his hands over his slim build. "Did you ask her how she broke her finger?"

Wayde lurched at his brother on the question, but the younger one escaped. "You can't trust Reid!"

"We're going to tell the whole story this time," Tom insisted. "Diana wouldn't have brought him if she didn't trust him."

"Maybe where he's concerned, Diana's got starry eyes and can't see straight."

Mitch felt a flush of heat rising up his neck. He stole a glance in Diana's direction where she stood beneath the apple tree. She colored lightly. And averted her gaze from the men to her hands. The late-afternoon sun streamed around her tangled hair, still caught in a braid at the back but now ruffled from the long ride and the wind.

Tom planted himself in front of his brother. "And maybe where Patty's concerned, you can't see straight, either."

Mitch jumped between them, glaring from one smoldering face to the other. "Are you finished insulting each other?" They looked up weakly. "Good. Then let's get down to business. Patty Upwood told me she slammed her finger in the till by accident when the robbery occurred."

"Did you ask any of the other tellers if they bandaged it for her? Or witnessed it?" Tom asked. "Because she didn't break it in the till. In an argument the night before, her husband broke it for her."

"Shut…up!" This time Wayde lunged and flung his arms around his brother's waist. They both tumbled to the ground. "Do you know what her husband will do to Patty if this gets out?"

Mitch let them fight. It might release their aggression, he thought. But Diana wouldn't let them. She tried to break them up, yelling in the process.

Mitch hollered into the air, stopping everyone cold. "That's why you wouldn't say what's been happening. You're protecting Patty."

The brothers parted and Wayde slowly rose from the ground. His mouth shook. "She's seventeen years old. Same age as me. Her father gave her away to a man who's close to fifty. Her husband's a drunk and a bully."

The brothers rose from the dirt.

"I didn't seek her out," said Wayde. "She boards her horse at Cedarville Stables, same place we deliver ours, and goes riding a lot with her sister. I've gotten to know her well. Her husband was the one who bought the mules from us the day before the robbery. I was so ashamed of having shook his hand on the deal instead of punching him out for what he was doin' to Patty, I had to see her and explain. And try to figure out a way to get her out of there."

"I've got a way," said Mitch. "When we get back to town—"

"No, sir," hollered Tom. "I thought you might be able to help us, but we're not going back to Calgary."

"It's the only way to clear your names."

"But the prints prove we were in the bank. We'll be hanged."

"If I find the owners of the remaining two prints, I'll solve the puzzle. In the meantime, you'll explain to your lawyer and the judge that you visited the bank the day before and why. You're in the right."

"No," said Wayde, taking his time to reply. "You don't know Upwood. He'll kill Patty. What's the use of bein' right, then?"

How was Mitch to argue with that?

As Diana tried to convince her brothers, Mitch cocked his head at a familiar thundering sound. "Do you hear that?"

They stopped and listened. "What?" asked Diana.

"Galloping horses. Several of them."

"Posse," Diana whispered, ashen at the growing sound.

Wayde swore. "I told you we couldn't trust him. He brought more men."

"Get into the cabin!" Mitch pushed them all inside. Whirling to find the guns that he'd ordered Wayde and Tom to drop earlier, he found them nestled in the grass. Racing, he tossed them inside the back door then tore his own guns from his holster and dashed to the front corner of the cabin, protecting himself from whatever might be coming.

Eight men rode up on horseback, some of the same faces who'd glared defiantly at Mitch at the livery stables hours earlier. Gritting his teeth, he noticed his *friends* high atop their saddles, sitting in the middle of the angry mob—Art, Quinn, Clay and Vic.

Quinn removed his six-shooter and slid off his saddle.

Mitch stepped out from the shadows. "I told you not to come."

Art drew his horse to the front of the herd. His weight hadn't slowed him, Mitch noticed. He still rode with the skill and ease of a man who'd been raised on a cattle ranch. But a strange thought raced through Mitch's head. Due to Art's massive size, his fingerprints would be visibly larger on examination.

"Maybe *I* should speak, on account of our friendship," said Art.

"What kind of friendship is this?"

Quinn was less skillful with words. "We've come for the Campbell brothers. All of us here have a stake in the Calgary bank, and we won't see our money taken without a fight."

Some of the men were handling their guns. In Mitch's mind, it meant they were through talking. He ran on instinct. "I could use your help."

"What?" asked Quinn.

"Now that you're here, I can see your logic, and could use you all. The Campbell brothers are inside. They're in my custody. Their sister's in there with them, trying to talk to them. I'm trying to force them to come back with me, but they're putting up an argument. But your arrival might be more persuasive." He grinned softly.

Then he shot his guns into the air. The bang sent a flock of crows flapping from the pines.

"You're surrounded," he hollered to Wayde and Tom inside. "Come out now."

He stood panting, surrounded by explosive men and explosive possibilities.

Slowly and quietly, Diana came around the back corner. With arms stretched above her head, she indicated she was unarmed. Tom and Wayde followed with their arms held high in the air. As they passed, all three looked at Mitch with such intense fear that it made him gasp for breath.

He hoped like hell his plan would work.

Chapter Nineteen

Mitch had done the honorable thing, thought Diana, but the two-hour ride home was difficult to take.

Galloping in the darkness beside her brothers, Mitch and the eight men, chilled beneath her cape to the point of constant shivering, Diana knew that by turning her brothers over to the posse and ensuring that he rode beside them under constant watch, Mitch had saved their lives.

One of the toughest-looking men demanded that her brothers wear handcuffs, and Mitch had relented. Her younger brothers, to whom she'd vowed to provide safety and security, were riding in shame back to a town she'd brought them to.

Wayde and Tom had tried to protect a young woman who couldn't protect herself, and in the end it might be they who suffered most.

Her stomach growled as she jostled in the saddle. She hadn't thought of food since noon when Mitch had stopped to offer her smoked beef from his saddlebag. The thought of food now added to her nausea.

The dim lights and sounds of Calgary amplified as

they drew closer to the outskirts. A few of the riders said goodbye, nodding their sullen faces and fading into black.

Soon, the remaining riders were headed toward the fort gates. Mitch proclaimed to the two awaiting guards, "I've got the Campbell brothers here." He tossed them keys to the handcuffs. "Lock them up."

Diana tugged back on her reins and watched her brothers ride away.

Turning back to the remaining men, Mitch thanked them.

To Diana, the activities blurred—arguments from Quinn and Art about the upcoming trial, Mitch insisting they go home and get a good night's rest, others complaining bitterly about justice being done and stolen money returned to the banks.

Diana turned away but Mitch reined his horse beside hers. "Slow down, I'll take you home."

Quinn turned in on her other side. "I'll take care of her."

Feeling trapped between them, Diana said nothing while they rode. Something else was going on besides their fighting over who would ride with her. After Quinn's display against her brothers, he was insane if he thought she'd have anything to do with him.

Yet keeping him close felt safer than keeping him at a distance. Why did he care so much about what her brothers did?

Her denim pants brushed against her mare. She directed her question straight at Quinn. "Do you fear for my safety as well as my brothers'?"

"You're not in any danger."

"But my brothers are."

"Not too much with Officer Reid on their side."

"I don't know if even Officer Reid can help justify their fingerprints."

Mitch shook his head at her in the dark, as if warning her to be silent, but it was too late.

Quinn's face flickered in the darkness as they rode past the noisy saloon. "Don't tell me their fingerprints have been found at the scene of the crime?"

Mitch shifted dangerously in his saddle. "I thought you didn't believe in fingerprints."

"Looks like I might be persuaded."

"Persuaded enough to let me take a sample of yours?"

Quinn stiffened. He glared at Mitch as Diana sensed a deep discord. Something was terribly wrong between these men. "You're joking, right?"

"Jack Sherman would have said yes just now. He would have done anything I asked. At one time, I believed you would, too."

"Jack's not here, is he?"

"Let me take a sample of your prints to prove that you don't believe in them. That my methods are flawed."

Quinn laughed. "Twenty-five years," he whispered in some secret message to Mitch, then jammed his heels into his horse and rode off.

"What's going on between you two?"

"Twenty-five years is the length of a murder sentence." They reined their horses into her narrow street. Lanterns and candles shimmered in the windows of passing homes.

"I've discovered the missing puzzle piece," said Mitch. "Quinn plays the banjo."

"What significance does that have?"

"We were all there the night of the swimming party. All eight of us, including Jack."

"You're going way too fast. Are you talking about the swimming party where Jack got hurt?"

Mitch nodded. "Quinn was playing the song, 'Five Miles to Home.' We were all humming the words."

Did the words mean something she should recognize? "I heard Quinn play that at your barbecue, but what do the words—"

"Inspector Reid!" The guard who Mitch had planted outside her home greeted them.

"Anything happening here?" Mitch asked him.

They dismounted, with the guard helping Diana.

"It's been quiet, sir."

"I want you to remain on guard," said Mitch. "I've called for another man to join you. You're to stay all night."

Mitch turned to her. "There'll be a lot of activity tomorrow, things you won't understand. You've got to hold tight. Hold tight on to that long-ago image you have of Calgary. Don't give up on me, Diana."

Mitch surprised her by dropping by the office the following evening at closing time. Diana was rearranging spectacles at the front counter, her mind flooding with the confusing rumors customers had been bringing in hour by hour.

The newspaper reporter, David Fitzgibbon, had come in trying to confirm the rumors with her, but she sent him away empty-handed.

At the sound of horses neighing, she peered through the darkening windowpanes to see the stagecoach coming in from the southern part of the territory.

Travelers disembarked onto the boardwalk in front of the boarding house, brushing dust off their suits beneath the lamplight, eager to have arrived. Not too long ago, she and her brothers and sisters had also been new arrivals. Circumstances had changed. She couldn't wait to board the stagecoach again to search for a place that might truly welcome them.

"Diana?" The bell on the front door tinkled. Mitch strode in wearing his red tunic and black breeches. Impatience emanated from every muscle of his lean body, causing every one of hers to tense. He removed his wide-brimmed brown hat, revealing a flattened crown of thick black hair. Jamming his rough fingers through it, he looked around the empty store.

Her chest squeezed at the sight of his dark imposing looks. "What is it? Is something wrong?"

"Your brothers are fine. They're talking to their lawyer. The truth is washing out and it can only be good for everyone. Is York in?"

Diana closed a tortoiseshell case. It slid across her palm as she replaced it in the glass display case. A ring of keys clanged from her fingers. Her skirts swayed about her old shoes and her braid clung to her chest.

"He went home early. I think—I think he's having dinner with the jeweler's daughter. She was in earlier and..." Diana fumbled with the keys "...I heard them talking."

Mitch sauntered to the counter, towering over it and filling the space between them with a muscled body hewn from years of training and riding. "He's not good enough for you. I'm glad he's having dinner with someone else."

Acutely conscious of his stare, she reached for the dusting rag and ran it over the glass. "You don't always have to say what you're thinking, especially if no one's asked you."

"I guess that's the difference between you and I."

His reply angered her more than the initial statement. "And what is that supposed to mean?"

He tapped the glass. "I'm more direct than you are."

"Good for you. I'll have Dr. York grind you a trophy and have it engraved—"

"*Dr.?* Yesterday you were calling him Emmit."

She tightened her mouth. "I'm calling him a lot of things today."

"Because he's seeing the jeweler's daughter?"

"It's irrelevant now. And I think you should leave if that's what you've come to say."

He turned and walked to the rack of spectacles. "Maybe I've come to be fitted for spectacles."

She lifted her chin. "Have you?"

"Yes, I think I may need a monocle."

He loomed over the rack, twisting at the waist to lift a gold-rimmed monocle and place it over his right eye.

She stifled a smile.

"How can you laugh at my plight? My eyesight is going."

She continued dusting and he replaced the monocle. "It's always good to see you smile, Diana." Then he found the painted sign in the window. He pulled it out and read. "Help Wanted."

Humiliation swept over her. The cuckoo clock picked that moment to come out and yell. Diana jumped at the chirping. Six o'clock and time to close the doors. She sauntered to the front door and locked it. "Dr. York wants me to stay long enough to train the replacement."

"I'm sorry." His voice was no louder than a hush and whispered over her skin. "I know how hard you worked to get this job."

"Maybe it'll be more appreciated at the next place." Wherever that was.

Dr. York had told her at noon today that he could no longer support an employee in her shaky position, that as much as he'd like to, he couldn't jeopardize the town's goodwill. Thank God she'd kept the job at the factory, that she still had a way to provide for the younger ones. The foreman had questioned her about her situation, but Charlotte and Winnie had defended her.

Diana's outward detachment didn't seem to convince Mitch. He came to face her, heat emanating from his body, darkness enveloping the two of them alone in the store. "It's always been a struggle for you, hasn't it?"

The honesty in his words affected her. "Don't worry what I'll be doing—"

"Why not?"

"Because I've got half a mind to rent a part of the mercantile next door and apply for the sole rights to the Bridgerton Catalog. They sell spectacles in the catalog and all I'd need to do is create a little space with a mirror and adjustment tools. I could double the sales Dr. York does in here, I know I could. As it is, folks recommend me to their relatives and they come asking for me here. I could sell other merchandise along with it, like gowns and bonnets from Ireland, and lamps from England."

The room had grown totally dark. Lighting from the street lamps outside filtered through the space onto her long brown skirt and worn white blouse. Her loose braid hung over the ridge of her breast.

"I'd buy my monocle from you."

His comment was so ridiculous, so useless while trying to be helpful, that she burst into a sob of laughter.

Not wanting him to see her falling apart, she hustled down the hall to the side door to lock it. "I've got to find a lantern."

When she spun around again, he was standing before her. His dark figure tightened beneath his tunic. She could see only the outline of his face in the darkness, the curve of his lips and pride in his stance.

"Is it true what folks are saying? Did you toss her in jail as an accomplice to the crime?"

"Mrs. Patty Upwood is there as we speak."

"And her husband?"

"He just dropped by, drunk as ever, trying to get her released and as furious as a bull in a ring."

"So what the customers have been telling me is true. You let the town know that she was seeing Wayde." Fear for her brother took hold again. He didn't need another strike against him in the eyes of the town.

"I told you. I'm more direct than you."

"How could you risk it?" she murmured.

He reached out with a mighty hand and braced the wall. "There's no safer place for Patty as the truth comes out about what she was doing with your brothers."

"They were only having lunch."

"That's not what Mr. Upwood's accusing her of."

"At least he can't hit her."

"I told him if he does, I'd hit him back."

Diana swallowed. "What's going to happen?"

"Mr. Upwood will sober up. My guess is he'll go home to bed soon. I'll keep his wife locked up as an accomplice to the crime for as long as he's angry."

"So the charges aren't going to last."

"They're more for the benefit of keeping her in protective custody. But that's just between you and me and the commander. She doesn't know it, either."

Diana pushed past him toward the cloakroom.

He pulled her back by the wrist. "Don't leave."

Her braid skipped along her breast. Her hand throbbed where he touched her. "We shouldn't be seen together. The judge might think you're not in control—"

"I'm *not* in control," he growled, yanking her closer, pressing the length of her thigh along his. "Not when it comes to you."

He struck a deep chord within her. No one else in town believed in her brothers as much as Mitch did. He'd been her one true friend in all of this.

"You better leave. Open that door and go." She tried to wrestle free but his grip was firm.

"I know who did it."

Her throat clamped. "Did what?"

"The robberies."

Her body stilled beneath his hold. Her heart, her mind, her hopes raced. "Tell me."

"Quinn Turner."

"Your *friend?*"

"I thought he was."

"Why?"

"I'm not sure, but it's got something to do with what's between him and me. And maybe it's a way to retaliate against his father." His voice lowered. "He has an accomplice, but I don't know who."

"How do you know Quinn's responsible?"

"I haven't proven it yet. That's why I'm here. I need your help."

"How?"

"I need a sample of his fingerprints. The judge says he can't order a suspect to cooperate with fingerprints because there's no precedent in the law. Prints have to be taken voluntarily. Since Quinn has already refused, I figure if I come across a sample on my own and they match the scene of the crime, the judge might reconsider."

"You haven't told the judge who you suspect, have you?"

"I don't want my suspicions voiced until I know for sure."

"Why are you telling me?"

"Because there's no one else I trust."

She allowed time for the throbbing in her heart to slow. "What can I do?"

"Spend time with him. Ever since he saw me with you at the barbecue, he's been competitive, so I know he'd like nothing more than to court you. I need a sample of something he touches. It can't be fabric or paper or anything that would absorb the oils from his fingers. It's got to be something smooth and hard, like a pair of spectacles or a drinking glass."

"Where is he? Take me to him."

"We can't make it obvious. I tracked him down and know he just stepped into the diner."

"Let me get my cape." She stumbled past him, breathing in his scent, aching for the fulfillment of touching him, longing for something beyond her reach.

"He'll be there awhile. He likes to take his time."

Anchoring herself against the wall beside the lantern, she withdrew a match from its box. She lit the lantern and adjusted the flame. A hollow swoosh filled the silence of the hallway.

"How could you choose York over me?" Mitch's words resonated with emotion.

"It doesn't matter anymore."

"Yes, it does. It matters to me."

She slid the lantern to her waist and hurried down the hall toward the cloakroom. Mitch followed, his long strides easily overtaking her in the doorway.

"Sacrificing what you want and need is meaningless. You went to York with open arms for your family's sake, to secure a future for them, but where did it get you?"

"At least I tried. Where does your self-sacrifice get you? You bury yourself in misery over the death of your friend when everyone around you wants to help."

Wary, he stepped back. "We'll not talk of Jack."

"Then how about Digger?"

Mitch flinched.

"I never knew Jack, but I believe he wouldn't have wanted you to sacrifice the carefree man who used to laugh and joke with your friends for the sullen one you are today."

"You never knew me then."

"Mrs. Sherman told me."

"With people like Quinn, it seems I can't trust my friends, though, can I?"

And neither could she, from the friends and servants who'd stolen her parents' fortune. She tilted her face upward. "We're both the same, then, aren't we?"

Dauntless, she dipped into the darkened corner of the cloakroom, resting the lantern on its wall shelf as she reached for her cape.

He asked, "And why do you suppose it is that whenever I come near you, the blood's pounding in me so hard I can barely restrain myself?"

Lifting an arm to reach her cape on the peg, she buried her face in her sleeve. She ached to touch him.

"Come closer and don't run from me, Diana."

Still turned away, she clung to her woolen cape. "Do you know how hard it is for me to look into your eyes and see the agony there, the unspoken hurt of losing your friend Jack?"

Mitch didn't answer. Then she felt him roping his fingers around her thick braid, skimming the fabric along her shoulder blades. She tingled beneath his touch, came alive to the man standing behind her.

The heat of his touch penetrated through her flimsy cotton blouse, reminding her of another night they shared that seemed as if it'd happened a century ago. A night that'd been passionate and exciting and one that she'd carry in her memory forever.

"It's not only the loss of Jack you witness in my eyes," he whispered. "It's the thought of losing you."

"Every time you touch me, I feel like my corset's done up too tight. I can't breathe. Stop this," she pleaded.

But he drew closer. She felt him press his legs against the back of her thighs. Then he was burying his face in the crux of her neck, inhaling deeply. "God, you smell good. Every minute we're together, I feel like I'm running a losing race. I couldn't stop what I'm thinking or what I'm about to do even if I wanted."

His hands slid up along her body, cupping her hips, her waist, her ribs. Giving in to her desire, Diana tilted her head back, resting it on his chin. She had an inexplicable need to say goodbye to Mitch by closing the distance between them again if only for one last, blissful time, to let him know she'd always remember his kiss, his murmurs, his body.

She felt so much for this man.

It couldn't end. Not tonight.

Mitch was losing her. He could feel it.

He wanted to pull Diana's heart and soul into his arms, but he felt her adrift in a sea of unspoken sentiment. They could start afresh, he thought, a new beginning. His lips opened as he bit into her neck, playfully sinking his teeth into the soft flesh. She arched her back against his front and he was instantly hard.

His right hand left her waist and traveled up her arm, squeezing the swell of her upper muscles before settling at the base of her warm neck. His other hand tugged at her velvety hair, releasing the clasp at the end of her braid. It pinged off the floorboards then must have lost itself in the rug.

He bit her earlobe, tongued behind her ear, kissed along her temple at the soft, downy skin that beckoned to be touched. She held firm to the wall facing away from him, palms planted against the wallpaper, allowing him to touch her wherever he pleased.

With a firm yank, he hiked the back of her skirt over the back of her bare thighs. His pulse raced, his breathing turned to panting.

She gasped, but he continued, clawing his hard hands along the top of her stockings that met with the bottom of her soft pantaloons. He tried to claw those, off, too, reaching around the waistline to the front, searching for a discreet tie that would unknot the package.

He found it and tugged. The pantaloons slid over her ample hips. From behind, he took the smooth buttocks into his massive hands and gripped her, pulling her body against the rigid center of his breeches.

She reached around and pressed her slender fingers against his shaft, trying to pull down on his breeches.

He understood her request and slid his pants down slightly, releasing his straining erection to the exhilarating rush of cool air, sliding it against the bare warmth of her plush behind.

By the low murmurs that escaped her throat, he knew she loved this, too.

With a physical abandon he'd never known, he pulled her by an arm, hauling her around to face him directly, keeping her skirt lifted to her waist, pressing himself against her awaiting thighs.

The musky scent of her drove him to a frenzy. The swooshing of the lantern echoed above her head. The heat from the flames warmed his face.

He stared down at the woman trapped in the circle of his arms. The lantern's glow flickered in her warm, green eyes. Half-hooded with sensuality, they gazed up at him as if she were an innocent young thing who had never experienced such ecstasy.

"We've shared this before," he reminded her. Pressing his mouth gently over hers, he knew he would take her here.

Chapter Twenty

While he kissed her, Diana felt the beating of his heart through his tunic. Mitch had surprised her with his swiftness, how quickly he'd swooped upon her in the cloakroom and how quickly she'd responded.

At first it was a penetrating kiss that seared through her mouth into her very existence. She wasn't afraid of him, but her body trembled beneath his as if in fear.

Her spine pressed against the cool wall, her back flattening in response to the onslaught of Mitch's firm body. She felt his cool fingers race along the edge of her waistband. He bunched her skirt in one boxy hand and explored the contours of her naked belly with the other. The grazing of his fingertips sent spiraling waves of pleasure through her stomach, making her wet with urgency, hot with need.

Then his lips pulled back slightly and she responded in kind, teasing and tempting him with her flickering tongue. It was a last goodbye, she felt, and so she had little to lose if she gave herself completely and enjoyed the fantasy of making love to Mitch one last time.

He'd been her first kiss. With anguish wrenching at

her heart, she knew she'd never meet another man like him. He was so many men rolled into one—dangerous, compassionate, humorous and melancholy. So much feeling in one single man.

She felt it now, the emotions thundering through his skin, his urgency and abandon as he kissed her mouth, her cheek, her throat, her neck.

Golden light from the lantern shimmered over his dark face, his black cropped hair, the muscles at his temples and the outline of his lips.

"I never knew I could feel this way," she whispered.

"Neither did I."

She soared when he said that, marveling that a man so experienced could find unique pleasure in being with her.

His grip on her bare hips tightened. She felt the hardness of his erection higher on her clothing and ached for it to come closer to her center. But entwined in a tangle of limbs, half-shed clothing, legs that couldn't move because of lowered breeches, it was difficult to get into the right positioning.

His lips wandered to her earlobe. When he bit it lightly, she caught her breath then forgot to exhale as he slid his warm mouth down her neck to the base of her lacy collar.

"Take this off," he murmured.

She remembered where they were. "It's rather dangerous to be doing this in here, isn't it? I mean, what if someone should walk in?"

"Both doors are locked."

"Yes, but—"

He smothered her protests with his mouth. She ran her hand up along his tunic and unfastened the bottom button. Then reaching lower, she stroked the silky skin of his shaft. He gasped into her mouth and pressed closer, indicating how much he enjoyed her touch.

But her nervousness grew. "It's not right to do this here."

"Tell me to stop, then. Tell me…."

She groaned. The doors were locked. She and Mitch were safe.

A wildfire coursed through her body, excitement that she could do this to Officer Mitchell Reid. Gone was the commander with a dozen men beneath him and in his place stood a man who couldn't stop touching and holding her.

Timidly, she dropped her hand from his shaft and moved it lower, cupping the warm, swinging flesh. He moaned. She loved the feel of him in her palm, the heady rush of what was happening between them.

"I want to kiss you everywhere," he whispered into her hair. "Everywhere."

His words sent goose flesh rising to her skin. She was quaking in his arms, her body fevered and aching for greater closeness. When she tore free of his mouth, she gazed into his brown eyes and saw the fire she'd lit inside of him. The same fire he stoked in her.

With a loud intake of air, his mouth closed on hers. His fingers gently unfastened the buttons at her throat and worked down toward her skirt. Without him holding it, her skirt slid back down her legs.

Her blouse parted. Gently, he curled the edges of the fabric over her shoulders and slid the sleeves over her wrists until the blouse fell free.

Taking a breath, Diana slid her lips from his and pressed her forehead against his chin. She kissed the thin scar along his jaw where his stitches had been removed.

They rocked together as he unclasped her corset. Lantern light fluttered over the swell of her rising bosom. The curves glistened like golden apples.

He took a moment to allow his eyes to linger on the vision. Without a word, he bent his dark head and kissed the top of each breast.

His movements were soft and gentle. Then with a firm grip and a sudden jolt, he ripped through the front stays of her corset, releasing her breasts to the taut, warm air.

"You've got beautiful tits."

The crude way he said it made excitement leap to her throat. Her breasts fell into his hot palms. He stared at the soft pink areolas, as large as plums. Bending lower, he licked the tip of one, then watched with a growing smile as it hardened. She yearned for more. He kissed the other tip ever so gracefully, making her quiver with unreleased tension.

She'd never before been so aware of what a man's kiss might entail. A kiss on her lips, on her breast, on her belly.

But it was her turn. She would tempt and tease him, make him savor the brink that they were exploring together, rolling along the edge of ecstasy, longing to release, yet longing to prolong the wonder.

With a sound so low coming from Mitch, almost a vibration that echoed in her ears, she unfastened his jacket. When the red wool parted, she splayed her hands along his undershirt and the warmth of his chest, feeling the layers of muscle and flesh cord beneath her fingers.

Roughly, she yanked his undershirt up and clawed her fingers upon the bare flesh of his stomach, loving the texture of the hair that rose up from between his thighs.

The side door rattled beyond the room. Diana shuddered. "Someone's coming."

"No, it's the wind." He laughed and gently lowered

her to the carpet, sliding her cape off the peg and pressing it beneath her body and the rug. He removed her pantaloons in one gliding motion.

Unable to look at her old shoes reminding her of who and what she was, she slid them off her feet. At this moment, she was simply Diana, lover to Mitch, and she had never felt so wanted.

Mitch didn't seem to care what she wore. He was hungry for her flesh and for her kisses. The wind gained speed outside and lapped at the boards, sending shivers through her spine.

"We'll be caught," she whispered.

"Um-mm." With a low moan of laughter, Mitch ran his hands along the length of her stockings from her ankles to her thighs. She closed her eyes and allowed herself the luxury of feeling every nuance of his touch.

"You're trembling," he said.

"That we'll be caught."

"It's the wind in the trees and the passing horses you hear. It's Mother Nature telling us she approves."

"And you, my dear inspector, are full of malarkey." She removed his jacket and peeled off his undershirt slowly, watching the light dip into the rippled muscles of his chest, over the band of hair along his belly.

Sitting upright with her bare breasts bouncing above him, her skirt hiked around her waist to reveal stockings but no pantaloons, Diana tortured him by slowly inching her body down toward his legs. With a yank and their soft laughter combining in the room, they removed his breeches and socks so he was totally naked.

His chiseled body was like a stranger to hers, naked in the room, yet she felt his aura as if he were her dearest friend. Relaxing for a moment to gaze at his long legs, lightly matted with hair and awash in a sheen of gold paint that blazed from the lantern, she swallowed hard at the vision. Then ever so lightly, she took his erection in her hand.

He was lost to her touch and the world around them. She loved giving him pleasure, the feel of warm clay in her hand. It was only a moment when she felt him pull away, groaning in unbelievable ecstasy but murmuring words of holding back.

"I want to be inside of you, Diana. I want to feel you around me."

"I want that, too."

Anchoring his massive hands beneath her arms, he pulled her to lie on top of him. Her naked chest slid along his torso. Their skin electrified on contact. He found her mouth, lightly and gently, and kissed her with such heated feeling she could barely breathe.

The evening and their time together had to end at some time, she realized, but pushed the thought from her mind. It remained like a looming whisper, driving her to force it from her thoughts with more urgent demands on Mitch.

He turned her over so that he was on top. Their mouths rolled together in a heated embrace, then he slid down lower to sample other parts of her body. He suckled at her breasts and she fed them to his eager mouth. He kissed her ribs, her belly button, then parted her thighs with the hot breath of his mouth.

She turned to him in surrender, doing what he asked, raising her bottom off the soft wool of her cape when his lips found the inner pink of her center.

His tongue felt like a warm, whispering breeze at first, darting softly along her folds, then gaining urgency and pressure as he found the spot that demanded attention.

She clamped her hands on either side of his head, running her fingers through the silky hair above his ears, urging him to continue.

But his head suddenly turned to kiss the inside of one thigh. Without a word, he was on his feet and lifting her. They stood up. Kissing her fully on the mouth, he wrapped his solid arms around her shoulders and walked her backward till she was once again pressed against the wall.

Lifting her left leg with a firm tug, he wrapped it up and around his naked hip, then thrust closer toward her.

His shaft slid along the wetness as he reached over and slid his hot fingers along the top of her folds.

"Mmm," she responded to the slick hot feel of his fingers.

His thick erection dipped inside of her, filling her with inches and inches of throbbing flesh. The combination of his fingers and his shaft seemed to touch and ignite every cell of hers that needed touching and igniting.

Powerless in his hands, she pulled him against her so that she was well anchored against the wall, then clung tightly to his shoulders with both arms and raised her other leg around his hip. He cupped her bottom with his hands, supporting her entire weight as they stood entwined.

"Perfect," he growled, sliding deeper inside of her. "You're perfect."

She lost herself in the feel of him and the pounding of her arteries. Her muscles, her heart, her mouth and everywhere he touched seemed to throb. His fingers slid back and forth, coaxing her to a new height she could barely absorb but desperately wanted to climb.

In a moment, she reached her peak, the muscles of her thighs clenching, the sweet ache of coming, the vulnerability of being held by Mitch and sharing with him something so intimate she couldn't speak. He watched her face as her muscles gave way to ecstasy, as she gave way to Mitch.

His cheeks flushed as he continued pumping, murmuring her name and kissing her in a thousand points. His grip tightened, his fingers dug into her flesh. He bit softly at her neck, closed his eyes and shuddered. As he released, she slid her hands up along his spine to the curves of his lower back and the warm tugging of muscles.

She adored this, with Mitch being inside of her and a part of her. When they were together, she felt as if the rest of her life was secondary. A wash of guilt crept to her face. Her brothers and sisters weren't secondary. She didn't want them to feel that way. Teetering on the edge of indecision, she buried her face into the bend of Mitch's neck and longed to know what to do.

"Mitch," she whispered.

"Yes?" He turned so that his face was touching hers.

She reveled in the warmth of his skin. How could she possibly tell him this was goodbye.

When Diana didn't speak, Mitch disentangled himself tenderly from her arms. "There's more to us than these interludes of lovemaking. I know you feel it, too."

Silently she scooped her blouse off the floor, looking suddenly shy. But she didn't have enough fabric to cover the swell of her breasts and the side of one naked leg. Enjoying the view, he smiled in the warmth of the glittering lamplight. How could she be shy with him after what they'd just shared?

He helped her collect her clothing from the rug. At her direction, he followed her into the room that had a water pump to clean up and dress.

Her black hair swayed at her hips as she buttoned her blouse. To his unease, she seemed distant again.

She was battling something. "What do we do about these feelings?"

He slid a muscled arm into his jacket, brimming with hopes for the future. "I want to take you out in the open, to show my family and the town the charming beauty I've discovered."

She spoke with a gentle frown, trying to understand him. "How is your reaction different to me than to any other woman you've been with?"

He groped for words. The frank look in her eyes dampened his confidence. He couldn't let her slip away. "I want to be with you all the time. You're all I think about."

She buttoned her skirt, her trembling fingers working rapidly at her waist. "Should we go *now*," she asked softly, "to tell your men and commander at the fort that we're a couple?"

"I was thinking we should wait until this business with your brothers is over."

"I see." She plopped her feet into her shoes. "I'm not a big believer in waiting, Mitch. To me, love and family always come first."

Towering above the counter and a ceramic bowl of water, Mitch washed his hands and thought about what she said. "I'm not good with explanations of how I feel. All I know is that you *are* different."

"It's not enough," she whispered.

He knew his offer wasn't enough. Diana had changed since he'd first gotten to know her. She'd gained self-confidence and she could attract the attention of any man she wanted.

What could he offer her?

Permanence? He'd never wanted permanence with a woman before. But it didn't mean it wasn't possible.

"Wait for me," he begged. "When this is all over with your brothers, I want to see you. I want to be with you."

Diana pushed the hair from her cheek. "I'd like to be with you, too, Mitch, but…I'm a hardworking woman from the poultry factory, who happened to win a hero for twenty-four hours at the fair. You'll never understand the desperation in my life."

Words clung to the inside of his throat. It was she who wouldn't understand the desperation in his. Was he strong enough for her? Strong enough? Could he take care of her family? He knew he couldn't make promises until his case was solved.

She lowered her head to adjust her waistband, ever so slight and graceful. "When this is over with Wayde and Tom, I've decided…my family's decided…it'll be best if we leave town."

Chapter Twenty-One

Affected deeply by the misery she'd caused him, Diana studied Mitch's lean dark face as she locked the outside alley door of Dr. York's office. She'd been honest with Mitch about her plans for leaving town, but her heart felt swollen, as if it were suffocating her.

There was a growing strain between them as they walked down the silent, darkened alleyway toward the light and bustle of a busier boardwalk. Her feelings for him had nothing to do with levelheaded reason, and everything to do with opening her mind and soul to a power bigger than the two of them. She was stunned by the gravity of what she felt for Mitch. Not the lust, but the passion.

She understood that Mitch was investigating her brothers and shouldn't be involved with her, that he wanted to wait until he cleared them, but she didn't understand why Mitch couldn't pledge his feelings and his promises for a solid future. If that was truly how he felt.

They approached the diner and her mood veered sharply at the thought of Quinn, and that he might possibly escape the reach of the law to leave her brothers exposed to a crime they didn't commit. She pushed her personal problems aside and thought only of her brothers.

"Are you sure you want to do this?" Mitch squeezed through the evening crowd that was heading toward the diner for the dinner hour. His bridled rage at his friend Quinn was evident in the way his lips thinned and his voice stretched. "Maybe what I'm asking you to do is too—"

"It's not. I can do this." She patted the canvas bag that she'd taken from the office—a bag where she could easily slide in a piece of evidence. She'd stuffed it with rags so that it wasn't empty and didn't look suspicious. It dangled off her wrist next to her faded drawstring purse. "You need just a simple piece of crockery, or a tin that he's touched, right?"

Mitch nodded. "I won't be far. I'll wait beneath the canopy of the livery stables." He motioned to the other side of the street. "I won't leave until I see you come out. There are lots of folks inside tonight." He peered into the front windows of the diner, still two doors down. Café curtains rose halfway up the panes to reveal tables full of dining strangers.

Diana flung the edge of her cape across her shoulders. The warm chinook that had been blowing from the west for the last little while had fled. South, like the geese.

She moved toward the diner, but stopped when she felt Mitch's hand on her shoulder.

"Diana," he said. Light cascaded from the street lamp above their heads, filling the contours of his face and making his dark eyes shimmer. "There's a crowd in there, so you won't be in any danger. Quinn's not going to do anything to raise suspicion now. A man's been killed at his hand and I do believe that was unintentional. But if at any time you feel in danger, I want you to get up and leave."

"I will," she said, nodding through an onslaught of emotions. She thought of Quinn and she'd never felt such burning hatred for someone since the day the banker had informed her, four years ago, that her uncle Desmond had sold their family home. He'd taken the money from the estate, tricking and shaming her to such depths that she'd spent two days sobbing before being able to explain to Wayde and Tom and the rest of the children how she'd lost their money, and that they needed to move out within the week.

A year after that, she'd heard from the police investigation that her uncle hadn't made it across the ocean with his money. He'd lost half of it in a game of cards, and the other half had been stolen from him at knifepoint. He'd landed in South Africa, penniless.

It brought her no comfort that he'd lost his stolen fortune.

But cornering Quinn and bringing him to trial might. It meant more to her than simply nabbing a criminal. If they—if *she*—could do this, it would somehow atone for her guilt in letting the ones who'd harmed her family five years ago escape.

"There'll be no crying this time," she whispered to Mitch, although she knew he couldn't understand.

He touched the bottom of her chin. "Sometimes, crying is natural."

The unknown kindness in his words, deeper than he could know, seared into her heart.

"You're strong," he added. "You've always been strong, and I believe in you. Take these coins." He stuffed two into her hand, squeezing her fingers together and cupping her fist. "Order a pie from the man behind the counter. That's all you need to do."

"But shouldn't I look for Quinn and his companions?"

"That would be too obvious. Ignore him totally. Just ask for a pie to take home to your family and wait at the counter for them to get you one. Pretend you're in a hurry. Quinn will do the rest."

She stared at the clasp of Mitch's hard fingers over hers, remembering how dearly he'd held her. Then with a whoosh, she spun around and lost herself in the folks walking along the boardwalk.

She entered the diner and walked straight to the display counter. She spoke to a short, round man with a bushy red beard. "I'd like...to order a pie."

"Sure, miss. Will you be eatin' it 'ere?"

Forcing herself to get into the spirit, she smiled. "That would be too much for one person. I'm taking it home to my family."

"What sort would you like? We can bake you any kind—raisin, pumpkin, apple, pecan."

"I'm in a bit of a hurry...what sort do you have made already?"

"Let me go to the kitchen and check. Wait right 'ere. Pull up a stool if you like."

She nodded stiffly, her nervousness beginning to show in the way her fingers were trembling on her purse. The man disappeared and she paced from the edge of the counter to the door, trying to pretend she was unaware of the glances being shot in her direction. She removed her bonnet and held it firmly between her fingers.

An older couple whispered something as they looked at her. She couldn't hear all the words, but made out a few. "...brothers...trial...a pity..."

In her peripheral vision, there was no sign of Quinn or his friends in the near vicinity. She didn't dare look deeper to the back of the restaurant for fear of giving away her hand.

She waited.

And waited.

No one came. She peered out the front windows and spotted Mitch across the road, leaning against the side of the stables and talking to one of the stable hands.

Folks passed by her, saying, "Excuse me."

She slid from the path of the doorway when the man behind the counter, carrying two urns of coffee, motioned toward her. "Peach or apple?"

"The peach sounds wonderful. One please." It would be canned peaches, not fresh, but a flavor she and her family hadn't tasted in years. If she actually got the pie that far.

"Brown sugar or cinnamon on top?"

"I think the children would like both."

"Comin' right up."

When he left and she was left to wait again, she worried whether Quinn was here, and if he'd noticed her. Maybe she should stroll out farther into the room—

"Well hello, Miss Campbell."

She glanced up to see him standing there. Her stomach twisted into a tight mesh at the grin on Quinn's face.

"Howdy," she replied.

"Your pie's 'ere!" The man behind the counter slid it across the countertop. He covered the golden-brown pastry with a checkered yellow cloth. "Please return the cloth and the glass plate tomorrow. We go through an awful lot of 'em."

"Yes, yes I will."

"Diana," Quinn repeated. "It's good to bump into you. Won't you join me for a cup of coffee?"

She smiled, but declined. "I'm afraid I'm in a rush to get home to the children. You know how it is when you've been away all day, working." She turned to the waiter. "How much?"

"Two bits."

"Allow me," said Quinn. "Put it on my tab."

"Oh, I really couldn't." Diana held out the coins.

Quinn reached out and pressed her hand closed. She felt nauseous at his touch. She wished he would have touched the coins instead of her hand, for maybe then he might have left a fingerprint. Then she realized if she could get him to lift the bottom of the glass plate, he might leave his prints there and she might be through with him quicker than she'd imagined.

"Thank you kindly." She smiled and tucked her coins into her purse, taking her time, hoping that Quinn would lift the pie.

"Leave it here behind the counter," Quinn said to the man. With a deadly smile, he gripped Diana by the elbow. "Please join me and my friends, won't you? Ten minutes surely won't make a difference to your family."

A shiver of disgust rolled through her. "Certainly, if only to thank you for the pie."

As she followed him through the noisy dining room, Diana wondered how two men could be so different. Mitch and Quinn had come from the same town, both raised on cattle ranches, friends during school and into their manhood, yet one had for some reason veered down a dark path.

Diana joined the table of men, saying hello to Art and Clay and wondering how and if they were involved. Mitch had said Quinn had an accomplice.

While Art and Clay grew preoccupied with the ladies eating at the next table, Quinn leaned over her side. "I'm sorry to hear your brothers are facing such a difficult time."

Gritting her teeth, Diana grasped the linen napkin in front of her. She unwound it, exposing a set of tin cutlery, then folded it across her lap. "Thank you," she murmured to Quinn, although she had a strong urge to slap him.

The waiter appeared and poured coffee for the four of them.

"Please don't mind me. Go ahead and finish your dessert," she indicated to the men.

Quinn bit into a crumbly piece of spice cake and talked with his mouth full. "What does your new lawyer think about the case?"

Diana felt her cheeks burning. She would in no way grovel to this man or admit a disadvantage. "That we've got a very strong case."

"Really? I'm surprised."

Biting her choked response, she glanced to her coffee. Lifting it gently to her lips, she tried not to tremble. "Why would you be surprised?"

An entire cake sat before them on the table. Quinn lifted his dining knife to hack another piece, pointing the blade at her to make his point, as if he were a brilliant teacher and she a failing student. "They say the fella who died in his coma whispered your brothers' names before he passed."

Her eyes flew to the plate he was touching, to the tin cup he handled. To everything she might confiscate to prove his guilt. "I've never heard that before."

"Oh…maybe I shouldn't be repeating it. Please, keep it under your hat. Your bonnet, so to speak." When he smirked, his mouth opened to reveal cake jammed between his teeth.

She wondered if he was starting a rumor he hoped would gain momentum, to confuse folks into believing there was truth to what he said. Mitch had told her Mr. Billings had died without saying a word, and she believed Mitch.

"With your brothers gone, you could do with a strong man about the house."

Do you know of any? she longed to ask.

"Cake?" he offered, balancing a piece on his knife.

She held up her hand, gesturing no. "Then I wouldn't have room for pie." She watched him chew. "You and Mitch have been friends for a long time, haven't you?"

He paused. "Long enough."

"What happened on the night Jack Sherman died?"

The question startled him. He set the remaining piece of cake on his plate, then sat back and looked at her.

She shouldn't have said it and now fear raced through her. "I'm sorry to have brought that up. I know Jack was a friend to you both." Dabbing her lips with the napkin, she slapped it to the table on top of his cutlery. Sliding out of her chair, she purposefully banged against the table leg, causing it to knock her tin of remaining coffee on its side.

While Quinn swore and jumped to his feet to soak up the mess, she apologized and slid the knife he'd been using into her canvas bag.

"Dear me, I'm so sorry. My apologies."

Art and Clay peered up from their conversations with the two other women. They nodded goodbye to Diana as she swirled past them.

"Let me walk you outside," Quinn insisted.

"Please don't trouble yourself. Thank you for the coffee and the pie."

"No trouble," he said, lifting her napkin to mop the remaining liquid.

He frowned at the table, then looked quickly to her

bag as if he realized she'd taken the knife but couldn't fathom why.

Her pulse kicked into full swing. "I'll just get my pie and let you men finish your meal." She dashed through the tables toward the front of the diner.

To her dismay, Quinn followed. "Not so fast. Here, let me get your pie for you." He nodded to the waiter behind the counter. "We'll take it now."

The man slid it across the counter. Diana waited three seconds for Quinn to lift it. Another set of fingerprints wouldn't hurt. But Quinn simply stared at it, waiting and gauging her reaction.

In the mounting pressure, he reached for a toothpick from the mason jar on the counter, pressing his coarse fingers against the round glass, then reached up and picked his teeth.

The rapid pounding in Diana's throat intensified. She stretched over the counter and scooped the pie into her arms. Her cape trailed behind her arms, over the mason jar of toothpicks, and along the floor. Her bonnet swayed between her shaking fingers. Could she scoop the mason jar into her bag without Quinn noticing? Glancing through the front windows, she watched in drumming terror as Mitch crossed the darkened street among the horses, wagons and pedestrians, focused on the diner. She wanted to flee out the door, but was the timing good?

Her beating heart rang in her ears. Things were about to collide.

Mitch was ready to rip the door down. They were so close to solving this crime he could feel the tautness in every muscle. He walked across the street, peering around a team of heavy oxen to the diner.

Gripped with nervous tension and wondering what was taking her this long, he caught glimpses of Diana through the front window. Inside, the crowd around her blurred into confusing shapes and colors. It was more the cape he caught sight of than Diana. When he reached the corner of the building at the alley, he squeezed into a shadowed alcove to wait.

Nodding to folks he recognized strolling on the boardwalk, he fingered the smooth leather holsters slung on his hips. A chilly breeze whistled past his face. His shoulders eased into the wide expanse of his red coat and his thighs clenched beneath snug breeches.

"Diana!" he whispered hoarsely as she whipped by.

He made the mistake of stepping out too soon. He came face-to-face with Quinn.

Mitch froze but his senses rallied to full alert.

Diana gasped at Mitch's unexpected appearance. Entangled by the wind, her loose hair flew over her shoulder. A covered pie teetered in her hand. The canvas tote sagged against her body.

Quinn's dark eyes widened at Mitch. He tugged harshly at Diana's elbow. "What's this all about?"

Mitch told himself to remain calm, that a fight wouldn't accomplish anything. Especially a fight pertaining to Diana Campbell, sister of two suspects in the crime he was investigating.

Mitch fought for a quick and logical explanation. "I'm escorting Miss Campbell to her home. She's under surveillance." He raised an eyebrow at Diana. "I see you've got the pie."

With a brisk manner, Mitch stepped up beside her, overshadowing Quinn. Taking the pie from her, Mitch gestured to the boardwalk stairs, indicating she lead.

"Good night," she said, glancing awkwardly to

Quinn, sliding her bonnet to her head and fumbling with the ties. When she raised her arms, the weight inside the canvas bag shifted. She was carrying something bulky, round and heavy, thought Mitch as he looked at the outline of the fabric. Good. He hoped Quinn's prints were pressed all over it.

Mitch relaxed slightly at the thought that they were free to run with the evidence, but then recoiled when he heard Quinn's footsteps following them around the corner into the alley.

"What I don't understand is why you took the knife." Quinn's cool voice echoed against the dark buildings.

Diana slowed her pace but Mitch gripped her arm and urged her to keep walking. The wind fluttered through Mitch's hair, leaving a cool wake.

Quinn bellowed, "Why did you take the knife?"

Mitch felt Diana shiver beneath his hand.

Turning around slowly, Mitch indicated she not answer. *He* would protect her from Quinn's wrath. Unlike how he'd been able to protect Jack the night he drowned. "What are you getting so worked up about, Quinn?"

"*She* knows what." Quinn's face and body were masked by competing shadows, harsh ones spilling down the alleyway from the street lamps, gentler warmer tones from candlelight flashing high above them in overlooking windows.

Diana slid up against the boarded wall of the diner.

They were so close in escaping, thought Mitch. Just a few more feet and they'd be clear around the corner. "She's got a plate of pie for the kids. That's all."

But Quinn came running at her. He tried to wrench the bag from her arm but succeeded only in twisting her wrist.

Diana yelped in pain but the bastard wouldn't release her.

Without blinking, Mitch hauled Quinn back by the shirt and punched him in the jaw. His knuckles sank into bristled flesh. "Keep your dirty hands off her! Take a swipe at me but keep your hands off her!"

He heard people on the boardwalk screaming. Boot steps trampled into the alley. Diana jumped out of reach but her bag tumbled to the dirt and a mason jar of toothpicks tumbled out.

Quinn jerked to his feet. "Toothpicks? What the hell is going on?" He swore loud and clear and threw himself at Mitch.

Quinn sank his fists into Mitch's lower back, thudding into his kidneys. It was an unfair blow.

Pain radiated straight down Mitch's legs. "Uhh." He kneed Quinn in the chest and shoved him. Quinn reeled backward into the dirt, cursing the whole way down.

On the ground, Quinn growled like an unfed boar. When Mitch pulled his gun and aimed it at his *friend,* the growling and the fighting came to a dead stop.

A cluster of onlookers gasped. "What did he do to you, Mitch?" someone asked.

"Looks like they're fightin' over the girl," answered another.

Mitch panted for air. He felt a taste of blood in his mouth and licked his lower lip.

Diana, speechless, collected her fallen items.

"What are you going to do?" wheezed Quinn. "Arrest me for using toothpicks?"

"You sang that song the night Jack drowned. 'Five Miles Away From Home.'"

"So what, you son of a bitch?"

"You're the only person I know who plays a banjo."

"I'll play it at your goddamn funeral."

"You developed calluses on your fingers, Quinn,"

Mitch said with sickening disgust. "From the banjo playing. Similar to a cigarette burn, but not quite. I thought I was looking for a smoker but I'm looking for you. I'll bet my life your prints match the ones taken at the scene of the crime."

The crowd hushed. Quinn's face darkened like a gathering storm. He glared at Diana, then down at the bag that held a mason jar and a knife, likely covered with his fingerprints.

Voices began to call. Questions were murmured. "My Lord," said someone. "Mitch's friend is the thief."

"But who was his accomplice?" said another.

Mitch watched it play out, deliberately not answering. He too wondered which one—or more—of their so-called friends had betrayed Mitch. He slid handcuffs from his belt and with the greatest of pleasure, clicked them on to Quinn's wrists. He hauled the traitor to his feet in a crowd that was getting louder.

"This has been a long time coming," said Mitch.

"There's no evidence against me." Quinn spat the words. "You can't take me in."

It was true enough. The prints still had to be matched. "Disturbing the peace. Accosting a lady and striking at an officer."

Quinn hurled more expletives.

Mitch clamped down on his jaw, scared if he let loose again, he might kill the man. "Why did you rob the banks?"

Quinn spat at Mitch but missed. He refused to respond and Mitch wondered if he'd ever discover how the puzzle pieces fit together. He yanked on the icy metal cuffs and pushed Quinn down the street with a gun pressed between his shoulder blades.

"The night of the party," whispered Quinn as they

turned the corner and more folks stopped to watch, "when you two were flying off for your damn mission and your damn celebration, it was you I was goading to dive into the water. Not Jack. It should have been you that drowned."

Mitch twisted away from Quinn's malicious glare, unable to comprehend such deep hatred, wondering if he could have done anything to save Jack. In a flash of self-awareness, Mitch realized he couldn't have done any more than he had. A burden lifted from his back, one he'd been carrying for over a year. He didn't have to be responsible for everyone and everything. Then he caught Diana's look of quiet sympathy.

Diana, who'd been here all along.

Diana, who accepted him and cared for him and made him feel as though he was enough, just the way he was.

Chapter Twenty-Two

He had to see her. Mitch exhaled in the early-morning sunshine. It was finally over, and as painful as the last forty-eight hours had been, taking Quinn into custody and then discovering his accomplice was Clay Hayward, Mitch had learned the entire truth. But the last two days had taught him something else he hadn't expected, and it had to do with Diana.

With a duffel bag slung over his shoulder, fringed suede jacket shielding him from the wind, off-duty clothes of denim pants and shirt hugging his body, Mitch stood on her front step and knocked on the door.

It was early but the children were already up and playing in the backyard, chasing each other through the laundry strung on the line. Seeing the shirts and socks flapping in the breeze made him recall the night when he himself had chased Diana on the hill. It brought a tender smile to his lips.

"You can't go in the house!" Margaret shouted.

"No strangers are allowed!" Robert added, rolling by on his unicycle. "They might hurt us!"

Mitch waved and nodded but his smile flitted to the

wind. That was why they'd kept him out. Protecting themselves from strangers who might harm them. The only time he'd set foot in the house had been when he'd barged in to tell Diana her brothers were under arrest.

There were so many things he hadn't understood about her, that he ached to know about her now. There were a few things he might even learn from this reserved family, from their quiet motto of hard work and no complaints.

Wayde and Tom appeared from around the corner, set free from jail yesterday and dragging an old trunk behind them. "Mitch! Good of you to drop by."

The men shook hands, not saying much, not needing to.

"What's in the trunk?"

"We're packin' up the outdoor stuff."

Mitch sobered at the reminder that they still planned to move.

Tom peered up at him with a strange look on his face. "Are you here to see Diana?"

"Yeah."

"She's in there. Just keep knocking."

Mitch spun toward the door and rapped again, wondering if she might ignore him as she had once before. Maybe it was stupid of him to come. Maybe—

The door flew open. "Mitch."

"Hi, Diana."

Her lips parted slightly, revealing a row of pretty teeth. Her hair smelled newly washed and tumbled over her shoulders, as if the shiny strands were a part of the glossy sun. A white lace blouse was tucked into her waistline, and Lord help him, she was wearing those tight denim pants. They outlined the curve of her thighs and made his pulse dance.

He snagged a breath of air, watching her.

She squinted in the sunshine streaming in from around his shoulders. "Good morning." Her voice caught in a swell of emotion. "I take it you've come to say goodbye."

He couldn't speak at the thought of losing her.

A sad smile drifted to her lips. "Won't you come in?"

She moved gracefully to the side of the hall and opened the door as wide as it would go. She was finally asking him in.

His throat tightened at the gesture. With the deepest pride, he stepped inside the cabin. The aroma of freshly baking bread wafted through the air to welcome him. "It smells good in here."

He turned to tell her, but the space was so tight he was practically standing on top of her. He liked how their bodies contrasted in shape and size. His was almost boxy, hers curved and round in all the best places. Towering inches above her hair, he inhaled the scent of soap. Her cheeks were scrubbed clean and her eyes were clear.

"I was just packing," she said awkwardly. Closing the door, she slipped from the pull of his gravity, then led him into the parlor.

"Packing." The word fell roughly from his lips. He looked about at the two scratched suitcases, the skirts flung over the rough sofa, the socks tucked inside out and lined up like obedient soldiers, waiting to be ordered to their positions. "Where are you going this time?"

She walked to her pile of clothing and gingerly folded a blouse. "Farther west. We've never seen the ocean. We're going to Vancouver."

Could he compete with an ocean? "I brought you something."

"There's no need. You've already given me the best

gift I could have hoped for with the release of my brothers. And please tell me what else you've learned about Quinn and the robberies. I've heard all sorts of rumors."

"In a minute." He placed his duffel bag on a chair and shoved his fingers into his pocket. He pulled out a coin and placed it in her hand.

She frowned. "A nickel."

"A return of your money. The five cents it cost you for the bachelor raffle."

Her eyes watered. She held the coin to her heart. "The best money I ever spent." Abruptly, she turned away and continued folding clothes, overtaken by sentiment.

"I'll remember you always," she whispered.

Her words tugged at a deep corner of his heart. He opened his duffel bag and placed his other gift on the sofa beside her.

She stopped moving and simply stared. Then gently, she traced the outline of the new brown leather shoes, her fingers touching the buckles and the buttons, her gaze taking in the high heels and stylish cut. "A brand-new pair of women's shoes."

"Winnie and Charlotte told me your size."

"Oh, Mitch…" Her eyes filled with dew. "How can I accept them?"

"You can put them on and show me how they fit."

"What can I possibly give you in return?"

"Come with me to visit someone."

"But I'm in the middle of—"

"Come with me, Diana. I'm going to see Mrs. Sherman."

She peered up at him with understanding, as if she knew by his soft inflection and the hesitant way he was standing that the impending visit meant the world to him.

"I'd like you to be at my side. And then after that, if

you still want to…if you're still determined… Let's not think about that yet. Please come with me."

He held out his hand and softly, Diana took it.

They raced uphill in the bright sunshine, Mitch steering them toward the old Sherman house, passing through town with its early-morning shoppers on their way to the harvest market. Fighting a storm of apprehension, Mitch knew that this morning's visit would be his one last shot at getting things right. Between himself and Mrs. Sherman; himself and Diana.

"Mitch!" Diana laughed, twirling through the air, her cape sliding over her pants, her blouse ruffled at her throat. Diana projected an energy that always drove him to distraction. "I've got new shoes! Every time I look down, I can't believe I'm looking at my legs!"

Laughing, he raced beside her. They wove around water troughs, boardwalk stairs and teams of horses already laden with squash, corn, crates of chickens, boxes of eggs and seed packets in preparation for the spring.

Someone else shouted at him by the nickname he'd recently been christened with. "Hey, *Fingerprint,* brilliant job yesterday!"

Mitch waved. Diana turned toward him and with a wrinkling of her eyebrows, smiled in the timid way that made him ache to kiss her. "Fingerprint. It suits you."

He nodded with rising pride. He didn't mind the name. He didn't mind the promotion he'd gotten along with it, either. On Monday, he'd start training the new recruits with the fingerprinting techniques he'd mastered.

"When are you going to tell me what happened?"

"As soon as we reach the house."

"Don't you think I should change into a dress for Mrs. Sherman? These pants—"

"Look wonderful. And I want you to stay as you are. I think Mrs. Sherman would appreciate the people around her being who they are…would appreciate me being honest with myself and the past. I've been trying to color the events to make it easier on her, but all it accomplished was to make it harder on everyone."

Diana listened, but Mitch knew she couldn't understand the depth of what he'd just sorted out for himself. He'd explain it at Mrs. Sherman's.

They turned the corner at the end of the main road and marched toward the grayed board-and-batten house.

Intimidating in its looming presence and the memories it held for him, the crooked house sat in a field of autumn wheat, surrounded by the things he remembered—the hiss of the wind rippling through the shafts, the buzz of flies, the scent of rich loam, the parched dry heat on his skin.

A collage of visions assaulted him. There was the dry apple tree in the front yard that had never produced a healthy apple in its lifetime, but had made an awfully good tree for building their forts. There was the big barn door that still had the markings of a hand-drawn bull's-eye he and Jack had used for practicing bows and arrows. There was the speckled mule in the back quarter that brayed incessantly at everyone's arrival, and who was braying at this very moment. And as they drew closer, there was the fifteen-year-old splatter of white paint on the door's threshold where he and Jack had accidentally toppled the can while trying to race for suppertime.

His heart pounded a rhythm at what he was about to face.

Diana's mood turned serious, reflecting his own.

When they reached the crooked front porch, he led them to the door and knocked. No one answered.

Then a familiar holler rose from behind the house. Mitch couldn't yet see Mrs. Sherman, but he could hear her. "Bessy, who in tarnation is here? With your brayin' you'd think the king himself has come to call."

Mrs. Sherman appeared at the corner. Wearing a bee-keeper's net that dangled off her floppy hat and over her face, and carrying a tin can with smoke billowing from its top, she was, Mitch realized, in the middle of collecting honey.

The warm eyes twinkled at him behind her spectacles and beneath the netting. Her mouth trembled slightly.

Please don't cry, Mrs. Sherman.

"You're just in time, Mitchell Reid, to help bring the honeycombs inside." She swallowed tightly. "If Jack were here..." Her old voice dwindled to a whisper.

A fly buzzed past his ear as they stood there admiring the sight of each other.

"If Jack were here," said Mitch, "he'd be wearing that crazy hat and half the honey would be gone already."

"Indeed he would. He was crazy about honey."

"No wonder you never made a penny from your business."

"It's grown into a fine operation."

"Jack would be proud of his dear old ma."

She smiled this time, instead of crying. Joy beamed from her face, washing away the wrinkles.

"I should have come sooner," he said, filling with shame.

She was silent for a moment. "I suspect you came as soon as you could."

A soft sob exploded from his throat. He hadn't realized it was there.

Diana pressed her hand on his shoulder and his pain subsided. "I know you've met Diana," he said.

"She helped me choose my new spectacles and she visited once before. How do you do?"

"Very well, thank you."

"Well, then, let me put my things away and I'll make you two a lovely pot of tea."

They'd made peace with each other, Diana observed quietly as she sipped hot lemon tea and listened to the tales passing back and forth between Mitch and Mrs. Sherman.

Diana shooed the flies from the sugar bowl but welcomed the crisp autumn breeze rolling through the propped backyard door. Although she loved listening to Mitch's childhood memories, he and Mrs. Sherman had been reminiscing for twenty minutes in the sunny kitchen but Diana hadn't contributed to the conversation. Perhaps she was intruding. The word outsider hammered away at her thoughts. She felt honored that Mitch had invited her, but tried not to read any more into it other than he wanted her here as a friend.

He'd found a place for himself, was reconnecting with dear Mrs. Sherman who obviously thought the world of him.

"…and then when you two came running out of the pond with reeds stuck to your head," said Mrs. Sherman, "you remember what happened. I thought you were ghosts coming to haunt me and screamed so loud that Bessy didn't stop brayin' for two hours."

Their laughter echoed off the ceiling rafters, fading into a soft hush.

Diana's curiosity deepened. She wondered when he'd finally get around to explaining what exactly had happened yesterday and how it related to Jack's drowning. She'd been wondering for what seemed like forever, but wanted to allow him the freedom to tell the story in his own time.

Mrs. Sherman set down her teacup. Porcelain clinked beneath her gnarled fingers. "Mitch, what happened on the night that Jack drowned?"

The pleading in her tone tugged at Diana's sympathies. Losing a son who'd been in the prime of his life was unimaginable. Diana still ached at the loss of her parents, but knew it would have been harder to understand the loss of one of her younger brothers or sisters.

Mitch rubbed his temple and shifted in his seat. The weight of his body caused the wooden chair to creak. "I know you've heard the story already from the investigating Mounties."

"I've never heard it from you."

Mitch looked from one expectant woman to the other. "Quinn had invited us to his ranch for a celebration a week before we were supposed to leave for Regina. I believe you know that."

Mrs. Sherman nodded.

"He told us it was in honor of our going away to Officers' Academy. Now we know that Quinn had also applied to the academy but the commander had turned him down."

That was news to both women.

"Why?" asked Mrs. Sherman.

"The commander told me yesterday that it was because of Quinn's character…that somehow he always managed to stir up trouble. Always exposing other people's weaknesses, only to get them riled up or to hurt them in some way. Quinn always claimed he was joking, that folks didn't know how to mind a good joke, but the commander didn't think it appropriate for the moral character of an officer."

"So he refused him entry," said Diana. "On the grounds of his moral character."

"That's right."

"The one thing Quinn couldn't change about himself," said Mrs. Sherman.

"Right again. If he was a poor shot, or a bad rider, he could have practiced and exercised till he overcame it. As it was, he'd always been the best athlete among the gang. The best runner, the best rider."

Mrs. Sherman peered at Mitch above her spectacles. "Did you ever like him?"

"One time...Mrs. Sherman, I never told you this and I doubt Jack did, either, but once when we were adolescents, we went hunting to the south ridge."

"You did that a lot. Duck hunting."

Mitch nodded. "One time, early on a Saturday morning, we heard horrible shrieking coming out of the woods. It terrified us. Jack and I snuck up on Quinn and his father. His father was beating the tar out of him for missing what he called an easy shot at one of the ducks. We just stood there, hidden behind the trees. The fighting stopped almost as soon as we got there, but we didn't help Quinn. We didn't know how. I think Jack and I both knew if we spoke up, it'd shame Quinn forever. We felt sorry for him and that's why we took him in to our gang of friends."

"Befriending him was an act of kindness."

Mitch scoffed. "Maybe it was an act of weakness. We didn't stand up to his father and we never suggested he should, either."

"An act of kindness," the woman whispered again.

Mitch's voice rumbled with shame. "But years later, I never stood up to Quinn when he grew into an adult. He became the same vicious bully his father had been. And look where it got Jack."

"But you've got to know—"

"Yes, I know. I'm not responsible for what happened to Jack. I hate what happened to him, but it's not the fault of *good* people." Mitch looked out of the window and they all turned to watch a bird fluttering in the trees. "Quinn taunted me that night. There were women at the barbecue and there was dancing later. After the women went home, a few of us kept drinking. Quinn suggested we go out on the raft and see who could paddle the fastest upstream.

"I didn't like the idea. I said no. He suggested the Mounties against the ranchers, two against two. He and Clay against me and Jack. Jack convinced me to go for the hell of it.

"Pretty soon we got into deeper water and it got darker. Clay had been drinking so heavily that he fell off right at the beginning and went back to the fire. I demanded we turn around and head to shore, too, but Jack and Quinn both…they both kept going. It was crazy. I tried to reason with them, but Quinn told me I was too cautious…that I was always too cautious…too cowardly…and that I'd never make a great officer…"

Diana nearly choked at how awful Mitch must have felt.

"My dog, Digger, was restless. He was on the raft with me and Jack. He started barking at things he saw in the water. Reflections of the moon slipping in and out of the clouds. The river started to toss. Then Quinn dived in for a swim. He goaded us to follow. Jack did but I didn't. Pretty soon I couldn't see him. Quinn swam to shore and watched from there. Digger dived in. I followed… I couldn't save either one of them…. For a long time afterward, I believed I *was* too cautious. That I should have dived in as soon as Jack had."

Mrs. Sherman reached across the table and planted

her hand over his. "Your cautious nature will save a lot of folks in your line of duty and *is* what makes you a great officer, from what I'm hearing."

"I agree," Diana murmured gently, marveling at the strength Mitch demonstrated in nearly everything he touched. He glanced into her eyes and she felt her chest tighten.

The emotional weight of the conversation held the three of them spellbound. "Where were the others?" Diana asked. "What were they doing?"

"They were back at the fire, pulling out decks of cards, getting ready for a final hand." He sighed. "I've always heard that drowning is silent. I never believed it. I thought a spectator would be able to hear the thrashing and the calling for help, but that never happened. There was no thrashing and no calling. Just a raised hand that slipped beneath the water."

Mrs. Sherman looked down at her tea. Tears washed down her cheeks. Diana knew no matter how difficult it was for Mrs. Sherman to hear, she wanted to hear the truth from Mitch and didn't want it sugarcoated. Diana reached over and patted her until she stopped sobbing.

"Two hours later and a mile downstream, we pulled out his body. He was still holding on to Digger. Digger had tried to save him."

Diana took a deep breath. "How did Quinn go from an ugly rivalry with his friends to robbing banks?"

"It wasn't just him. Clay was his partner."

"Clay?" said Mrs. Sherman, grasping at her throat.

"So the rumors I heard yesterday were true," said Diana.

Mitch nodded. "Clay apparently did it for the money. He's the one whose cards they kept leaving behind at every hit. Clay's the type of man that once you get him liquored up, you can convince him into doing anything. He'd always been the quietest drinker among us, but you never knew what he was thinking. Yesterday he looked so desperate, pleading for another chance."

"It's out of your hands, Mitch. It's up to the judge." Mrs. Sherman sank back into her chair and nodded over and over. It was comforting watching her, thought Diana, being with her.

Mitch continued, his voice strained and rough. "Quinn never came up with a good response to why he'd gone to robbing banks, but I suspect it was the gritty competition he felt with me and Jack. Jack was gone, but Quinn could still prove he was smarter and more wily on his feet than me, as a new officer."

"Or so he thought," said Diana, knowing how difficult it must be for Mitch to have lost both Quinn and Clay as friends. "And maybe in some cruel way, robbing banks was something Quinn did to get back at his father. His father owns the Calgary Bank and Loan. Clay said it was next on their list."

Mrs. Sherman gently adjusted her teacup. "You're likely right about that."

"Quinn used his father's hairpiece during the robberies," said Mitch, shaking his head in disbelief. "The red strands match the hair fiber taken at the scene. And the bullet imbedded in the wall of the bank has the same rifling marks as bullets from Clay's gun. There was other physical evidence but it was incidental and irrelevant. Broken brown glass and dripped flecks of red paint. Boot prints that matched Quinn's size but nothing distinct."

"What about Art?" asked Diana. "He always struck me as an unusual sort of fellow. I never knew whether to trust him or not."

"Sometimes I felt that way myself. But Art's been the real gem behind this awful business. He came to tell me yesterday he was sorry for everything that had gone down and that he wasn't aware of any of it."

"Somehow, I think you already knew that."

"I knew his fingerprints wouldn't match any of the ones I'd taken at the bank. He's a heavy man and his prints would have been recognizably larger."

Mitch was a remarkable man, thought Diana, her stomach squeezing at the thought that they'd soon be saying goodbye. Mitch sighed as he watched her, the lines around his eyes creasing, his dark gaze inspecting hers.

Mrs. Sherman broke their stare. "Can I show you something outside?"

"Sure." Mitch rose to his feet and loomed over the other two. "What is it?"

"Something I've been saving. Hoping to give to you when you stopped by."

Mitch rubbed his neck self-consciously. "Folks have been telling me you've got something to give me."

"Come have a look out in the barn."

"Out there? I thought you wanted to give me something of Jack's."

"Nope. Follow me."

It felt splendid to walk in the sunshine, thought Diana, following alongside Mitch and a smiling Mrs. Sherman, knowing that their chaotic lives had somehow fallen into a peaceful order. If only she could find the same peace in her own life.

"Diana, I wanted to commend you on the handling of your brothers." Mrs. Sherman poked her head around Mitch's wide shoulders.

"I thought I'd done so poorly with them, Mrs. Sherman. They didn't confide in me about Patty Upwood."

"But they did what's right in protecting her. It's only been a couple of months that you've lived here, but you've blended into the community so well. Why, everyone I know talks highly of you. And your brothers… You know I've raised three sons of my own and it's not easy to raise boys. Two words come to mind. Wild and worrisome."

Diana smiled.

"If you ever need a listening ear or advice of any kind, please allow me…please don't feel it a burden if you knock on my door. Your oldest brother, Wayde, the protective but stubborn one, he reminds me of Jack."

There were so many things that the woman seemed to know, details she observed about Mitch and about Diana. If Jack had been anything like his mother, it was no wonder Mitch had been his friend.

By the tenderness in her clear blue eyes, Mrs. Sherman looked as if she was expecting a reply. Diana swallowed the heaviness in her throat and nodded. "Thank you."

When they heard animals yelping, Mitch stepped into the darkened corner of a stall.

"Puppies?" Diana hoisted herself onto the stall boards and looked down at the wriggling, delightful bodies.

Four yellow puppies fought for space at their mother's belly. Two slightly larger ones played in the corner and chewed at some biscuits, apparently weaned.

Mitch laughed softly. "It's feeding time."

"The mother is Digger's sister." Mrs. Sherman opened the door wider so they could enter. Straw rustled beneath their boots. "The pups are ten weeks old and I wanted to give you first pick of the litter."

"So this is the surprise you've been saving for me." With a tenderness Diana had forgotten he possessed,

Mitch gently lifted one of the two larger mutts into his arms. It squirmed in his palm, looking as if it weighed no more than two pounds. Mitch smiled and Diana felt powerless to resist watching him as he spoke to the golden puppy. "So that means Digger would have been your uncle."

Chapter Twenty-Three

The sounds of a beautiful autumn, as Diana and Mitch walked toward town accompanied by a small yapping pup, would have seemed welcoming in times of contentment, but on this midmorning only intensified Diana's feelings of isolation.

Farmers shouted to each other in their fields. Golden hay swished in the cool wind and beneath the sickle's blade. Horses rumbled as they plowed soil. And the constant drum of Mitch's footsteps beside her in the rutted road vibrated against the blazing blue sky and the mournful, silent beating of her heart.

She was leaving in less than a week. She'd already informed the poultry factory, packed most of their household items and given notice to their landlord.

The only major thing left to do was to say goodbye to Mitch. The hardest thing she'd ever have to do.

Leading the pup by an old rope, Mitch bent down and scooped him up. The dog immediately lapped at his master's chin.

They stood in the open road. A man in a wobbly cart, pulled by an old mare, rolled by. They nodded in greeting, the man frowning down at Diana's pants. Although perturbed by his silent disapproval, she ignored him and he soon passed.

Mitch pulled the puppy away from his dark, bristled jaw. "What do you think I should name him?"

"Harvest," Diana replied with a wistful sigh. She pushed back the hair that had fallen against her cheek.

Mitch laughed. "Why Harvest?"

"Because it means all things good. Because it's a season for reaping what you sow. Because all the time and love you invested in Digger and Jack and Mrs. Sherman have come back to reward you in your new little friend."

And because she and her family had never been a part of a bountiful harvest, as they had in Calgary.

For seconds neither of them spoke. He studied her beneath the brim of his remarkable leather hat, his features darkly crisp and distinct against the brilliant sky behind him. Lines grooved his face around his mouth, and years of experience shone through his fascinating brown eyes.

She gripped the belt buckle that looped through her pants.

Mitch squinted. "I was thinking more like Butch or Bones or Rufus. Something powerful and doglike."

He set down the dog.

Mitch's humor couldn't sway Diana's somber mood, although she wished the tension would ease between them. "Maybe I'm being too serious. I'm very opinionated, in case you haven't noticed. I really should work on that. It—it always causes everyone around me grief."

Diana turned and continued walking, briskly this time.

"It's not your firm opinions that need to be softened. It's your seriousness."

She shrugged her shoulders, her white lace blouse billowing at her elbows.

"Diana, please stop and listen to me."

"It's getting close to noon. Time to make everyone lunch."

"They can do without you for half an hour."

She increased her step.

He pulled her to a stop by yanking on the back of her belt. She nearly lost her balance.

Panting, she squirmed but he held her firmly by her belt. "Let me go. You're making this very difficult."

"What's difficult?"

"To say goodbye."

His Adam's apple tightened. His mouth narrowed, then he released her. "I've been wanting to say something to you ever since the first time I saw you in those pants."

She paced herself a good distance away, beyond his reach. But not beyond his searing gaze. The way he looked her up and down, with the corner of his mouth slightly raised, made her body flush with unexpected warmth.

"They're hand-me-downs, and I've—I've decided they're so comfortable to wear around the house, I don't care what anyone says about them."

"I've never seen a woman look more...worth having...than you in those pants."

Worth having? "In faded old trousers more than ten years old? The direct sun is affecting your thinking."

"When I look at the outline of your legs plastered against the grass, and the round of your behind going up and down when you walk, all I think of is..." His eyes penetrated hers. "You know what."

Indeed, she did. She felt her face turn crimson.

"We're in the middle of the road, heaven forbid, in the middle of the day, and what you should be thinking of are your manners."

She turned and nearly ran. He caught up quickly.

Her words tore from her breast. "And that part of our lives is definitely...definitely...over."

"Are you really intending to say goodbye?"

She nodded, conscious of the ache in her throat.

"Why, when everything you're feeling, I'm feeling?"

They drifted to a slow stop. He planted his hands roughly on her shoulders and turned her to face him.

He searched her face. "I know you feel it. Do you think I can't see it in your eyes when you look at me? Do you think I don't notice the sweet friction between us when we touch? Do you think I can't see your pulse fluttering at your collar this moment?"

"Maybe someday, Mitch...someday when the children are older..."

"Then what? You'll allow yourself the right to enjoy your life?"

"I *do* enjoy my life."

"Not fully. You're sacrificing the depth of what you might really feel if you allowed yourself...what you know you want."

She closed her eyes, so used to shutting out the world for five years that she no longer knew how to let it in. "What I want is..."

"...*me*...." He whispered it so earnestly, so softly, she wasn't sure he'd said it.

Slowly opening her eyes, she ran her gaze over the creased lines around his eyes, the determined arch of his lips.

"Tell me you want me," he breathed.

"It's hard," she whispered.

"All you have to do is reach up and wrap those lovely arms around me, Diana, that's all you have to do. Then I'll know and I'll find a way for us."

She couldn't move for the torture of standing so close to Mitch, the anguish of breathing in the same air, seeing the same pain reflected in his face. But she felt adhered to the ground, her arms glued to her sides. For the few short weeks she'd known Mitch, she'd come to life. He'd brought her back to the land of dreams and hopes and possibilities. Without him, she was as parched as a fistful of dust.

"Aren't you lonely without me?" he murmured. "Don't you feel as scared as I do when you tuck yourself into your bed at night, wondering if you'll be tucking yourself in alone forty years from now?"

She swallowed past the tight ball of tears that threatened to spill, still unable to give him what he wanted, to reach up and prove how she felt.

With a wounded moan, he released her. His mouth trembled, barely in control. "I see. I thought you felt the same as I did. Evidently, I was mistaken."

Gathering his tattered pride, Mitch pulled away and tugged on the pup's leash. "Did you know your brothers are upset that you're moving to Vancouver?"

She frowned. "How do you mean?"

"I mean have you asked them, and really listened to their answers about moving? Or have you alone decided that you need to do this? Maybe your older brothers are just going along because they think it's best for you this time."

As she struggled to absorb this, the dog barked. Thrashing his tail, he jumped at a fluttering moth. Mitch followed, holding the rope loosely between his fingers.

Diana stood enthralled, watching the breadth of

Mitch's shoulders as he walked away from her. The massive size of him in comparison to his two-pound dog touched her tenderly.

She found her words and shouted after him. "Do you know how hard it's been to keep away from you? I think of you a hundred times a day. What you're doing and who you're doing it with."

At her choked voice, he spun back to face her. His looming figure, rich and masculine, draped in a backdrop of the Rocky Mountains, stood solid in the wind. His face, tinged brown from the sun and the weather, seemed invincible.

She pressed her palms together, feeling the tension ripple up her arms. Things needed to be said, and then maybe…

"I've been thinking, Mitch, ever since our talk with Mrs. Sherman. She believes I've made a home for myself, a place for my family, here. She made me feel welcome, like I've started to build something for my family in Calgary. I've never taken a step back before to look at myself from someone else's viewpoint."

"Mrs. Sherman can see farther than most. I wish I had remembered that when I first came back from Regina. She's right. What you've done for your family has been amazing." He paused. "And I think that you might not recognize it, but maybe Wayde and Tom are ready to stand on their own two feet now. You've done enough for them."

The sob that burst from her throat was one of clear astonishment. How had Wayde and Tom grown into two fine young men without her recognizing it? In the past few weeks, they'd made decisions on their own. Maybe not the wisest choices, but who was she to judge? Their decision to protect Patty had come from a spirit of true kindness and responsibility.

"You're so different than what I thought you were the first time we met, when you stood on my threshold berating my brothers. You're a more compassionate man than I gave you credit for."

"After Jack died, I swung too far in trying to suppress who I was. I suppose I sacrificed a part of myself, too, just as you had for your family, for the sake of Jack's memory. I thought I needed to be tougher and not the cheerful, joking Reid brother everyone has always called me."

Mustering her courage, she spoke honestly. "I love that part of Mitchell Reid."

His eyes glistened. His body tensed. He waited and watched. The puppy barked on his leash. "I've got a new dog and a new promotion. What this happy picture is missing is a partner by my side. A wife, if she'll have me."

Her heart trembled, saturated with the love she had for this great man. *Love.*

She looked at him with newfound amazement. Perhaps she'd known it all along. She was in love with Mitchell Reid. "Will any woman do?"

A smile flitted across his lips, and in that instant, she knew that they'd be all right.

"I'm looking for one with six brothers and sisters. Do you know of any?"

With a moan of joy, she dropped her hands and ran toward him.

He laughed as he caught her. Trapped in his embrace, she kissed his neck. He stroked her hair at the right temple while his other hand reached up across her blouse and closed along her spine, sending tremors within her. His thumb toyed with the soft skin at her ear. He touched his lips to her eyebrow, her eyelid, her cheek. When her breath caught, he whispered into her hair.

"I love you, Diana."

She murmured without words, grasping his waist with one hand and riding her hands up along the muscles of his chest.

"What are we going to do, Mitch? How is this going to work?"

He kissed her mouth, the breath racing out of him in soft gasps. "You're going to marry me."

She whispered in wonder, "Oh…"

"Do you want to?"

"Yes," she breathed.

"Do you love me?"

The adoration she saw reflected in his face, reflected in her heart. "Um-hmm," she whispered. "I think I fell in love with you that night outside the forge. When you kept saying, wait for me."

"And I think I fell in love with you at the harvest fair, the first time we played the alphabet game."

"That soon?"

"Yeah, that soon. We feel right together. I was never thrilled about marriage because I'd never met you, Diana."

She let his hands play over her back, marveling at the tingle they immediately caused in her stomach. "And now?"

"And now," he said as he devoured her throat and filled her with splendor, "and now we'd better find a minister."

Epilogue

The harvest fair, one year later

"My word, they're raffling off men."

The woman speaking was anonymous in the crowd, but her tone of amazement caused Mitch to turn and share a smile with Diana. As organizers of the charity game this year, the two stood on the platform, a foot above a gathering throng. Stepping across the planks, Mitch wove a loose arm around his beautiful wife and tugged her back to protect her from an oncoming splash. The newspaper reporter clicked his camera as another Mountie plunked into the water.

"I love it when that happens," Diana whispered.

Her warm breath at the base of his neck reminded him of the kiss she'd planted there early this morning. Making love to Diana at the break of sunrise was a powerful way to rouse him from his sleep.

Pinching the brim of his leather hat, Mitch kissed her warm forehead. She stepped out to give the wet officer a towel and introduce him to the woman who'd won him for the next twenty-four hours. With a stream of sunshine outlining her new rose-colored blouse and long navy skirt, Diana swung her dark braid over her shoulder. The widow's peak of her hairline framed the tenderness in her eyes and the smile that rushed to her moist lips.

With good humor, Mitch watched her give instructions to the couple. He clapped the middle-aged officer on the back. "I hope you have as much fun as I did."

"But I heard yours ended in matrimony."

"I had to pluck a few chickens first."

"Whatever you do," Diana told the quiet young woman, "don't let him organize the day. It's up to you to make good use of him."

While the couple asked more questions of Diana, Mitch let his gaze drift over the crowd. He had a good view from atop the platform. Horses neighed to the left of the dirt midway, and to their right, the wooden carousel creaked.

Diana's brothers and sisters were walking toward them as a group. Wayde has his arm slung around Patty Upwood, and Tom had his around his girl, Patty's sister Abbie. The youngsters stopped at a dart game and begged their older brothers to play. Wayde, working full time at the stables, was now one of the foremen, earned a decent wage and had just proposed to Patty. Last year, after having heard her complaints against her brutal husband and her request for a divorce, the judge had granted her one.

Mitch loved being part of a big family. He loved providing for them, giving them advice when they asked, and along with Diana, filled with pride when they did well in school.

When Diana and Mitch had married, Wayde and Tom had insisted on staying where they were and renting the cabin on their own. Mitch had built a fine ranch house on his father's property for the rest of them. Diana loved the company of Mitch's extended family—Travis and Jessica with their twins, and Shawna and Tom with their son. Mitch felt secure leaving her and the four youngsters behind when he traveled in the territory on police duty. The ranch house also gave Diana a good base for her new catalog business. Much to Emmit York's displeasure, she was strong competition.

As for Mitch's old gang of friends, Quinn and Clay were serving their time in prison, and surprisingly, the experience had brought the rest of them closer in friendship. Art and Vic had promised to help Mitch at tomorrow's barbecue in handling the steer roast, while Mrs. Sherman had promised to bring a dozen jars of honey.

People cheered at a booth ten yards away, pulling Mitch from his thoughts. Adjusting his hat, he observed with a smile that some excited soul had just won a small plaster prize.

Diana nudged him. They were ready for another contestant.

"Next!" Mitch hollered to the lineup of men.

They watched as David Fitzgibbon, the reporter, stepped up to the plank and sat down. His straw-colored hair poked out from beneath a plaid cap. Technically he wasn't a Mountie, but he was infamous in town due to his intrusive nature, and many here would enjoy seeing him get soaked. The commander's wife had been after David for three years to volunteer.

Holding the red rubber ball and raising her arm in the air, Diana shared a laugh with Mitch at the boisterous scene.

"One shot for a nickel and three for a dime!" she hollered.

"Put your money right here on the platform, it's all for a good cause!"

Mitch caught the mischievous sheen in her gaze. N,O,P. He was very much aware of what they were doing.

"Quality, folks!" Diana shouted. "Look at the caliber of this reporter! Why, he could write letters home to your family, or write a story about your life in Calgary!"

"Right, or he could compose a pretty poem for the woman who wins him!"

That generated the most response. Three ladies immediately came forward to pay Diana. Sliding beside her, Mitch raised a gentle hand to her shoulder then ran it up and down her arm. He could never get enough of the feel of her.

With a sparkle to her green eyes and laughter in her voice, Diana peered up at him. "Should we tell them there's no transfer of prizes?"

"They'll find out soon enough." With the hooting and cheering of the crowd around them, Mitch lowered his mouth to hers and kissed his wife softly on the lips. He heard a loud splash, water trickled on his boots, then the crowd roared.

* * * * *

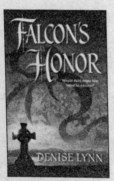

If you enjoyed what you just read,
then we've got an offer you can't resist!

Take 2 bestselling love stories FREE!

Plus get a FREE surprise gift!

Clip this page and mail it to Harlequin Reader Service®

IN U.S.A.	**IN CANADA**
3010 Walden Ave.	P.O. Box 609
P.O. Box 1867	Fort Erie, Ontario
Buffalo, N.Y. 14240-1867	L2A 5X3

YES! Please send me 2 free Harlequin Historicals® novels and my free surprise gift. After receiving them, if I don't wish to receive anymore, I can return the shipping statement marked cancel. If I don't cancel, I will receive 6 brand-new novels every month, before they're available in stores! In the U.S.A., bill me at the bargain price of $4.69 plus 25¢ shipping and handling per book and applicable sales tax, if any*. In Canada, bill me at the bargain price of $5.24 plus 25¢ shipping and handling per book and applicable taxes**. That's the complete price and a savings of over 10% off the cover prices—what a great deal! I understand that accepting the 2 free books and gift places me under no obligation ever to buy any books. I can always return a shipment and cancel at any time. Even if I never buy another book from Harlequin, the 2 free books and gift are mine to keep forever.

246 HDN DZ7Q
349 HDN DZ7R

Name	(PLEASE PRINT)	
Address	Apt.#	
City	State/Prov.	Zip/Postal Code

Not valid to current Harlequin Historicals® subscribers.

Want to try two free books from another series?
Call 1-800-873-8635 or visit www.morefreebooks.com.

* Terms and prices subject to change without notice. Sales tax applicable in N.Y.
** Canadian residents will be charged applicable provincial taxes and GST.
   All orders subject to approval. Offer limited to one per household.
   ® are registered trademarks owned and used by the trademark owner and or its licensee.

HIST04R   ©2004 Harlequin Enterprises Limited